THE COVER UP AT
BEVERLY HILLS HOSPITAL . . .

He had no idea how long he had slept, when he again awakened with that odd sense of apprehension, again feeling that someone had come into the room. This time he was certain that a door had opened and closed, but he could see no one in the light or in the shadows. He could hear no sound of movement.

He waited for a moment, watching and listening, and then, cursing himself audibly, forced his eyes to close.

When they opened again, he was sure that it wasn't simply his imagination; there was someone in the room with him. Victor was certain that there had been some sound, some movement. Something in the room had altered, but he couldn't determine immediately what it was.

Then he saw it.

The intravenous bottle was swinging on its pole — and it was empty! There was none of the precious life-sustaining plasma at all.

Victor reached for the buzzer to call the nurses' station.

It was not there.

He groped frantically around the edge of the bed, desperately searching for the small plastic box, for the cord that held it. It had been there earlier in the evening. Someone had obviously taken it away, just as someone had obviously emptied the IV bottle.

. . . INCLUDED MURDER

COVER UP

COVER UP

HOWARD A. OLGIN, M.D.

PaperJacks LTD.

TORONTO   NEW YORK

AN ORIGINAL

PaperJacks

COVER UP

PaperJacks LTD.

330 STEELCASE RD. E., MARKHAM, ONT. L3R 2M1
210 FIFTH AVE., NEW YORK, N.Y. 10010

PaperJacks edition published January 1988

CDN ISBN 0-7701-0833-4
US ISBN 0-7701-0756-7
Copyright © 1988 by Howard Olgin
Printed in the USA

For Aviva,
for my parents, Joseph and Miriam,
and for Dr. Bill Rubinson, a good friend.

COVER UP

Chapter One

Dave Berger eyed his tape recorder nervously. It hummed softly, the red signal light flashing as the professor's voice boomed from the podium.

"You are all here to get your union cards . . . the certificate that will allow you to work as surgeons. All of your years in medical school, internships, residencies, fellowships, and private practice have now come down to this: You cannot practice your specialty in medicine — indeed, you cannot survive in medicine in the 1980s — without your boards. That's the state of the art."

Dave shifted uncomfortably and looked around. There were seven hundred and ninety-two candidates in the room and, Dave noted with some surprise, there were more than a few from the Middle East, Africa, Asia, even a few Iranians. Dave sniffed; a foul odor came from the Iranian sitting on his right.

"An M.D. degree isn't enough," the professor was saying. "It's board certification, or nothing."

Dave knew the statistics. They weren't reassuring. Nearly fifty percent flunked the board exam the first time, and of those, only half would pass on later.

The professor continued: "You have all passed part one of the boards, the written section, so we know you have the knowledge. It is the day-to-day decisions in your own community practice that we wish to test here.

How your mind works. How sharp your surgical judgment is. We can teach a monkey how to sew and staple tissues together, gentlemen, but surgical judgment — knowing when to operate — is more subtle.''

The professor switched speeds and began to talk about the three rooms each candidate would visit for his boards. For Dave, those rooms would be in a fancy motel in Palo Alto, California. Others would be called to hotels in New York, Miami, Tucson, Arizona, and Billings, Montana. The American College of Surgeons played the game of boards across the entire country, and the candidates had to be prepared to go anywhere at any time to take them. "Let the board know you're willing to go to Idaho or Colorado or even North Carolina to be examined," the professor said. "An opening may develop at any time.

"Impressions are important. Always carry a handkerchief. Everyone experiences the adrenaline response — sweaty palms, from being scared shitless. Before you go into a room and shake hands with the two board-certified examining physicians, I would recommend you first wipe your hands with a handkerchief. A limp, wet paw will not make a good impression.''

The candidates looked nervously at one another. It wasn't just medical knowledge but the *art* of taking this test that was important.

It wasn't enough that Dave had gone to med school, completed his internship and residency, served in the army, and been in practice for three years. What mattered was that he wasn't yet a board-certified surgeon.

When Dave had first gone to work at Beverly Hills Hospital, he had just passed the written boards and was about to take the orals. That was two tries and three years ago. He had failed both times. But everyone was given five years to pass the boards, so he was permitted to work in the emergency room and take his turn on the surgery panel while he continued to study.

While Dave worked shifts in the ER and supplemented his meager income with surgery panel calls, the wealthy patients and those with insurance always went to the other surgeons — the board-certified ones. Dave got the three A.M. calls and the welfare cases.

He turned his attention back to the professor. "The important thing is to listen to each question and answer it. Do not answer another question, or the question you think you heard.

"Some of our friends who did their medical training in other countries, or who were born in other countries, will have trouble just understanding the English. We know that . . . and we sympathize." Dave glanced at the Iranian sitting beside him. "If you don't understand the words to a question, please ask the examiner to repeat it."

If he didn't pass the oral boards this time, he would have to go back for a year of graduate training. He'd have to give up his practice, however meager, and go back to residency, to thirty-six-hour shifts. He would also lose the little status that he had fought so hard to attain at Beverly Hills Hospital, where most of the other doctors looked down on him and excluded him from their social activities.

Suddenly his tape recorder clicked off. As he inserted a fresh cassette, the Iranian muttered, "Should have got ninety-minute tapes." Dave gave him a dirty look. What was worse, now his hemorrhoids were bothering him. He tried desperately to concentrate on the professor.

"A few words of advice . . . little things. One: Don't fight the examiner. I know a candidate who went in and started telling the examiner who was an expert on burns that the burn cream the examiner was using in his own private practice shouldn't be used. He then went into the ten reasons why not. Obviously, this didn't endear him to the examiner.

"Point two: While it doesn't matter what you wear to

the test, I would advise you to leave your sandals, sunglasses, beads, and gold chains at home. You are trying to make an impression. In general, the board examiners are quite conservative.

"Point three: You do not need to know everything. Seventy-five percent is enough. There's no one who knows everything. Even I couldn't answer every question. So if you miss one, don't be discouraged.

"Finally, do not guess, unless you're invited to. A guess can bring on the wrath of the examiner.

Keep a sense of humor. And balance. For example, on a melanoma question last year, a candidate was told, 'You have a patient with a deeply invasive level-three malignant melanoma of the arm. How wide an excision would you perform?' 'Five centimeters' was the reply. 'Okay. Now, suppose that same cancer is in the middle of the forehead. Would you take out both eyes and the nose, just to achieve five centimeters' margin?' The candidate finally muttered, "Well, nothing is etched in stone, sir. I suppose I'd have to modify my margin on this patient, and leave in the eyes and nose.'

"Again, some common sense, and a little sense of humor. Try not to sweat or faint or fight with your examiners. Dress nicely. We want you to pass. We *really* want you all to pass.

"State of the art," the professor concluded. "This course hopefully will make you better surgeons."

Chapter Two

Beverly Hills, November 12 (Seven Days Before Boards)

When Dave arrived at Beverly Hills Hospital late Monday night, he was depressed, impatient, and irritable. It was raining, so several of the nurses and orderlies on the eleven o'clock shift were late. It took half an hour to get things organized before he could see his first patient, an overweight woman who had mistaken indigestion for a heart attack. He was as curt with her as he was with the staff.

Dave knew he was allowing his preoccupation with the boards to get the better of him. As soon as he had left the hospital yesterday, the dark mood had begun to descend. It wasn't the first time he'd contemplated failure; he had only to think of his first two attempts to pass the boards.

What distressed him wasn't that he made mistakes or misdiagnosed illnesses, but that after three years of working the emergency room at Beverly Hills Hospital, he had rarely been allowed to undertake any case in which mistakes were even a possibility.

Occasionally, on weekends, there were so many emergency cases and so few surgeons on call that the hospital relaxed its rules and allowed him to take some panel surgical cases. But for the most part he functioned more like an intern, taking histories and physicals, making preliminary diagnoses, and referring surgery cases to the surgeon on panel.

Dave had spent Sunday evening trying to evaluate his situation. He understood the problem: The hospital was run by a group of self-serving doctors, all of whom were part owners, and most of whom regarded him as an "outsider" without boards.

He'd begun to think it had been a mistake to move to California. He felt he didn't fit in with the people or the life-style. And he was sure that others sensed this.

Dave didn't understand why he had failed to fit in. Was it just because he hadn't passed the boards? The doctors at Beverly Hills Hospital had certainly wanted him when he had been interviewed for the position. Dr. Winston, who ran the emergency room by contract from the hospital, cared deeply about the kind of doctors he hired. Their success meant his success. "I want you, Dr. Berger," he had told Dave. "Of all the doctors I've interviewed, I feel you have the greatest potential."

Dave had liked Dr. Winston instantly. He was of the old school, in contrast to the number of young and slick doctors at Beverly Hills. Dave had no idea how old Winston was, but he doubted the man was under sixty. Whatever, he was dignified, a real gentleman, and Dave admired him.

For the last three years, as Dave tried — and failed — to find the promised career opportunity, Dr. Winston had continued to encourage him. But Dave was still in the emergency room. At least he worked the midnight shift only half the time now; a new doctor had come in last year to occupy the lowest rung of the ladder.

Dave had almost no personal life and only a small private practice. His cramped office on Wilshire Boulevard was still furnished with rented equipment; by the time it finally belonged to him, it would be completely worn out.

Dave's patients knew he wasn't a success; it showed in the way they looked at him, the way they talked to him, and in the hesitant, almost apologetic way they referred their friends to him — on the rare occasions when they actually did refer them.

He didn't blame his patients for looking for the superficial signs of success. What else would tell them that he was an excellent diagnostician and surgeon?

By the time he had gone to bed last night, he had decided that his failure was due to his attitude, so he resolved to change it. But he had awakened without the conviction he had taken to bed. He was tired, it was raining, and he felt no place could be more depressing than Los Angeles in the rain. It wreaked havoc with traffic and turned drivers into maniacs.

It was not an auspicious way to begin a day, much less a week. Within an hour of arriving at the hospital, he was in a foul mood — spiteful, and arrogant.

He certainly wasn't ready for Jaspar Jarvis, a young black with two bullet holes in his belly. Jarvis had had the poor judgment to give a truck driver the one-finger salute on the freeway.

It was three A.M. as the nurses and techs started two large intravenous needles in Jarvis's arm and Ringer's lactate solution wide open.

Dave snapped. "Six units, type- and cross-match whole blood, and get me some stat lytes, CBC, BUN, and liver panel. And call the GP and surgeon on panel. Who is it?"

"Dr. Curtis, family practice, and Dr. Stein is on until eight A.M. Then Dr. Collins comes on," replied one of the nurses.

Joe Curtis was the first panel doctor to arrive, about ten minutes after the call. "Throw in an amylase!" he shouted as he leaned over Jarvis. "Jeez, it's bad," he muttered as he listened to Jarvis's chest and abdomen with a stethoscope.

Dave wondered what the hell Curtis thought he was doing. It was obvious that the patient needed exploratory surgery to determine the extent of the internal injuries.

"X-rays show the bullet near the lumbar spine," Curtis pointed out. "No neurological defects. I guess it missed the spinal cord. Blood pressure is ninety over sixty, pulse is one twenty. He's breathing shallow."

At that moment Dr. Stein arrived. "Let's not guess at anything," he said after examining the patient. "I want a neurosurgeon's note on the chart, stating clearly that there are no hints of paralysis, and I want it on before we get into the operating room. Got it? That's defensive medicine, Curtis. Cover your ass."

As a nurse ran to the telephone to summon the neurosurgeon on call, everyone turned to look at Stein. He was the surgeon — the board-certified surgeon.

"Dr. Berger, your intravenous line is okay for the emergency room," Stein said easily, "but we'll need a better CVP setup."

Dave took care of the CVP, then watched Stein prep and swab Jarvis's neck and right shoulder with betadine solution and stick a large bore needle into the big blue vein under the surface of the collarbone.

"Central venous line," Stein said quietly. "Now we're covered. The patient is young and has a strong heart. He shouldn't need a Swan Ganz."

Dave felt like kicking himself. He should have had the

line put in before Stein arrived. He felt — and had performed — more like the intern on the case.

"What will you do about the bullets?" Startled, Dave whirled around as he realized one of the police officers was addressing him. "Will you be taking out the bullets? We'll need them, if possible."

"I'm not the surgeon," Dave said, "only the assistant here. Ask Dr. —"

"We'll try to get the bullets," Stein cut in. "Exactly what happened?"

"Jarvis was driving along the San Diego Freeway south to Beverly Hills. A truck entered on the Sunset Boulevard ramp and cut him off. Jarvis swerved into the next lane. Then he apparently opened his window and gave the truck driver the finger as he passed. The truck driver caught up with Jarvis, forced him off the freeway, then started smashing his car with a lead pipe."

Dave watched Stein probe the rigid muscles in Jarvis's belly; the bowel sounds were fading fast, which meant there was plenty of trouble internally.

"Jarvis got out of his car and punched the truck driver in the stomach," the officer continued. "The driver went back to his truck and returned with a gun. Then he blasted Jarvis twice, right in his guts, in full view of a couple of people."

"We'd better get him into the OR quick," Stein said.

"His belly's pretty rigid," Dave offered. "I'm sure he got his liver and spleen."

"And maybe the pancreas," Stein added, as the neurosurgeon arrived and quickly put the note on Jarvis's chart that they'd been waiting for.

"Shave his belly!" Stein shouted to the emergency room nurse. "Get the blood going as soon as you can. We'll meet you in the OR."

Curtis and Dave were joined by Dr. Stein as they hurried to the OR. Stein, who was in his second year as general surgeon and had an office in Dave's building, had come to Los Angeles a year after Dave. He was on a first-name basis with most of the country's leading surgeons. He was state of the art in medicine, right up to his ass in certificates. He also wrote articles in medical and surgical journals. He had passed his boards just six months ago, when Dave had failed for the second time.

Dave, Stein, and Curtis stopped in the waiting room, where Jarvis's family was gathered. "He's gonna be very sick," Stein told them quickly. "We'll do our best, and we'll talk to you right after."

As they entered the scrub room, Stein said, "I usually make it sound much worse. I always tell them the patient is probably going to die. We've got to cover our asses. We could be sued in a hundred different ways in a case like this." Looking pointedly at Dave, he added, "Boards or no boards, we've all got to protect ourselves from the patients."

"Defensive medicine," said Curtis. Though he was just beginning family practice, Curtis was going to be second assistant. Curtis, too, had his boards.

As the three approached the operating table, a nurse was prepping the patient, sloshing betadine solution over his abdomen. Then towels and sheets were placed over the patient so that only the abdomen was visible. Stein took his place at the right side of the table, while Dave stood on the left with Curtis at his elbow. The two bullet wounds stared up at them.

Stein picked up a scalpel and cut into the midline from the xyphoid process to the pubic areas, opening the entire belly, and from there into the linea alba, the white tendon sheath that opened into the peritoneal cavity. He was greeted by a spurt of dark clotted blood.

"Pressure, eighty over forty!" shouted Horowitz, the anesthesiologist.

"He's full of clots," Dave said.

"Must have gotten the spleen, maybe the liver."

Stein and Dave scooped out the clotted blood into a special bucket as Curtis muttered, "God, the kid isn't gonna make it."

"Don't be too sure," Stein retorted.

They scooped out three bucketsful of clotted blood and suction took care of a fourth. Then Stein reached down and delivered the spleen with his right hand. There was a bullet hole the size of a small golf ball through the center, and the splenic artery was pumping briskly. He quickly put two clamps over the splenic blood vessels.

"Scissors!" he called.

After a few minutes, the situation appeared under control, the spleen resting in a bucket, yet Stein continued to probe Jarvis's belly.

Dave stared at the spleen. Not exactly state of the art, he thought. The professor at the Chicago course had said, "Don't take out the spleen if you can help it. If you must remove it, document on the chart and in your operative note that you damned well spent a long time, even several hours, trying to save it. Document it for the patients, the doctors, and the lawyers. Cover your ass."

Dave had written on his outline in bright red letters, "Whatever you do, leave the fucking spleen alone!"

Dave knew the spleen had to come out. It was shot to hell, right through the middle. But Stein was board-certified and so could get away with it. If Dave had done it, he'd be looking at some very deep trouble.

"Another fucking Z-number — no insurance," Curtis whispered to Dave. "My fifth this week. I got out of bed at three the other morning for a heart attack patient. Again, no insurance. At five, a drug overdose came in. I worked on him from five to seven; as soon as the guy came out of it, he told me to fuck off and signed out of the hospital, against medical advice."

"Come on, Dave, hold back the fucking retractor!" Stein bellowed. "I have to see the pancreas."

The pancreas, especially the tail, was disintegrated. It looked like mush where the bullet had pierced it.

Stein scooped out as much pancreatic tissue as he could. Then, using a large hemoclip and stitches, he tried to get control of the oozing tissue. After five bottles of saline irrigation, the left upper quadrant became a little clearer. Another nick in the left lobe of the liver was seen, and was briskly sutured with heavy chromic ties.

Dave glanced at Curtis. The guy looked so tired. He was a general practitioner with three years of residency in family practice, but that didn't help much. During Curtis's first month in private practice, he saw eight patients; seven were on Medi-Cal, and four of them had forgotten their stickers.

Stein was now looking through twenty-odd feet of Jarvis's intestine. "There's a leak!" he shouted suddenly, as putrid greenish fluid oozed out of a ragged hole in the center of the intestine. He lifted the area out of Jarvis's belly entirely and said, "We'll have to resect," then ran the rest of the bowel to make sure there were no other holes.

Stein put a clean blue towel around the damaged area, clamped the blood supply and the intestines, and removed them from the field. Two ends of intestine faced him — two empty tubes that had to be sewn together in two layers.

As the silk stitches were passed from scrub nurse to surgeon, Stein got into the rhythm of it. Curtis held the intestine in balance. Stitch, tie, hold, stitch, tie, cut.

Dave looked across at Stein's face and saw that sweat was beading on the surgeon's forehead. He immediately thought of a fairy tale he'd written as a child.

Little Duck and Big Camel were walking down the

road in Animal Land. "I think it's better to be big," Big Camel said.

"I think it's better to be little," said Little Duck.

Dave liked that — instant conflict.

Stitch, sew, cut, stitch, sew, cut. Gradually, Jarvis's small intestine was coming together. Curtis reminded Dave of Big Camel and Stein of Little Duck. Maybe it was their size, or the way Curtis hunched over the OR table, while Stein seemed to be waddling through the case.

Dave thought of Little Duck and Big Camel coming to a high wall; on the other side of it was a large apple tree. Little Duck couldn't reach the apples, but Big Camel could. "See, I told you it's better to be big," said Big Camel, chewing on the apple.

"Oh, nuts," said Little Duck.

"Chomp, chomp," said Big Camel.

Big Camel smiled, while Little Duck went into an acute schizophrenic depression.

Stein finished the anastamosis and irrigated the belly more.

All of a sudden Curtis wrinkled his nose. "I smell gas," he said quickly. "Shit!"

And there it was, a large hole in the left colon where the bullet had ripped the splenic flexure.

"Shit!" Curtis said again.

"We'll have to bring the proximal end out as a colostomy on his abdominal wall," Dave said. "I think we can bury the distal end and come back later, if there is a later."

The colostomy was accomplished quickly, the distal end was closed, and Stein irrigated the entire belly with saline and antibiotic solution. The surgeon began to relax as he closed the peritoneal layer with a running chromic and asked for a large retention suture for the anterior abdominal wall.

"Give him another gram of Gentomycin IV and add some Cleocin," Stein ordered. "We might as well cover him with all guns. If he makes it through the first twenty-four hours, infection call kill him as well as anything."

Dave thought of Little Duck and Big Camel again. This time they came to a tree with even bigger, better apples than the first. This time the wall was so big that even Big Camel couldn't reach over it. But there was a little door in the wall, and Little Duck scooted through it and picked up an apple that had fallen to the ground.

"See, I told you it's better to be little," said Little Duck, chewing on his apple.

"Oh, nuts," said Big Camel.

"Chomp, chomp," said Little Duck.

"Six tubes and drains," Curtis groaned, as Stein went about putting Jarvis back together. "Six is a bad sign."

Even Dave knew that any patient who left the OR with more than five tubes, drains, or needles hadn't much chance of surviving.

Chapter Three

Dave returned to his emergency room duties at seven twenty-five A.M., while Stein and Curtis worked on closing up Jarvis's belly.

He was only a few feet from the emergency entrance when a woman ran in and screamed, "There's been an accident in the parking lot! It's Dr. Winston! He's badly hurt!"

"Get a stretcher, stat!" Dave shouted at an orderly, then ran out to the parking lot.

Dark clouds swirled past the sun, casting strange shadows on the puddles on the ground. A small crowd had already begun to gather around Dr. Winston, who lay on the wet pavement in the emergency drive. Blood flowed freely from the side of his head, staining his silver hair and mixing with the puddle of water under him. His arms and legs were twisted in unnatural positions.

"It was an ambulance," said someone in the crowd. "Didn't even see him, it was going so fast."

"Where's the ambulance?" Dave demanded.

The woman who had come rushing into the emergency entrance answered flatly, "It didn't stop. The driver seemed to be in a big hurry, even though he didn't have his siren on."

Dave shook his head slowly before kneeling to examine Dr. Winston. He was alive, but barely. His injuries were very serious. Besides a concussion and numerous contusions, there probably were fractures and, most critical, internal injuries that might be hemorrhaging.

Dave barked orders to the nurses and orderlies hovering around. Emily Harris was among them; he'd snapped at her several times at the beginning of the shift.

"Who's the surgeon on panel this morning?"

"Dr. Collins," she replied testily.

"Call him! And see that he's got an operating room!"

As Emily rushed back to the emergency room, Dave turned to another nurse. "Get an IV started!"

He didn't trust the orderlies, so he helped lift Winston onto the stretcher himself, and he stayed with the stretcher all the way into the hospital. No one said much. They had all seen patients come into the emergency room in much worse condition than Dr. Winston, but this accident had occurred on the premises and affected them personally.

And it had been caused by someone who worked with them, who had been charged with the responsibility of saving lives but who was clearly too reckless to care. Dave vowed to find out who had been driving that ambulance and to see that, at the very least, he lost his job. But for now Dave had to be concerned with saving Winston's life.

While Dr. Winston was being X-rayed, Dave grew increasingly anxious. He had asked Emily to call the surgeon on panel, but no one had arrived. Winston had to be operated on soon, or there would be little chance of saving him. His heartbeat was erratic and his belly appeared to be swelling, a sure sign of internal hemorrhaging.

Dave located Emily as she was coming out of the ladies' room. "Did you call Collins?" he demanded.

She bristled. "No one knows where he is. His service insists he's here at the hospital. I've paged him, but he hasn't answered."

"Well, page him again!" Dave snapped. "There isn't much time!"

She turned and stalked off toward the nurses' station.

Dave called after her, "Do we have anybody as back-up, in case Collins isn't available?"

"There's Dr. Whitaker," she replied, "but he's in surgery and isn't expected out for at least another forty-five minutes. Otherwise, there's just you and Dr. Nino. And Stein and Curtis are still involved with that Jarvis gunshot case. Besides, Stein is off duty now. He's been up all night, and has a gallbladder to do at another hospital, which he's late for already."

Nino was the new man, even less experienced than Dave. It would be a greater breach of hospital protocol for Nino to operate on Dr. Winston.

Dave was barely acquainted with Andrew Collins, the son-in-law of Tony Manchester, who was chairman of the board of the hospital. But he knew him by reputation; Collins was the most successful young surgeon at Beverly Hills.

Andrew Collins was in his early forties. His patients were movie stars, politicians, and leaders of business and industry. Photographs of Collins and his beautiful wife appeared regularly in the society pages of the newspapers. When movies or television shows needed a medical consultant, it was Dr. Andrew Collins who was called. He also owned a sizable piece of stock in Beverly Hills Hospital.

He wasn't the sort of person Dave would have crossed intentionally.

But after he had checked with Emily twice more and

she had shrugged and told him, "Still no word from Dr. Collins," Dave took a deep breath and made the decision to take Winston into surgery himself, with Dr. Nino assisting — at least until Collins arrived. If there was any trouble later, he would have witnesses. After all, he reasoned, it was Collins who was being irresponsible. When a surgeon was on emergency room call, he was supposed to respond immediately.

"Let's start our antibiotics now, before surgery," he said to Emily. "Eighty milligrams Tobramycin — that ought to get the gram negatives. And six hundred milligrams Cleocin IV — for the anaerobes."

Emily gave him a strange look. "I'm sorry if I'm out of line, Dr. Berger, but I've worked in the ER long enough to know that to give aminoglycoside, which is potentially nephro-toxic in the face of possible damage to the kidney and shock that —"

"Just do what I tell you," Dave said brusquely. "I'm the doctor here."

As Emily scurried off to start the IV's, Dave thought back to the course in Chicago and a lecture titled Antiobiots: State of the Art. On potential abdominal trauma, with rupture of the intestine or possible damage to the liver or pancreas, the surgeon was faced with two possibilities: to start the patient on a broad-spectrum antibiotic like cephalosporin, or, if he anticipated trouble in the belly, an aminoglycoside, and a second antibiotic to cover the anaerobes, which were so plentiful in the colon.

Dr. Winston's life was on the line. Dave suspected at least liver and colon injuries, maybe small intestine and pancreas, and perhaps more. He looked around again. Still no Andrew Collins.

He went over the X rays with Dr. Nino, who pointed out multiple pelvic fractures. "Maybe we ought to get a cystogram to evaluate the bladder and urethra."

"I have a urinalysis," Dave said. "It's clear. I don't think we need the cystogram."

"How about a one-shot IVP?"

"Don't have the time," Dave said. "It's a judgment, and we'd all be more comfortable knowing how the kidneys, ureters, urethra and bladder look, but —"

"I think it would be a good idea," Nino interrupted, "particularly since Collins hasn't arrived yet. This way we could have it all ready for him."

"But Winston's in shock!" Dave cried. "I don't want him to die in X ray."

Over Nino's objection and a second look from Emily, the one-shot IVP was bypassed. Dr. Winston was given his two intravenous antibiotics and taken to the surgery suite.

"Hemoglobin is slightly down. I'd expect that with some internal bleeding and those pelvic fractures," Dave said to Nino. "Must have lost a unit or two in there."

"The white count and amylase are up, too," Nino replied.

Dave hesitated for a fraction of a second, then instructed Emily to have Winston prepped for surgery, and he went in to scrub.

Chapter Four

The traffic on the wet, slippery freeway was moving at about twenty miles an hour. Andrew Collins swore as he switched lanes, trying unsuccessfully to maneuver his way ahead of the other cars.

Normally, Collins wouldn't have been concerned about being late to the hospital, but this morning was different for several reasons, not the least of which being that he wasn't coming from his home. His wife and his answering service believed he had spent the night in his office at the hospital, but he had stayed at Lina Lathrop's apartment in the valley.

He didn't feel guilty about his affair with Lina, nor did it bother him that he might be hurting his wife. Alice had gotten over her jealousy about two years and twenty women ago.

What bothered him was how he would look walking into the hospital over an hour late. He knew that he looked haggard and that his clothes looked as if they had been slept in. He would have to remember to leave a change of clothes in Lina's closet. He had already left a toothbrush and razor in her bathroom.

Collins wondered if he should go to his office and freshen up before checking with the emergency room. Appearances mattered to him because they mattered to other people. He had worked very hard at creating an image, and he would not allow anything to spoil it.

Thirty years ago, Andrew Collins might easily have been a movie star. He was tall and lean, with a perfect tan, which he kept all year and which made his eyes seem bluer and his hair blonder. When he smiled, his cheeks dimpled, and he flashed perfectly even white teeth, which, he was proud, had not even been capped. He was forty-four, but with women he admitted only to thirty-nine.

He dressed impeccably — Gucci loafers, Bill Blass slacks and jacket, Cartier tank watch. And he had a beautiful and celebrated wife, who complemented him perfectly at social functions. However, as a singer who had been something of a celebrity, she was recognized by few people today. She had given up her successful career to have a baby, then had insisted that she preferred the life of a wife and mother. After fourteen years away from the spotlight, her public had forgotten her.

At the time, Alice had insisted that singing meant nothing to her. She had taken it up after college simply to have something to do. Because she was Tony Manchester's daughter, it had been easy for her to get a recording contract and nightclub and television bookings. It was nothing special to her. She had grown up surrounded by show business, and she viewed it simply as work. What she really wanted was a husband and children.

Or so she thought fourteen years ago, maybe even ten years ago. But now she regretted her choices. She and Collins had not been happy together for a long time, and she had quickly grown bored with her domestic life.

Collins had encouraged her to go back to singing, but she refused. And, finally, she had turned on him. "Why do you want it so bad? Do you think my being famous will bring you more patients?"

That had angered Collins, mainly because he knew there was a certain amount of truth in her words. He didn't need the patients, but he liked the prestige of being married to an entertainer. Still, he hadn't brought the subject up again. They went on with keeping up the appearance of being the perfect couple, showing up at all the right parties and events, entertaining regularly in their elegant Spanish-style mansion, which was listed in the Hollywood tourist map along with the names of each of the famous film stars who had owned it.

Collins was aware that all of this could crumble. People loved to talk — especially people who worked at hospitals. They thrived on gossip, the more malicious, the better.

If anyone at the hospital found out about Collins's affair with Lina Lathrop, the image he had worked so hard to achieve would be blown to bits. And images were what Beverly Hills was all about.

Collins's most serious problem was that Lina didn't fit into his plans at all. She was an accident. She should have been like all the other women Collins had been involved with since his marriage — she should have left his life as quickly as she had come into it. But he hadn't wanted her to go. He had never known a woman to hold his interest for so long, and he feared that he might be in love with her.

Collins had met Lina on the set of "The Medicine Man," the new television show for which he was the technical consultant. A Tony Manchester production, it was Lina's first major acting job. While she had only a small part, it was an important role, a continuing character who appeared in almost every episode. Collins had noticed her on the first day of shooting. More importantly, she had noticed him. In fact, she had made the first move.

Lina was beautiful. She didn't have that willowy thinness or the half-starved look that so many actresses cultivated. Instead, Lina was luxuriantly voluptuous, and her sexual appetite insatiable. But it was Lina's attitude that made her endlessly intriguing. She seemed so much more in control of herself than other women; she never demanded beyond the moment.

It had been she, not he, who had set the limits on their relationship. "I don't like possessiveness. When we're apart, or when we're working, we don't owe each other anything. But when we're together, I won't allow anything to interfere with us — not even your work. Your emergency beeper has to be turned off from the time you come in my door until the time you leave."

With a start, Collins realized he had forgotten to turn his pager back on after he had left Lina's place. He was easing onto the Wilshire Boulevard off-ramp as he reached into his pocket to turn it on. Instantly it began the irritating beeping sound. He switched it off again. There was nothing he could do about it now; to stop and find a phone would only delay him more. Since he was on panel this morning, it was probably the hospital paging him, and he couldn't possibly get there any faster.

The traffic on Wilshire Boulevard was as bad as that on the freeway. Everything seemed to be conspiring against him today. He hadn't even wanted to go to work this morning. It was the kind of cool, rainy day when he would have loved to stay in bed with Lina, dozing between the lovemaking. He thought about how she looked when he'd left, her soft pink body wrapped in the sheets, and he sighed; he could still smell her delicate fragrance.

It was at such times that he ached to have her forever.

He thought about divorcing Alice and marrying Lina, but this always brought him up short, abruptly ending his reverie. There was no way he could divorce Tony Manchester's daughter without losing everything he had gained at Beverly Hills Hospital. His entire medical practice was dependent on his part in the hospital partnership, and there was no woman on earth for whom it was worth giving up everything.

The traffic eased a bit as Collins neared Beverly Hills Hospital. The great facade of white marble and tinted-brown glass was impressive, and each time Collins approached from this direction, a thrill of pride, and possibly of possessiveness, gripped him.

It was the best-equipped hospital west of the Mississippi, and its executive wing was the most luxurious in the world. For patients who could afford it, there were suites with plush carpeting and French-provincial furnishings, and the finest catered meals, served on the best china, silver, and crystal.

Collins looked forward to the day when he would no longer have to deal with Medicare and welfare patients, emergency rooms and questions of insurance coverage. He had always had to steel himself to face his emergency room duties and to perform surgery on patients for whom he felt nothing but disdain or revulsion. It wasn't so much that he disliked being reminded of poverty and suffering as it was that he could not bear having his life taken up by people for whom he felt no commitment.

As he hurried through the chill rain toward the emergency entrance, the image of Lina Lathrop flashed into his head again. It was the word *commitment* that had brought her to mind — the way she had looked as he slipped into her bed last night, her soft warm body, naked, honest, and vulnerable. Collins wanted her to commit her life to him as he wanted to commit himself to her. The fact that he couldn't frustrated him.

The insistent beeping decided him; he would not go to his office to change. If anyone noticed his appearance he hoped they would attribute it to the rain.

But as he approached the nurses' station and saw that Emily Harris was on duty, he was assailed by doubts. She was an incessant gossip and was always coming on to him with a flirtatious manner that invited an advance. Collins had always kept his distance, knowing she would take even the slightest show of friendliness as something to talk about with the rest of the staff.

As soon as she saw him, Emily got up from the desk, her eyebrows raised, her lips pursed. "Where have you been, Dr. Collins?" she called in a voice that was unnecessarily loud. "We've been trying to reach you for almost an hour. We've got an emergency."

"I got the message," Collins lied, "but I was on an emergency of my own. I got here as quickly as I could. What's the case?"

Emily gave him an odd look. "If you got the message, you should know," she said. "It's Dr. Winston. He's already been wheeled into emergency surgery."

"Dr. Winston?" Collins asked incredulously. "But who's going to operate?"

"Dr. Berger," Emily said with a smirk. "With Dr. Nino assisting."

"Jesus!" Collins almost winced. With a patient as important as Dr. Winston being operated on by a lowly emergency room assistant, there were bound to be questions. The surgery committee would want to know why the surgeon on call hadn't been available.

"I know it's against regulations, but Dr. Berger insisted on doing the surgery himself," Emily explained.

She continued to talk, but Collins was no longer listening. The first rule of surgery — "cover your ass," which he had learned years ago in med school — was all he could think about. He knew he couldn't possibly come up with an excuse that the surgery committee would accept. All he could do was get to the OR as quickly as he could, and pray that he would arrive in time to take over.

Emily was still trying to explain what had happened as he sprinted off down the hall.

The doctors' locker room was empty, which meant that Berger had already suited up for surgery. Panic gripped Collins. What if he was too late? He grabbed a fresh green suit, struggled into the pants, and, with the shirt half on and the cap and mask in his hand, rushed out into the scrub area.

Berger, who had just finished scrubbing, was standing outside the OR, talking with Dr. Nino, Dr. Horowitz, the anesthesiologist, and one of the nurses.

As soon as Dave saw Collins, he reached up and pulled down his mask. "Dr. Collins," he said weakly, "you're just in time."

"It's damned lucky for you that I am! What the hell do you think you're doing, Berger?"

"Phil Winston is in b-b-bad shape," Dave stammered, his face reddening. "I had to act fast. If he doesn't have —"

"You're only an employee here," Collins said coldly. "You're supposed to call the surgeon on panel, not take cases yourself. You don't have the skill to handle a difficult case."

"Dammit! Collins, we tried to reach you! There wasn't any time. And besides I'm board-eligible —"

"You've flunked the oral exam twice, Berger. We all know that. Remember those tests? They're designed to show how you react under pressure, in emergency situations like this, to show how *safe* a surgeon you are. I'm going into surgery; you get back to your job."

"But I want you to understand that I was simply trying to —"

"Tell that to the hospital committee," Collins shot back. "Right now, I've got work to do." He turned his back on Dave and began scrubbing. When he had finished only the nurse and Dr. Nino remained, waiting for instructions.

"What's Winston's condition?" Collins addressed Nino. "Heart attack?"

The young assistant stared at him. "You mean you don't know?"

"Of course I don't know! I just got here!"

Spots of color appeared high on Nino's cheeks. "He was hit by an ambulance. He's still unconscious, and his condition is critical."

An accident? Collins's mind whirled. But of course it wasn't an accident. Collins had been so preoccupied that he had forgotten the political situation at the hospital. *The final meeting was to have been this morning.* Winston obviously hadn't changed his mind, so this was their only alternative. Now Collins wished he had let Berger go ahead with the surgery.

Collins saw that Nino was staring curiously at him. Self-consciously, he cleared his throat and said stiffly, "Let's get moving."

The rest of the operating team was in position around the table. Winston had been shaved and prepped, the iodine smeared across his belly almost hiding the tire mark just below the rib cage. The body hadn't been draped yet; and, despite the lacerations on the face and the tube that had been inserted into the throat to help his breathing, it was clearly Phil Winston.

Collins surveyed the people around the table. They were all looking at him. *How much do they know?* he wondered. *Do they suspect?*

His head was spinning and he felt nauseated. He knew his hands were shaking, so he kept them at his sides.

"Let's . . . let's . . ." His voice cracked. "We'd better

get to work." With a sense of relief, he thought, *Winston can't possibly survive.* He turned to the head of the table. "How's his blood pressure?"

The anesthesiologist shook his head. "Weak. Very weak. Pulse is sky-high, too. We've got three IV's running wide open, plus an arterial line."

By the time Winston was draped and only a two-foot section of his skin was visible, Collins was in control and ready to begin. His actions were automatic. With the knife held firmly in his rubber-gloved right hand, he made a neat incision from the rib cage to the pelvic area, baring the thin yellow layer of fat beneath the skin. Another quick cut along the same line and he was inside.

Dark blood began to spurt over the pale flesh, flowing freely into the crisp white towels.

"Suction!" he barked. "And sponges!"

His skill notwithstanding, Collins knew that Phil Winston's chances were very slim. "Liver's been lacerated," he said to Nino, eyeing the eight-centimeter cut across the right lobe of the liver, from which bright red blood was pouring. With Nino's assistance, Collins quickly sutured it.

He then searched the abdominal cavity and found two holes in the small intestine, which he sutured.

"There were multiple pelvic fractures," Nino told him. "And look at the size of that hematoma around the kidneys! Talk about three pints of pure clot!"

"What did the cystogram and IVP show?" Collins asked. "I assume you got one in the emergency room?"

Nino hesitated. "Well . . . Dr. Berger thought there might not be time."

"What do you mean? That's mandatory. Any patient with pelvic fractures has to have a film of the kidney and bladder, to show that his urinary tract, not to mention the fucking urethra, is intact."

"Berger said the urine was clear, and . . . the X ray wasn't necessary — there wasn't time. And he didn't want the patient to die in X ray."

"Damn him! I can't tell shit from piss in here — everything's one big bloody mess."

Collins continued to explore and found a deep cut in the dome of the left kidney.

"See that? This kidney was almost sliced in two. It would have helped to know that before surgery."

Finding the rest of the kidney and urinary tract intact, he quickly sutured the kidney.

"Let's put the patient on something for anaerobes," he said briskly. "Now that we know the full extent of the trauma, broad-spectrum isn't enough."

Collins was still muttering under his breath when he saw blood gush from the area of the right kidney.

"Quick! Let's get control of the renal pedicle," he said to Nino as blood poured into the wound, covering Winston's belly and soaking into the doctors' uniforms.

"Quick!" We're losing him on the table!"

"No blood pressure," Dr. Horowitz said glumly. "Forty over twenty, now zero, now zero over zero."

Collins and Nino moved feverishly to try to get control of the kidney.

"I can't do it," Collins said finally. "I can't stop the bleeding. He's not going to make it. That goddamned Berger! The IVP would have shown . . . we could have —"

"No heartbeat, no heartbeat . . . cardiac arrest," Horowitz interrupted.

"Adrenaline, stat!" Collins yelled.

The scrub nurse handed him a full syringe and he injected it directly through the diaphragm into Winston's heart.

The operating team worked without letup for the next two hours, trying to control the hemorrhage and bring Dr. Winston back to life.

Chapter Five

The officer had treated her like a silly old fool, but Melissa Baxter was accustomed to that. It was the way almost all young people behaved toward women of her class and age, and Melissa accepted it. In fact, she did more than accept it: She worked it to her advantage.

Melissa Baxter was no fool, but playing the fool was her way of surviving in a tough, competitive business that was dominated by men, and generally, men who were much younger than she. These were the men who would tolerate a sweet motherly woman who usually knitted while she discussed business. Their suspicions suspended, they granted her the kind of concessions they would deny one another.

But Melissa was tempted not to play the fool with the police officer. She was even tempted to tell him everything she knew, but she very wisely resisted the temptation. It would hardly do Dr. Winston any good now. Everything she told the officer was true, of course; it just wasn't the whole truth.

She was the only eyewitness to the accident.

"Dr. Winston and I have been friends for a great many years," she explained. That was true. "We arranged to have breakfast together in the hospital cafeteria before the board meeting this morning." She did not tell the officer that someone else had suggested the breakfast.

"What time was that?" the officer asked.

"It was very loose," Melissa said evasively, surprised by the direct question. "We said 'about nine o'clock.' "

"Okay. Go ahead."

"I must have arrived only a moment or two after he did," she continued. "After I got out of my car, I saw him walking across the parking lot toward the entrance to the hospital. I called out to him, but he didn't seem to hear. I was hurrying to catch up with him when I saw the ambulance." She paused, aware that she had to very precise. "It was moving toward him very fast, but I assumed he would see it, or that the driver would turn on the siren, or stop, or something. It was almost on him before I screamed." Again she paused, trying to calm the trembling of her hands and voice. "He turned, but he barely had time to see the ambulance before it hit him."

"Did the driver slow down?" the officer asked. "Or try to stop at all?"

Melissa shook her head. "No. But I'm sure he must have known what happened because he increased his speed to get out of the parking lot onto the street."

"Did you see the driver's face?"

"No," she answered honestly. "There wasn't time to look. All I could think of was to get a doctor quickly, so I ran into the emergency room."

The officer went through her story again and asked for more details, but Melissa had done her part. Finally, he left her to question others and to look into the problem of the ambulance. An alert had been put out for it as soon as the police arrived at the scene, but there was a problem: So far no one had been able to account for its presence at the hospital.

Melissa glanced at the large clock on the wall, aware that she should go upstairs to the boardroom soon, but she was reluctant to leave the emergency area until she knew what Dr. Winston's condition was. She was also afraid to face the board meeting now.

So she was there in the emergency waiting area when Dr. Collins had rushed in, uncharacteristically disheveled. She was sitting quietly in a corner, working at her knitting, and so she heard his exchange with the nurse and saw him hurry off toward the OR. She thought she understood Dr. Collins's place in the scheme of things, but she wasn't entirely sure. His arriving late at the hospital, and his behavior, didn't quite fit.

She had felt better about having that young Dr. Berger looking after her friend, and she prayed that Dr. Collins would be too late. Melissa had never met Dr. Berger, but Phil Winston had told her much about him, and she had simply been waiting for the proper moment to enlist him in her program. Winston had great regard for Berger's medical skill, but, more important to Melissa, Berger was having a difficult time getting a practice started.

Soon after Collins rushed off to the surgery suite, Berger stormed into the emergency room. She wouldn't have known him but for his nameplate, but she liked what she saw. Berger was tall, with a squarish build. Dark hair framed a ruggedly handsome face that now wore a deep scowl. Melissa was most taken with his eyes, which were very dark, very intense, and which, she suspected, made some people very uncomfortable. Melissa doubted that he'd talk now, but she had to find out what Dr. Winston's condition was.

She got to her feet quickly and moved toward him,

taking her knitting with her. "Dr. Berger," she called, "could I speak to you a moment, please?"

He stopped and stared at her, his scowl indicating that he had no idea who she was. As she drew near, she could see that he was making an effort to submerge his anger.

"How is Dr. Winston?" she asked, aware that her voice sounded shrill and nasal.

"Are you a member of the family?" Berger responded, looking at her curiously.

"No. My name is Melissa Baxter." She paused, waiting to see if her name prompted any recognition, then continued: "Dr. Winston and I have been friends and business associates for a long time."

A slightly incredulous look crossed his face, and he almost smiled. She often had that effect on doctors when they met her for the first time.

His response was to be indulgent with her. "Dr. Winston's condition is very serious," he said gently, "but he's in very capable hands. Dr. Collins is operating on him right now."

"That's not very reassuring," she muttered.

"Pardon?" He looked at her in surprise. "He's one of the very best surgeons we have here."

"I know who he is," Melissa said sharply and was immediately sorry when she saw anger and confusion collide on his face. She smiled. "I'm sorry. I'm very concerned about Phil. You know, he's told me a great deal about you. He says you're one of the finest young doctors on the staff. I think, if he had any choice, he would have preferred to have you performing the surgery."

Dave stiffened slightly. "The hospital has its rules and regulations," he said. "I had the shift last night. We should be grateful that Dr. Collins arrived in time."

"Yes, of course." Melissa nodded. "I understand." She paused, trying to decide how frank she could be with Dr. Berger. There was much she wanted to know, but she didn't want to cause him to wonder about her. Finally she asked, "Tell me, Dr. Berger, if *you* were operating on Dr. Winston, what would you say his chances would be?"

He tried to give her his best bedside smile. "Don't worry. I think he'll be okay."

"No." Melissa shook her head. "He won't. I just wondered if you thought you might have saved him."

By now she had so confused and disarmed Dave that he relaxed and said quickly, "His chances are not good, I admit. But I can't speculate on what I might have done."

She smiled sweetly. "Thank you, Dr. Berger. That's all I wanted to know. I don't want to take up your time right now. . . ." She paused to rummage in her plastic knitting bag and said distractedly, "But if you don't mind, I'd like to talk to you again in a day or so."

She finally came up with a business card, a little bent from lying beneath her knitting, and handed it to him.

Dave started to reach for his wallet to return the courtesy, but she stopped him. "That's not necessary. I know where your office is. The only reason I haven't seen you before is that it's such an inconvenient location." She smiled brightly. "But we can change all that."

He looked down at her card. "Maturity Medical Services?"

"Yes, that's my business. Senior citizens who need doctors come to us, and we find them doctors who need patients."

Dave laughed. "You really are a business associate of Dr. Winston's?"

"Oh, yes," she said easily. "Now, I really have taken up too much of your time, and I must be getting upstairs to the board meeting. We'll talk again soon."

She was aware that Dr. Berger stared after her as she

walked down the hall to the elevators. She didn't mind. She derived a certain pleasure in taking people by surprise.

She wasn't looking forward to the board meeting, but she had to attend, if for no other reason than for Phil Winston's sake. She owed him at least that much loyalty.

From the very beginning Dr. Winston had helped her to make Maturity Medical Services work. He had been the first doctor to take on her patients; and when the program had gotten off the ground, he had helped her to buy stock in Beverly Hills Hospital.

Of course, she was only a limited partner — the general partnership was restricted to doctors — and her vote meant nothing on issues such as the sale of the hospital, which was the critical matter before the board right now.

Melissa Baxter and Phil Winston had opposed the sale of Beverly Hills Hospital to the Betco Corporation, but only Phil Winston's vote mattered. On something as important as this, the vote of the general partners had to be unanimous. Phil Winston had been the only doctor who would not benefit from the sale, for Betco refused to guarantee continuation of his emergency room contract with the new management.

Melissa had backed Winston out of personal loyalty, although she suspected that a change in the hospital administration could affect Maturity Services adversely.

Melissa's company supplied a `necessary and beneficial service to the elderly, a service that the government should have provided but didn't. Medicare was supposed to guarantee medical care to the elderly, but in reality it didn't always work. It was difficult enough for young people with private insurance to find a doctor when they needed one, but it was virtually impossible for someone who was old and sick and couldn't afford to pay more than Medicare paid.

She had made that discovery six years ago, when her

in-laws had retired and moved to Los Angeles to be near her. Because Melissa had worked in the billing department of Beverly Hills Hospital for a few years, she had been able to find them a doctor fairly easily, but then her friends at the senior citizens' recreation center had begun to solicit her help, and even offered to pay for her services.

In the beginning, Melissa hadn't expected it to grow into a profitable business; she hadn't realized how many desperate old people there were or how many doctors were in need of patients. Within five years, she had accumulated a list of more than fifty thousand patients and scores of doctors covering every possible specialty. She was able to provide her patients with any kind of doctor they needed at a moment's notice, and that doctor would charge no more than Medicare allowed.

Melissa was just about to step into the elevator to go upstairs when she heard someone call her name. Turning, she saw the police officer she had spoken with earlier. "If you can spare a moment," he said, as he approached her with long, hurried strides, "I'd like to talk to you some more."

"Yes, of course," she replied.

"It's very important," he said gently. "I want you to try very hard to remember anything you can about that ambulance driver."

Melissa studied his face. "I told you I didn't really notice anything about him," she said. "So what's up?"

"We've found the ambulance, but not the driver. You see, it was stolen."

"Stolen," she repeated slowly.

"The ambulance was found abandoned about twelve blocks from the hospital. Some drugs were missing from it, so it's fairly clear why it was stolen. It isn't the first time an addict has done this sort of thing. But we have no clue about the man's identity, and you're the only person who might have seen his face."

Melissa found it difficult to conceal her amazement. It was the perfect crime, made possible by creating the perfect accident.

"Do you remember anything?" the officer pressed in response to her long silence.

"No," she said shaking her head. "I'm sorry, I wish I could help."

She walked into the elevator, barely aware of what she was doing. For the first time, she was afraid for her own safety. How far would they go? She was perhaps the only person who was not with them. Would she, too, have to be eliminated?

She shuddered.

Melissa had no real proof, but she knew enough to be suspicious. She couldn't even be sure who was behind it or how many of them were involved. In fact, she had only one reason to question the situation at all.

On Wednesday of last week, the talks between Betco and the hospital had broken down completely, the question of Phil Winston's emergency room contract being the sole obstacle to agreement.

Yesterday, Tony Manchester, the chairman of the board, had called her at home to ask her to try to persuade Phil to change his mind.

"Before the meeting tomorrow, have breakfast with Winston," Tony had urged. "You've got to make him change his mind. It's very important."

Melissa was easily intimidated by Tony Manchester, but she had managed to protest weakly. "You know I couldn't do that."

"Couldn't?" he asked, his voice oily. "Or wouldn't?"

"Dr. Winston is a dear friend of mine, Tony. I wouldn't want to betray that friendship, and I don't think I could make him change his mind even if I wanted to."

Manchester had cleared his throat. "I'm sure neither

you nor Dr. Winston would want any trouble. I know how important Beverly Hills Hospital is to Maturity Medical Services.''

She had made the breakfast appointment with Phil Winston, if only to tell him about Manchester's threat. It hadn't occurred to her that something like this might happen. After all, it was perfectly natural for the two of them to meet and talk before a board meeting.

As she walked down the hall toward the boardroom, past the doors of the executive offices, Melissa's steps were hesitant, irregular. She knew her appearance was incongruous with these surroundings. The lush gold carpeting resisted the pressure of her feet, springing back at her with a firmness and confidence she didn't feel. The gleaming wallpaper, with its splashes of gold foil amid the shades of brown and rust, confused her as it blurred before her eyes. The expensive paintings in their gilt frames and the delicate, ornate French furniture called for silks and satins and laces, not the simple cotton housedress Melissa wore. With the cheap plastic knitting bag bumping clumsily against her hip, there was no way Melissa could even pretend she belonged in such surroundings.

She hesitated before the door of the boardroom, trying to gather the courage to make her entrance. She never liked to call attention to herself in these meetings and always chose an unobtrusive seat away from the table, preferably deep in a corner. Once settled, she took out her knitting, listened quietly to what the others had to say, and never spoke herself.

She listened at the door, but she couldn't hear anything; the door was too thick to permit sounds to pass through. There was no way she could prepare herself. She grasped the doorknob and pushed the big door open.

Either the meeting had been adjourned, or it hadn't begun. The board members were talking and laughing among themselves. The fluorescent lights lent a greenish glow to the room, creating reflections on the highly polished conference table and making it look as if everything was underwater.

It was Tony Manchester who noticed Melissa standing just inside the door.

"Mrs. Baxter." He moved toward her with a pleasant smile. "You're late. Where's Dr. Winston? We've been waiting for him to start the meeting."

Was it possible that Manchester didn't know? Melissa couldn't tell from his manner. Of course, Manchester had been a fine actor at one time.

Melissa frowned, then chose her words carefully. "Dr. Winston is in surgery."

She thought she saw anger flit across Manchester's face. She couldn't tell if it was genuine. "He should have notified us if he had an emergency," he said irritably. "We've been waiting almost half an hour."

Several of the others had stopped talking to listen to them. A few had moved in closer. Now all eyes were on Melissa.

"He isn't performing surgery," she announced. "He's the patient. He was run down by an ambulance in the parking lot this morning."

She was sure that Manchester's response could not have been faked, no matter how good an actor he was. His face turned pale, his eyes glazed over, and his lips trembled.

"An accident?" he repeated. And Melissa knew that, like her, he was wondering if Betco was involved.

"What's his condition?" someone asked from across the room.

Melissa turned and saw Victor Dawson, the head of Betco, watching her intently.

When Melissa didn't respond immediately, he asked, "Was Dr. Winston seriously injured?"

"His condition is critical," she answered finally, her

eyes returning to Tony Manchester. "Dr. Collins has the case but Dr. Berger told me the chances were fifty-fifty."

"Who's this Dr. Berger?" Dawson broke in sharply.

Melissa looked at him again. His eyes had almost disappeared into the folds of flesh surrounding them, but she could feel them burning into her. "Dr. Berger is the emergency room doctor who admitted Dr. Winston and examined him."

Victor Dawson scowled and reached into his jacket pocket for his cigarette case. "I guess there's no point in our meeting today." He lit his cigarette. "No point in anything until we know if Winston comes out okay." He began picking up his papers from the conference table and stuffing them into his alligator attaché case.

The other men looked at Dawson uncomfortably. Melissa was sure they were all thinking the same thing. Victor Dawson had little regard for human feelings, even for human life. He wanted Beverly Hills Hospital for Betco Enterprises, and he appeared to be impatient for Phil Winston to recover or die so he could finish the negotiations. They were all beginning to see the very thing that Phil Winston had suspected from the start: Victor Dawson and Betco Enterprises were not noted for their gentle approach.

Briefcase in hand, Dawson approached Tony Manchester and said brusquely, "I trust you'll inform me when we can meet and resume negotiations?"

"Yes." Manchester sounded almost vague. "I'll call you."

With a brisk nod, Dawson and Bill Benedict, the Betco lawyer, left the boardroom.

Chapter Six

Victor Dawson was a short man, but he could dominate a roomful of giants. The power that emanated from him could not be attributed to anything physical, though. He was paunchy, and his heavily jowled face made him look like a bulldog. His skin, which bore the harsh effects of the sun, was wrinkled and tanned to a leathery hardness. He had a prominent nose, and his small, dark eyes were surrounded by circles of flesh. His black hair, with only a trace of gray, was slicked straight back.

Victor knew that he wasn't as attractive as he had been some years ago. Although he wasn't vain, he was sensitive to the toll that time, hard work, and dissipation had taken on his body, so he tried to make up for it by dressing well. Even in California, where everyone dressed casually, he wore a neatly tailored suit of dark blue with a tiny gray pinstripe, and a crisp white custom-made shirt. His nails were manicured and polished, and he wore several heavy rings, the only loud note in an otherwise conservative appearance.

He knew it was tasteless for a man to wear diamonds and rubies, especially large ones, but he wore them as a symbol of his power. On Victor's small, almost delicate hands the rings attracted people's attention, distracting them from his face. Distracted, they were so easy to surprise.

The sun was threatening to shine as Victor Dawson left Beverly Hills Hospital and walked to the curb, where his chauffeur waited. There was still a damp chill to the air, however, and Dawson didn't want to stand around talking.

"Wait here and let me know when Winston's out of surgery," he instructed Bill Benedict. "I'll be in the car."

"Is that all, sir?" the lawyer asked, his tone almost mocking. "Just let you know he's out?"

Dawson's eyes flashed. "Dammit! Of course I want to know whether he's alive or dead! Otherwise, that's all."

"And then?" Benedict's voice was positively oily.

Dawson exploded. "And then go back to the hotel! Do nothing! Wait for me there!" He turned and climbed into the limousine.

But Benedict stalled, preventing the chauffeur from closing the door. "You do want me to proceed with drawing up the papers?"

"No. Just sit in the hotel and wait for me." He motioned to the chauffeur to close the door.

"Excuse me, sir," the chauffeur said to Benedict, firmly edging him out of the way.

Sometimes Victor Dawson wondered if he had been wrong to hire a lawyer as young as Bill Benedict. The man knew his business, though, of that there was no doubt; he was probably the best lawyer Betco had ever had. But Benedict was like the rest of his generation — soft, servile, and soulless.

Bill Benedict's appearance made him indistinguishable from a lot of his peers. He sported a mass of dark wavy hair styled and blow-dried to cover the tops of his ears and just barely reach the top of his collar; full but neatly trimmed moustache; and dark, steady eyes that masked the lack of sincerity behind them. Generally he wore slacks and a blazer with a garishly colored polyester shirt and no tie, several gold chains around his neck, and a gold bracelet on his wrist.

As the limousine pulled away from the hospital, Dawson reminded himself to be patient with the younger generation's faults — if that's what they were. He knew that he was getting old when he started resenting younger men just because they were younger.

As much as Bill Benedict's manner annoyed him, Victor had to admit that the young lawyer had more to recommend him than most young people. By "most young people" Victor usually meant his three children, Roger, Phyllis, and Margot. They had all been a great disappointment to him. Roger was now in his forties and had never done anything useful in his life. Victor had long ago dismissed him as a playboy and a golf bum.

The last time Victor had heard from his daughter Phyllis, she had been living in a commune somewhere in Arizona. Although he disagreed violently with her whenever they spoke, he grudgingly granted her a degree of respect. She was the only one of the three who did not depend on him for support.

His daughter Margot called him almost every week to ask for money. She lived in New York, where she claimed to be a sculptor, making strange-looking things out of odds and ends she picked out of other people's trash.

None of them had ever been interested in Betco. That

was why Victor had hired Bill Benedict. When he died, his children would inherit his stock, but none of them was capable of looking after their own interests. And Bill Benedict was capable; he could manage things and hand out the money the way Victor always had.

Victor instructed the chauffeur to drive around town for a while. There was no better place to be alone to think than the back seat of a limousine. The tinted windows made the isolation even more complete. The traffic mattered not at all; Victor could simply light a cigar or a cigarette, lean back, relax, and think.

He had a lot to think about. He wasn't happy about this latest development at the hospital. In fact, he was furious, but it was necessary that he keep his thoughts and feelings to himself for the moment. Until he knew precisely what had happened and what the outcome would be, the less he said, the better. He had faced similar situations many times, and he had learned long ago that when a man was taken by surprise, silence and careful thought were more effective than hasty words or actions.

And Victor *had* been taken by surprise by Dr. Winston's accident, but he was sure everyone would automatically assume he was behind it. When "accidents" like this happened in any of the companies associated with Betco, it was always assumed that Victor Dawson was responsible. He'd been fighting that reputation for years, and he was growing weary of the burden of his name. In fact, he had been looking for something that might redeem him, and he had hoped that the takeover of Beverly Hills Hospital might be it.

Victor Dawson was not getting any younger, and his health was poor. His doctor back home in Chicago had warned him to give up smoking and drinking and had advised him to get more rest and relaxation. For Dawson, the pleasure of living was already over. Some people turned to religion later in life; Victor hadn't gone that far, but he had developed a bit of a conscience, and he wanted to leave one pure, unsullied accomplishment behind him. He had wanted the hospital deal to go through fair and square, with nothing shady or underhanded about it.

Victor didn't apologize for his life; he had done what he had had to do to survive. He had never known who his father was, and his mother had died when he was a kid. He had been too young for legitimate work, but a bootlegger friend of his mother's had found things an innocent-looking boy could do. During Prohibition, nobody had much respect for the law. The "good" people had become smug and self-righteous, and Victor had found more genuine human kindness among the members of the syndicate. People did favors for one another, and favors were always remembered and repaid.

When he was old enough, Victor had worked the numbers; and when a friend needed a bright young man to manage a casino in Havana, he had gotten his first big opportunity. The hotel and casino were the first of the Betco Enterprises. It may have been different from other wartime corporations, but after the war it grew as the others did, gradually acquiring one subsidiary after another, the corporation itself standing as firm as the Rock of Gibraltar, while the power plays of its personnel broke against it like waves.

Although many large corporations had suffered rumors of connections with organized crime, the rumors about Betco had been more persistent, given the nature of the companies and businesses Betco had acquired — racetracks, casinos, hotels, resorts, a hospital catering service, a linen supply house, a recording company, a film company, and a newspaper-and-magazine distribution service.

The United States Department of Justice and the crime commissions of half a dozen states believed Dawson and Betco had ties with organized crime, but no one had ever been able to prove it. The reputation had been built entirely on rumors and speculation. While that hurt Victor personally, it had been good for business.

Victor had been called in to testify time and time again before investigative bodies. His phone had been tapped, not always legally; he had been hounded by the Internal Revenue Service; and he had learned to smell an FBI agent three blocks away.

Victor considered himself an honorable man. He played fair with those who played fair; rough with those who played rough. The tactics he had used against others were no different from the tactics the federal government used against him, and he had never used them against an honorable man.

The chauffeur had chosen to leave the busy streets of Beverly Hills in favor of a typical Los Angeles street, lined with a meager collection of unambitious shops and restaurants that were ninety percent flashy advertising. It was a strange and unreal world to Victor Dawson. The people who owned and managed these places and the people who patronized them were ciphers to him. These were the people who would remember him as either good or evil when he was gone. He told himself that it didn't matter what they thought, as long as he was remembered as powerful and successful, that it was really more important what he thought of himself, how satisfied he was with his own accomplishments.

He also tried to convince himself that it didn't matter what happened to Phil Winston; that the only important thing was taking over Beverly Hills Hospital, reorganizing it, and setting it on a sound financial course.

But it did matter to him. If Winston died, the take-over would be considered dirty, and Victor Dawson couldn't live with that.

The limousine slowed, and Victor glanced up at the chauffeur, noticing that he had picked up the telephone receiver. A moment later, the driver's voice crackled over the intercom. "Mr. Dawson, Mr. Benedict calling.

Benedict's voice came rushing at him. "The surgery's over. Winston died on the table."

It was what Victor had expected, but he felt nothing at hearing it confirmed. "All right," he said simply. "Thank you."

"Mr. Dawson," Benedict said rapidly, "any special instructions?"

"Just go back to the hotel," Victor said irritably. "I'll meet you there."

Chapter Seven

The confrontation with Andrew Collins had been humiliating for Dave. His pride, already weakened from months of frustration, had been dealt a severe and painful wound. He was aware that it was simply a misunderstanding, but it was nonetheless painful that another doctor — or anyone — would assume that his motives were less than honourable.

It was a question of human dignity. Dave was beginning to perceive that as the constant wound he had suffered. Had human dignity disappeared from all of modern life, he wondered, or just from the little island of Beverly Hills?

The frustration pursued Dave, and his rage continued to simmer. It took all his effort to maintain a professional attitude toward his patients and not to vent his feelings on them. Every case he was assigned annoyed him. The old man with the ulcer didn't speak English; the fourteen-year-old girl with gonorrhea was insistent about having gotten the disease from a toilet seat; the parents who had brought in their battered infant insisted that the child had fallen down the stairs, when it was clear to Dave that the child had been beaten.

Dave was in no mood for another confrontation with Andrew Collins, whom he had begun to regard as symbolic of everything that was preventing him from achieving success. But as Dave left the battered child and his parents, he saw Collins waiting for him near the emergency room desk, an angry scowl on his face.

Dave didn't change his course, but stiffened in anticipation of a verbal assault. It came before Dave even drew near.

"Berger!" Collins shouted, his blue eyes icy. "You're through at this hospital."

Dave knew that everyone in the ER area had turned to stare at him. His sense of injustice and humiliation was overwhelming; the only way he could keep from lashing back at Collins was to say nothing.

But it didn't stop Collins. "Dr. Winston is dead," he said viciously, "and I'm holding you responsible. You'll be lucky if you still have your license when I get through with you. That kidney X ray, that one-shoot IVP you conveniently failed to order, the one you said we didn't have time for —"

"The only thing we didn't have was the surgeon on panel call," Dave retorted.

Collins clenched his fists and continued. "The X ray, the IVP we didn't have time for — the one that would have shown nonvisualization of the left kidney and prompted us to get an angiogram, or at least be aware of major damage to the kidney blood supply . . ." Collins paused, aware that all eyes were on him. Dave shifted his weight from one foot to the other. "So that when we were up to our elbows in blood and shit and piss, we could see what we were doing and know Winston was bleeding to death from his renal artery and vein that had been torn off the kidney . . . The one simple test that may have saved Dr. Winston's life, Dr. Berger, you failed to order!''

Dave was more shocked by the announcement that Winston was dead than he was outraged by Collins's threats. "If Winston is dead," Dave said dully, "then your bungling killed him."

Dave stood a good five feet away from Collins, but now the man advanced on him.

"We'll see what the surgery board has to say about that," Collins growled. "You've been so damned eager to make a name for yourself that you've broken every rule in the book."

Dave's voice was steady. "There was no time for the IVP. I didn't want him to die in X ray. I was trying to save a life." And then it was all too much for him. He shouted, "What the hell was I supposed to do when you didn't respond to your call, let him die?"

"I responded, but you tried to get him into surgery before I could get here. And you handled the whole thing like . . . like the asshole without boards that you are."

Suddenly Dave saw what Collins was up to: To save himself, he was going to make Dave a scapegoat. Dave knew what his chances were against the successful and influential surgeon. "You son of a bitch!" he whispered, and delivered a clenched fist to Collins's jaw.

The senior surgeon stumbled backward under the blow. But he recovered quickly and lunged at Berger, sending him sprawling to the floor before a security guard and two orderlies intervened.

The two orderlies escorted Dave to his office, while the security guard took Collins by the arm and ushered him to the elevators, but not before Collins jerked around and delivered the parting shot. "I've got your ass, Berger! Remember that!"

As Collins stormed out of the emergeny room he told himself he knew Berger's weaknesses — where all the pimples were.

He well remembered the dean of his medical school announcing on that first day so long ago, "Gentlemen, you'll all need a coat of armor to survive out there. You'll need it to protect yourself from the patients, from the attorneys, and most of all from your fellow physicians. A coat of white armor."

How true. The surgery committee had assigned Collins to proctor Dave Berger, and report back on his performance. The message had been clear: "Fine Dr. Winston had hired Dave Berger and he was good, but keep him down. Keep him away from the private patients and private practice and out of the operating room. Let him diddle in the emergency room but keep him out of the way."

Andrew had done his job well. Now, three year later, Berger was still confined mostly to emergency room work. He had a small and very limited practice and he was totally under control. Andy knew that the general surgeons were relieved. There was no need for another surgeon, especially one with Berger's exceptional pair of hands, competing with them for cases.

On the surface Andrew and the others had all the advantages, the background, the training, the boards, but Dave Berger had one thing they would never have — the hands.

He had seen Berger suture in the ER and had observed Berger a few times in the OR doing a routine gallbladder, a hernia, a breast biopsy. Berger was good, too damned good. The movement and the rhythm were there. Berger was one hell of a technical surgeon. Lucy, the head of the operating room, had probably put it best. "That son of a bitch can sure operate."

Well, Andrew smiled grimly, no use calling attention to Berger's skills. Once the nurses started gossiping about his slick surgery, GP's, internists, and primary-care physicians would catch wind of him and start referring cases to the young surgeon.

No, Andrew Collins had done his job well. Dave Berger was no closer to making a dent at Beverly Hills Hospital now than he had been three years ago. The surgery committee had shown Andew its appreciation. He was appointed chief of surgery, the second most powerful position in the hospital next to chief of staff, and word had it that he was being groomed for the top spot.

Dave sat alone in his office for a long time before he returned to duty. He was more shaken than he had ever been in his life. Not only was he deeply anguished at having lost control of himself, but he believed that Andrew Collins could make good his threat.

Phil Winston had been Dave's only friend at Beverly Hills Hospital. Now, all Dave had on his side was truth, and the truth meant nothing when weighed against power. Andrew Collins had all the power on his side. When jobs were at stake, witnesses might conveniently forget what they had seen.

Dave knew that he would be lucky to get out of this mess without losing his license to practice — though, he reflected bitterly, the meager practice he had was hardly worth fighting for.

He was lost in thought when Emily Harris knocked at his door. "You've got three patients waiting, Dr. Berger," she announced breezily, "and they're backing up in the waiting room."

"All right," Dave said dully, staring at the nurse but not moving from his desk.

Emily stared back at him, a strange look on her face. She was not an unattractive woman. She had short sandy hair, catlike green eyes, a pert nose, a small but seductive mouth, and large breasts that seemed to protest the confines of her uniform. It was her manner that made her seem offensive. She always appeared to be struggling to conceal knowledge of impending disaster — a disaster that would give her great joy to observe unfolding.

After an uncomfortable silence, she said hesitantly, "Dr. Berger, I don't want to get mixed up in this trouble, but I think you did everything you could to save Dr. Winston." She paused, avoiding his eyes. "If I'm asked any questions, I'm not going to swear to anything. But there's one thing I think you ought to know." She looked at him again. "Dr. Collins is trying to hide something."

"What?" Dave asked distastefully.

"Well," she said slyly, "I don't think he slept at home last night. When I couldn't find him here at the hospital and couldn't reach him through his service, I tried calling him at home." She paused, prolonging her point, then announced with obvious satisfaction, "His wife didn't have any idea where he was."

Clearly, Emily expected Dave to be pleased at this revelation. When he just stared at her expressionlessly, she began to fidget.

He understood what she was getting at, but he didn't care for her snide implication. "I appreciate your trying to help," he said curtly. "But what Dr. Collins does with his personal life is his business. What's more important is that he wasn't on call when he was supposed to be. And I'm expecting you to confirm that if I'm brought before the committee."

Emily stiffened. "Well, like I said, I couldn't swear to anything. I left messages with his office, his home, and his service. When he got to the ER, he said that he'd gotten the message from his service."

Dave felt his anger surfacing again, but he managed to keep it under control. "When the matter comes up before the committee, I'm sure you'll tell the truth as you see it."

He rose from his desk. "Now, those cases I've got waiting. What's the first one?"

A flicker of annoyance creased Emily's brow, and then her manner changed entirely. For the first time, she looked at him with what appeared to be honesty and sincerity. "You're making a terrible mistake." She sighed. "That's not the way the game is played."

Chapter Eight

Victor Dawson's behavior puzzled Bill Benedict to no end. The Betco lawyer had expected the old man to be pleased by the day's developments, but Dawson had been silent and withdrawn — almost morose — since he'd learned of Dr. Winston's accident.

The talks with the hospital board had been going on for months, the past few weeks consumed by intensive and exhausting negotiations. Only twenty-four hours ago, facing what appeared to be certain defeat, Dawson had fought as if the battle was his. Now, with the longed-for victory a certainty, he looked like a defeated man.

After more than two years of working at Dawson's side, Bill had grown accustomed to most of the old man's moods. In fact, he secretly admired the qualities that others deprecated — his ruthlessness, his volatile spirit, his cold and dispassionate determination to have his own way in everything. Dawson was mean, crusty, obstreperous, vain, and he could be a cold-blooded killer when he had to be. If he hadn't so many obstacles to overcome in his life, Bill believed, he could have been a great lawyer, or at least a successful politician.

However, there had been a gradual change in Victor Dawson over the past few months, a weakening of the old man's will. Bill thought he knew why. It was something no one else knew. Dawson was having to face the fact that he was no longer invincible. He was not, strictly speaking, a dying man, but he was having to face the prospect of death.

On his last visit to his doctor in Chicago, Dawson had been given a clean bill of health. Yet, while Bill didn't know the details, he had been given strict instructions to monitor his boss's consumption of food, alcohol, and tobacco, and to watch for attacks of acute abdominal pain. The strong-willed old man could no longer be trusted to look out for himself.

Bill Benedict always referred to Dawson as "the old man," but not in a derogatory way. He looked up to Dawson as if he were his own father, and he felt that Dawson looked on him as a son.

Bill had never been close to his real father, a weak and ineffectual man who had drifted from job to job, spending half his time being unemployed. Bill's parents had divorced when he was five years old, and the role of stepfather had been filled by a succession of men, none of whom had ever commanded Bill's respect.

Bill's own marriage had failed after little more than a year, and he had vowed never to remarry. He felt that his living arrangement with Erica, after three years, was better than any marriage could be, and would go on indefinitely as long as there were no children. Neither he nor Erica wanted children.

Erica got along very well with the old man. In fact, she had been responsible for bringing Bill and Victor Dawson together. She worked for the architecture firm that handled the Betco hotels, casinos, and offices.

Individually and together, Bill and Erica had become very important to Dawson's health and well-being, and they looked after him as his own children should have done.

For that reason, Bill was perturbed by the old man's unexpected mood today. After informing Dawson of Dr. Winston's death, Bill had returned to the hotel and waited, as he had been instructed. Dawson had arrived half an hour later, clearly upset about something. He had remained uncommunicative, refusing to answer Bill's questions and frequently going to the window to stare out over Beverly Hills.

When the old man finally spoke, the question caught Bill by surprise. "What time is the next flight to Chicago?"

"I don't know," Bill answered, bewildered. "I'll have to check."

"Please," Dawson said.

Bill went to the phone and began to dial. Halfway through, he hung up and turned back to his boss. "There's no point in my calling unless I know when you want to leave."

"As soon as possible," Dawson said, a trace of weariness or sadness — Bill wasn't sure — in his voice.

"Do you mind if I ask why?"

"Because I want to go home. Isn't that a good enough reason?"

"Not if it's not the real reason," Bill said.

A suggestion of the old familiar spark returned to Dawson's eyes, and a trace of a grin stiffened his lips. Bill knew the old man liked a fight. "After today," he said, "you've got the hospital, and you've got it entirely on your terms."

"I don't want it anymore," Dawson said quietly. "Not this way."

Having gotten the old man to open up this far, Bill

decided to press his advantage. He didn't like this sign of conscience, this determination to accept defeat.

"What does it matter how you get the hospital, as long as you get it?" he demanded. "Winston did you a big favor by stepping out in front of an ambulance and getting himself killed. What's the big deal? It was an accident."

"It wasn't an accident!" Dawson snapped. "I know you're not stupid enough to believe that!"

For a moment, Bill feared he had pushed the old man too far. "It wouldn't be the first time you've gained control of a corporation by accident," he risked saying. "I don't know why it should bother you so much."

The old man glowered at him. "I didn't cause this accident."

"Do you have any idea who did?"

"I think so," Dawson said wearily.

"Who?"

The old man stared at Bill for a long time, then turned to look out the window again. Bill had almost given up on getting a response when Dawson answered.

"Either Tony Manchester or that son-in-law of his," he said so softly Bill almost missed it. "Or the two of them together."

Bill walked over to stand next to Dawson. "I don't see why you should let them stand in the way of what you want," he said.

"Oh, I'm not worried about them," Dawson said sadly.

"Then what are you worried about?"

Dawson sighed. "You're right. I have nothing to worry about. Forget about calling the airline."

Chapter Nine

It was only nine minutes by car from Beverly Hills Hospital to the Collins home in Trousdale Estates, but the problems and concerns of the hospital rarely reached Alice Collins. Very little of anything unsettling ever reached this quiet, insular community that clung to the hillsides above Beverly Hills. A stranger driving through the maze of short, twisting streets might have concluded that he was visiting a ghost town, a strange collection of large and stately mansions that were uninhabited but were somehow kept in pristine condition.

There was an unearthly quiet about it. There was no one to be seen; indeed, in most of the areas there were not even sidewalks. No children played on the lawns; and, though there were numerous swimming pools and tennis courts, they never seemed to be used.

Alice Collins felt that she had been buried in Trousdale, or, more accurately, entombed. Entombed in a three-million-dollar marble-and-glass mausoleum, with five bedrooms, three baths, gymnasium, double tennis court, swimming pool, and a magnificent view of Los Angeles. Entombed with only her thirteen-year-old daughter, Jennifer, for company. There was a maid, of course, but Alice didn't count her; she was an illegal alien and spoke no English.

Alice saw Andrew for only a few hours in the evening, if she saw him at all. Two or three times a week, he claimed to spend the night on the couch in his office, but she didn't believe that story any more than Andrew expected her to. She had known for a long time that he saw other women, but his affairs were never serious. Andrew had married her because she was Tony Manchester's daughter; and for that reason, he would never leave her for another woman.

But this was little consolation to Alice. She had considered leaving Andrew, but was unable to do so because she was frightened of what her life might be like without him and because she kept hoping that he would change.

Unfortunately, Alice loved her husband.

So she kept up the appearances that were so important to him, and she patiently endured the evenings when she knew he was with another woman. She did everything she could to make his home life pleasant and appealing. She kept herself attractive, and at thirty-nine she was still a beautiful woman. Her hair was a lustrous auburn, her eyes were distinctly baby blue, her complexion was smooth and unblemished, and she had kept her figure trim and firm, with softness in just the right places.

A few lines were beginning around her eyes, but she managed to conceal them. Some wear and tear still showed, though. Her lonely life wasn't easy. Andrew had left to her the entire responsibility of bringing up Jennifer. While he provided all the physical necessities and spoiled her with more luxuries than any child should have, he gave nothing of himself to his daughter, and that had created serious problems over the years, especially now that Jennifer was approaching adolescence.

Alice was constantly being called in to talk to the teachers at Jennifer's private school, where Jennifer had gained a reputation as a troublemaker. She'd already been threatened with expulsion several times. Drugs were a serious problem at the school, and Alice knew that Jennifer often smoked pot, and suspected that she had tried stronger drugs as well. There were also signs that Jennifer was no longer a virgin, and she certainly had a great many boys trooping through the house.

Jennifer had been accused of stealing things at school, but Alice could not believe that of her. Why should Jennifer have to steal when she had so much?

Andrew wouldn't even discuss these problems with Alice. "The household is your responsibility," he said. "I come home to escape from responsibility and from problems. If I can't do that, I don't see any point in coming home at all."

Andrew could always be counted on to take Alice out to dinner at the chic restaurants and to the social functions that were so necessary to their status. On the rare evenings he was at home, he usually spent his time in the gym, keeping his body trim. Occasionally he sat with her and watched television. If he was at home on a Saturday or a Sunday, he sunned himself by the pool to keep his tan. If they talked at all, it was only about trivial things.

Alice could only assume that life at the hospital was an unchanging routine. What little she knew, she learned from her father. Several months ago he had mentioned that Betco was interested in buying out the stock, but the subject hadn't been brought up again. Such a sale was of no concern to Alice; as far as she could see, it wouldn't affect her life.

After all, her father's film company had been bought by Betco and there had been no change. His stock had simply been exchanged for Betco stock, and he had continued to run the company. He was also the principal stockholder in Beverly Hills Hospital, and she assumed this merger would be a repeat of the earlier one.

Alice Collins adored and respected her father. Tony Manchester was a creator, a builder, a man who set out to achieve things against incredible odds, never doubting that he would succeed. He had built three distinctly different careers, and had made two successful marriages, both of which had ended in tragedy.

From his appearance, it was difficult to imagine how he had made a name for himself as an actor. He was extremely tall, considerably over six feet, and while his frame had filled out in recent years, he had been thin and lanky at the time he ventured into the movies. He had a great beak of a nose and glittering black eyes that always seemed to be laughing at some secret. He had lost most of his hair in his twenties, but he wore a toupee only when a role required it.

He possessed no real talent, but he became one of the best-loved character actors of the thirties and forties, taking advantage of the humor his appearance inspired. Alice's mother had also been in films, a great beauty with a promising career ahead of her. Alice's parents had been very much in love; Alice still treasured the timeworn fan magazines that extolled their relationship, one of the great love stories of Hollywood.

Her mother had died when Alice was born, and Tony had been devastated. Later, when he was forty years old, he set up his talent agency and remarried. Within three years, his talent agency was one of the most successful in Hollywood, and Alice's stepmother was dead of cancer. The grief-stricken Tony threw himself into his work. Within a few years he formed a production company and made one hit picture after another. He invested his money in a variety of businesses, but the investment that meant the most to him was the hospital. He never discussed the reasons for his interest in medicine, but Alice knew. They were the same reasons he hadn't married a third time.

Tony had been very pleased that Alice had married a doctor. He had never really liked Andrew, but for Alice's sake he had done everything he could to help Andrew's career. He would do anything to ensure his daughter's happiness.

That was why Alice had never let her father know how unhappy she was in her marriage. She kept up a good front for him as well as for the public, resorting to outright lies when necessary.

Tony almost always called before dropping by to see her and Andrew, so she was greatly surprised that Monday evening when he just appeared at her door.

The dusk was just darkening into night, and Alice had made herself a drink and was sitting in a chair by the wall of glass that overlooked the city, watching the lights come on and wondering if Andrew would be home tonight. He hadn't called to make an excuse, so she assumed he would be. She had even told Maria to expect him for dinner.

Jennifer was out. When the doorbell rang, Alice went to answer it herself, thinking it must be one of Jennifer's friends.

She was not only startled but embarrassed to see her father standing there.

"Sorry to pop in like this, honey, but I've been wanting to talk to Andrew. Is he home?"

"N-not yet," Alice stammered. "But it shouldn't be too long. Come in, Dad."

She couldn't hide the drink in her hand, so as she ushered her father into the large living room, she said, "I'm just having a drink before dinner. Will you have one?"

"No, thank you." She knew that her father rarely drank, and never when his mind was on business. "How are things?" he asked, as he folded his big frame onto the low, modern sofa.

"Fine," Alice answered, trying to smile.

"Where's my granddaughter?"

Alice forced a laugh and a shrug. "Oh, off with her friends somewhere. She should be in soon. I can't keep up with her at this age."

"Have you talked to Andrew today?" Tony asked. His tone suggested there was something more than pleasantry behind the question.

"No," she answered cautiously. "I suspect he's been very busy."

Tony nodded, then said, "Yes."

He was looking at her in a way that made her feel uncomfortable. She knew there was something troubling her father. Since he had come to the house to speak to Andrew, she assumed that it was personal rather than business. Had he heard something about their marital trouble?

She couldn't stand uncertainty, so she asked outright, "Is something wrong?"

"It's just business," he said, smiling patiently. "Nothing to trouble you with." Then he got to his feet and said, "I think I'll have that drink after all. Okay if I make it myself?"

Alice laughed, relieved. "You know where the bar is."

He was standing behind the bar when Andrew came in. Andrew was startled to see his father-in-law, but no more startled than Alice was by his appearance. He looked awful, with dark circles under his eyes and his clothes unkempt. Most startling of all was the bruise on his cheek.

Whatever the "business" trouble was, Alice knew immediately that it was serious.

"Well, Andrew," Tony said with a wry smile, "I see that it wasn't just hospital gossip. When you didn't return my calls, I feared it would be worse than this."

Alice set down her drink and hurried across the room to her husband. "What happened?"

Andrew scowled. "Hasn't your father told you already?"

"I don't tell tales out of school," Tony said easily. "You know that. Especially when I don't know if they're true or not." It was impossible to tell whether he was angry or amused or both. "I think you need a drink," he said cheerfully, reaching for a bottle of Scotch.

Alice said impatiently, "I wish one of you would tell me. I don't like being the only ignorant one in the room."

"Oh, you're not that, my dear," Tony said with a touch of sarcasm. "Not by any means."

Alice guessed that that was an even more private joke because her father was the only one who laughed.

"Stupid I may be," Andrew said, sipping his drink, "but ignorant I'm not." Then he turned to Alice, embarrassment reddening his face. "There was a slight altercation between me and another doctor at the hospital today. But I was defending myself, not brawling for the fun of it."

"Is it true that you were arguing over the Winston case?" Tony asked sternly.

Andrew nodded.

"And that you've asked for an investigation by the surgery committee?"

Again Andrew nodded.

Tony sighed and shook his head. "I hope you know what you're doing."

Alice noticed a strange look come over her husband's face and knew then that there was somthing going on that she knew nothing about. Andrew stared down at the glass in his hand. His jaw was rigid, and a vein throbbed in his forehead. He glanced at her before he spoke.

"Berger's actions were totally out of order," he said defensively. "He tried to operate on Dr. Winston without authority."

"And who the hell is this Berger, anyway? I thought he just worked in the ER. A kind of pleasant fellow, I always thought, and —"

"An incompetent!" Andrew cut in, then swallowed most of his drink. "Never passed the oral part of his boards, not even goddamned board-certified."

"I know," Tony replied. "I've been over his records. He's scheduled to take the orals this year . . . in fact, in less than a week."

"And" — Andrew refilled his glass quickly and gulped it down — "I'll nail the bastard but good on this one!"

Tony glanced at Alice, then turned back to Andrew. "Are you sure your action under the circumstances will stand up to scrutiny?"

"What do you mean?" Andrew shot back.

"From what I've heard," Tony said quietly, "you were a bit late responding to the emergency call."

"That's absolutely untrue. Who told you that?"

Tony shrugged. "It's just a story going around the hospital."

"Damn!" Andrew got up and moved to the bar. "Berger's already working on his defense. That's all the more reason for me to take this matter before the hospital committee."

Something about Andrew's manner told Alice he was lying, that he was hiding something. And she was beginning to suspect that she knew what it was. Andrew had been late getting to the hospital because he had spent the night with some woman. But that couldn't be the whole story. There was something else bothering him, something more serious. She knew him well enough to spot that.

As Tony rose and followed his son-in-law to the bar, Alice felt there was something mysterious about his manner as well; *menacing* was what came to mind.

"Boards or no boards, that's really not the question. You and I know the value of the boards, Andrew — the *political* value, that is. They don't make a man a better surgeon, but it's an important document, a 'right' paper to put on your wall." He paused, then asked sharply, "What was Winston's condition when you took over?"

Andrew studied his glass for a moment, then looked up, his expression solemn. "He didn't have a chance. Legally, he wasn't dead, but he might as well have been."

"Can you prove that?" Tony asked angrily.

"No one can prove otherwise."

"I hope you're sure of that." Tony smiled enigmatically. "I don't think anyone would be happy having a controversy at the hospital right now."

Chapter Ten

It was unsettling for Andrew to awaken to find himself nuzzling a warm luxuriant body in bed beside him, only to discover that the body belonged to his wife. He almost panicked, wondering, *Did I say anything in my sleep? Did I speak her name?*

Obviously he had said nothing, because Alice seemed very happy in his arms. He distinctly remembered her wearing a nightgown when she had gone to bed, but now she was naked, as he was, and she had managed to fit herself into the curve of his body. She was fondling his erection, and there was a grateful little smile on her lips.

Andrew's face must have reflected his dismay, because Alice's smile faded quickly, and she stiffened.

He resented that look, believing there was accusation in it, and in self-defense he would have to make love to her. He rarely did so anymore, though he was aware that she wanted it. When he did, it was out of a sense of duty. He had felt little passion for her in recent years, though he still acknowledged that she was one of the most beautiful women he had ever known.

Actually, Andrew's resentment had little to do with Alice herself. It was her father he resented.

Andrew had thought he knew what he was doing when he married Alice, but he had been extremely naïve. Those facile comedies about the "boss's daughter" gave no indication of the subtle exchanges that took place among real people. He admitted to himself that he had been attracted to her only partly because of her beauty and her personality; there had been the added attraction of her father's power. Beverly Hills Hospital was new when they met; and her father was chairman of the board. Andrew had seen a tremendous opportunity to make a name for himself quickly and easily.

It hadn't been as easy as he had thought. He had considered only what he would gain from the connection, never suspecting that Tony Manchester had more to gain than he did.

Andrew had risen very quickly. He had attracted a distinguished list of patients, he had bought into the hospital partnership, and he had profited greatly. But Tony Manchester acquired through Andrew a power within the hospital that he had not possessed before. Although Tony was chairman of the board and owned the largest share of stock, he was not a doctor, and therefore only could be a limited partner. On certain issues that came before the board, he had no vote. Through Andrew, he had gained that vote.

There was no doubt in Andrew's mind that his father-in-law controlled him. Tony gave orders, and Andrew obeyed them. Andrew had never even considered refusing; it was the sort of thing one didn't do. It would be like asking for the return of a piece of merchandise sold long ago and worn out by now. Andrew had gotten what he had wanted out of the arrangement; he could not cry about the cost.

More accurately, he felt he should not. But he couldn't help resenting the situation, nor could he help directing that resentment toward his wife, who was guilty only of loving her father as much as she loved her husband.

Andrew made love to her this morning, as she wanted and expected, but the act was born of rage rather than passion. When he kissed her, he bit her lips; when he embraced her, he held her too tightly, his fingernails digging into her soft flesh. And when he rhythmically thrust into her, it was more to give her pain than pleasure.

Alice tried to stifle her cries, to disguise them as moans of pleasure, but Andrew knew, and it was confirmed when, after their lovemaking was done, Alice began to cry softly.

Andrew felt remorse, but could do nothing to comfort her. Resentment remained the dominant emotion in him. He ignored Alice's tears, rose from the bed, aware that her eyes were on him, and went to the bathroom to get ready for work.

His resentment was particularly acute this morning. His confrontation with Tony last night had been extremely unsettling. For some reason — a reason Andrew had not yet figured out — Tony wanted him to withdraw his complaint against Dave Berger. He wanted the entire matter hushed up.

Of course, there was the obvious explanation: If there was an investigation into Dr. Winston's death, the Betco sale could be thrown into jeopardy. But, from what Andrew had heard of Betco, they had never let that sort of thing stop them.

Hell, Andrew thought as he stepped into the shower, if they were worried about a scandal, they wouldn't have gotten rid of Winston that way.

The more Andrew thought about it, the more sure he

was that it wasn't Betco's reaction Tony was worried about. It was something more than that. As he soaped his body and allowed the hot water to flow over him, he relaxed and let his mind wander.

It was while he was rinsing himself, with his face turned directly into the shower head, that the thought occurred to him: *Tony is behaving as if he, and not Betco, is responsible for Phil Winston's death.*

Quickly, he turned off the water, opened the shower door, and reached for a towel. He began to whistle as he dried himself. The thought of his father-in-law being in such a position pleased him. It even excited him.

It was Tony who had brought the Betco question before the board some months ago. To Andrew's knowledge, Tony had been acquainted with Victor Dawson as far back as the early fifties. And Tony Manchester Productions, Tony's film company, had been bought by Betco more than ten years ago. Tony hadn't been particularly happy about that merger at the time, because it meant he would lose a degree of control, and that fact had misled Andrew into believing that Tony would not be entirely happy about relinquishing the control of Beverly Hills Hospital.

Andrew grinned at himself in the mirror as he shaved. *Tony is out to get control of the whole megillah*, he reflected. *Victor Dawson's an old man. He can't live forever.*

This knowledge made Andrew feel less helpless in his relationship with his father-in-law. The knowledge that gave one power wasn't necessarily the knowledge gained from books; in the modern power structure, it was the knowledge of human weakness and vulnerability.

Andrew smiled grimly. He did not have that weakness and vulnerability. He did not have that chink in his coat of white armor.

He had not listened to any of the dean's lies or swallowed any of his professors' nonsense. They had told him and his classmates to become super specialists, to work for the university, to go into pediatric allergy or nephrology and be honored to get a little cubbyhole in an office at the university and work for fifty thousand dollars a year at best.

All lies, and he hadn't swallowed any of them.

Andrew knew that his classmates and others who had swallowed the lies — now fifteen to twenty years after medical school — were all disillusioned. They were locked in their cubbyholes while the GP's and the young family practice guys — the guys like himself doing general surgery, the bread-and-butter stuff that occurred commonly — were out there cleaning up, making nearly forty or fifty thousand dollars a month or more and laughing all the way to the bank.

Sure, he, Andrew Collins, had the best of both worlds. An appointment at the university where he made academic rounds once a week plus a lucrative private practice plus a lock-in at Beverly Hills Hospital — plus a wife who was the daughter of Tony Manchester.

Yes, Andrew thought, he had it all. He thought again of Dave Berger. Berger was the dangerous one. Berger had the hands. Andrew thought of another of his old professors' lies; "You can teach a monkey to operate in six months, but the judgment, *when* to operate on a patient, the million subtle things that go into making a complete and mature surgeon — that is the art of surgery."

Bullshit! After all these years, Andrew knew it was bullshit. What counted was being able to operate to get the patient through surgery with no complications, which, in turn, kept the GP's and the internists happy and out of trouble. One needed the hands for that, and Dave Berger had the hands. . . .

Andrew whistled happily as he left the bathroom, aware that Alice took this as a personal encouragement.

He kissed her gently and promised to call her from the office later in the day.

Before leaving for the office, however, he went to his study to phone his service for messages. There were several calls that Andrew decided could wait until he reached the hospital, but there was one that he considered very important, requiring an immediate call back. He had expected it. It was from Lina.

Andrew usually called Lina at least once a day, but yesterday he hadn't. There had been no time.

It was unlikely that Alice would come into his den; when she got out of the bathroom, she would head straight for the kitchen and a cup of coffee.

Andrew called Lina immediately. As soon as she answered, he began to apologize. "I'm sorry I couldn't call you —"

But Lina interrupted anxiously. "Is something wrong?"

This was so unlike her that Andrew was taken aback. There was a moment of surprised silence before he could respond. "No . . . at least nothing that you should be troubled about."

"You're not losing interest in me, are you?" she asked coyly.

"No. Not at all." Again he paused. "It's just hospital business. I'll see you later today and tell you about it."

"I don't know about today. I'm scheduled for shooting this afternoon, and it might run late."

"What about after you've finished shooting?" he pressed.

"I don't know."

If it had been any other woman, Andrew would have thought she was trying to punish him for his neglect, but Lina was always direct and straight about everything.

"We can leave it loose," he suggested. "Whatever time you're free."

"Okay," she said. "I *do* want to see you, because I've got a surprise for you."

The playfulness had returned to her voice, and it made Andrew feel good. A warm, intimate glow pushed back the irritation and resentment he had been feeling since last night. "What is it?" he asked softly.

"I don't want to tell you. I want it to be a surprise. But I can tell you this — you're going to like it." She laughed sensuously, and a shiver of anticipation, of wild and exotic sexual pleasures, tingled through his body.

"I can't wait," he said huskily. "I'll come by the studio after I finish at the hospital, hang around till you're through, and then take you home. About six o'clock, okay?"

"See you then. I'm crazy about you."

Lina never said the word *love*, and she refused to let Andrew say it.

"Crazy about you," Andrew echoed.

He hung up, then turned around and saw that he wasn't alone.

His daughter, Jennifer, was standing in the doorway, staring at him with a sullen, insolent look. He had no idea how long she had been standing there or how much of his conversation she had heard. From the look on her face, she had heard enough.

Andrew would have been less flustered if it had been his wife.

"The door was open," Jennifer said accusingly. "What was I supposed to do?"

"I wasn't . . . it wasn't what you think it was," Andrew stammered.

"How do you know what I think?" his daughter challenged. "And why should you even care?"

"What's that supposed to mean?" Andrew demanded.

She shrugged. "You're the one who claims to know what goes on inside my head."

"Sweetheart, I know I haven't been home much lately. Things at the hospital have been rough. Maybe we'll do something together on Sunday, just the two of us."

"I've got plans for Sunday."

"How about Saturday?" he tried.

"I'm busy."

"Okay," Andrew said irritably. "We'll make a date some other time." He looked at his watch. "I've got to get to the hospital."

"Sure." Jennifer said, a knowing smile on her face. "See you around."

Chapter Eleven

Dave was relieved that he didn't work the emergency room on Tuesday. He hoped that a day away from the hospital would ease the tension and perhaps give him — and everyone else — some perspective on the situation. He regretted having lost his temper with Andrew Collins. Obviously, Collins had wanted him to do something rash so that he could divert attention away from himself.

Dave had thought about it all evening alone in his studio apartment. He had told himself over and over that the best defense was a good offense, that he should approach the hospital committee with his own charges before Collins got too far with his. But he hadn't been firm in his resolve. His sleep had been troubled, and he had awakened as confused as ever. No wonder. Boards in less than a week.

He drove early to his office on Wilshire Boulevard, determined to think practically about his future. He intended to look over his financial records and his calendar of appointments for the next few weeks in order to decide whether his small practice was worth fighting for. It might be more practical to admit defeat, count his entire stay in California as a loss, and look for another place to set up practice.

He had nothing to keep him in California — no personal ties, no particular affection for the place, no investment of anything more than time.

Arriving at his office early in the morning did nothing to lessen this feeling. The suite he rented was on the third floor of an old building that probably had been unimpressive even when it was built. It had no lobby at all, only an entrance hall to the elevator, which made strained sounds of protest as it rose, giving its passengers plenty of time to study the graffiti that adorned its walls.

Dave had done everything he could to make his office pleasant, but with his limited funds it had been difficult. His waiting room was small and cramped, with room for only five chairs and two small tables. He'd tried to brighten it up with a few prints. The waiting room furniture was rented, along with the rest of the office furnishings and medical equipment.

Martina, Dave's receptionist, wasn't in yet, so he sat down at her desk to look over his books. A quick review of his finances and his prospects confirmed what he had suspected. He would be no worse off if he packed up and returned to New Jersey or New York, where he had family and friends.

When Martina arrived, Dave retreated to his office. He had nothing to do for the next two hours, when his first appointment would arrive — nothing to do, that was, except think.

He was startled when, ten minutes later, Martina ducked into his office to tell him he had a patient.

"It's a Mrs. Baxter," she explained. "She doesn't have an appointment, but she says she knows you."

He couldn't recall any Mrs. Baxter. "What does she look like?"

Martina closed the door behind her. "Sort of ordinary," she said. "Short, plainly dressed, graying hair, in her fifties. Carries her knitting with her."

Suddenly he knew. "Oh, yes." He smiled. "Melissa Baxter. Show her in."

"I apologize for not calling and making an appointment," Melissa said briskly as she entered Dave's office. "But there really hasn't been much time for formalities."

"That's quite all right," Dave said pleasantly. "Won't you sit down?"

Melissa Baxter was a very curious woman. He didn't know quite how to respond to her. Clearly, she had been a friend of Dr. Winston's, and she deserved respect. But, because of her appearance, it was difficult to accept her claim of being a businesswoman.

"I take it you'd like to talk about Dr. Winston," Dave said, as the woman settled into the chair across from his desk. "I'm afraid I don't really know any more than I told you yesterday."

"No," she said sadly. "There's nothing either of us can do for Dr. Winston now. Except to mourn his passing." Then she fussed with her knitting absently, as if trying to recall her last stitch, and continued: "I'm sure it will seem unfeeling of me to discuss such things so soon after his death, but life must go on. And I do have to think about my patients."

"Yes, of course," Dave said politely, thinking that there might be two or three old people who subscribed to her service.

"Some of the patients I had placed with Dr. Winston are really very badly off," she went on. "They need almost constant attention. I believe several are in intensive care at the moment."

"Several?" Dave asked. "Intensive care?" His bewilderment was obvious.

"I'm sorry. You don't really know what I'm getting at, do you?"

"No," Dave admitted, "I don't."

She blushed self-consciously and laid aside her knitting. "This has all happened so suddenly that I'm all turned around." She took a deep breath, as if to collect herself, then tried to explain. "Dr. Winston was one of the important subscribers to Maturity Medical Services. I didn't supply his entire practice, of course, and I can't be concerned about his private patients — they'll have to look after themselves. But I do have a duty to those who have signed contracts with me. There must be no interruption in their medical care."

She paused, to see if Dave understood so far. He nodded.

"Dr. Winston had a great deal of faith in you," she said matter-of-factly. "I think he would approve of your taking over his patients — that is, if you're interested."

"Certainly," Dave said politely. "I'll be glad to do what I can." He was still thinking in terms of one or two patients, so he expressed no enthusiasm. "You know that I'm still taking my boards?" he ventured hesitantly. "I mean, you know I'm not yet board-certified?"

"Yes, yes, Dr. Berger. You can count on me; today I've done my homework." She regarded him carefully for a moment, then added, "I'm aware of your past performance, and I and the other medical people I've spoken to are fully confident you'll pass your boards this time around. But if you can't take all the patients at this time, I'll understand. I know the boards are important to you for many reasons. And you've been studying hard. But I would appreciate it if you could take those who need immediate attention, like those who are under hospital care."

Dave was growing impatient. "How many patients would be involved?" he asked finally.

Melissa Baxter's eyelashes fluttered. "I'm ashamed to admit that I don't know the exact number at the moment; there hasn't been time to bring my records up to date since yesterday. The latest figure I had available was two thousand, three hundred and eighty-four."

"What?" The woman had to be a kook. She couldn't possibly control so many patients.

Melissa smiled. "I realize it's rather a large number to take care of all at once," she said apologetically. "I could ask one of the doctors to take some of them, but most of their lists are fairly full already, and it would be much simpler if I could just have a truck deliver all the records to one place."

Dave's head was reeling. Melissa Baxter was offering him what amounted to a full practice! It was too good to be true. She was probably just teasing him.

"Oh, I think I could handle that many," he said with a chuckle, "though I'm not sure my office space would be adequate."

"No," Melissa said seriously. "You would have to get a larger office."

Dave leaned forward and asked bluntly, "How many doctors subscribe to your service?"

She blushed again. "I'm afraid I don't have the exact numbers at hand, but it's somewhere between sixty and eighty, I think."

"And how many patients do you have in all?"

"Again, you have me at a disadvantage, without my records in hand. But it's somewhere around sixty thousand." She fussed again with her knitting. "You have to understand, at their ages, there's considerable turnover.

Once people reach retirement age, they don't hang around very long — what with heart attacks and strokes and all.''

Dave sat back in his chair, laughing. When Melissa Baxter looked offended, he explained, ''You have to forgive me, I don't mean to be rude, but this all sounds so unbelievable. Suddenly, you look like the fairy godmother.''

Melissa smiled understandingly. ''I know I don't look like a businesswoman, but you see, that's why the senior citizens like and trust me.''

Dave was beginning to perceive that he was dealing with a very shrewd woman. That thought sobered him. By patronizing her, he had let down his defense. ''What do you get out of this service?'' he asked. ''I mean, what sort of fee do I have to pay you? I'd better warn you that I'm in hock up to my neck. And,'' he added, self-consciously, ''other problems —''

''Oh, I know that. Old news, I presume. Dr. Winston told me all about you. But we're not here to discuss old news. There's no fee, at least not for the doctors. You simply have to agree to accept only the amounts that Medicare pays. The patients take care of my fees. It really wouldn't be fair of me to charge the doctors. Medicare doesn't pay enough for that.''

''I don't mean to be impertinent, but these people are entitled to this care for free. What do you need you for?''

Melissa smiled patiently. ''That's what I thought at first. But if you were old and sick, and had no way of getting around, how would you go about finding a doctor who would accept you? It's terribly demeaning to go knocking on doors, getting turned down time after time. It's worth it to them to pay my little fee, and they're assured of getting any kind of doctor they need at any time.'' Suddenly she sat up. ''That reminds me. Doctors don't refer my patients to other doctors. If they need any kind of care at all, whether it's a dermatologist or an anesthesiologist, I'm obligated to supply it from my list. Do you understand?''

Dave nodded. The woman was amazing. He had no idea if what she was doing was legal, but she had thought of everything. She hadn't told him what her fee was, but even if it was only ten or twenty dollars a year, with sixty thousand patients she would be doing very well.

''There's one other thing you have to be aware of,'' she said hesitantly. ''It shouldn't affect you, but I feel I should tell you. Not all the doctors I deal with are affiliated with Beverly Hills Hospital, so not all my patients are there. However, Dr. Winston's patients all used Beverly Hills, because he had a special contract, not only to supply the emergency room with doctors but to keep one-third of the beds at the hospital filled at all times. Of course, you can't be bound by his contract, but you should know that the patients who are there now are under a quota.''

Dave frowned. ''I don't think I understand.''

''It's just as well that you don't, but if there's any question when you begin to release patients, let me know.''

Chapter Twelve

Victor Dawson felt more kindly toward his lawyer after a night of sleep, but he was no more communicative than he had been the day before. In deciding to go ahead with the merger, Victor had also decided to keep quiet about what he intended to do. It was the sort of thing his lawyer would probably advise him against. On anything questionable, lawyers always advised doing nothing, although Benedict had generally been more willing to take risks than other lawyers with whom Victor had dealt.

There was another reason for Victor's silence: He didn't yet have enough proof to act. He needed more information.

To avoid questions, Victor told Benedict he was going into Beverly Hills to do some shopping, and he gave him instructions for work to be accomplished before he returned around noon. "Most important," he advised, "is to get in touch with Tony Manchester to find out where we stand. Are we to move ahead immediately? If so, I want you to make sure all the papers are in order and ready for signing. But if he wants them signed today or tomorrow, don't commit yourself; tell him you have to get back to me. If he wants to delay, however, give him the impression that we're anxious to get everything taken care of and get home to Chicago. You know the sort of thing — keep him on the defensive."

Victor knew that this was what Bill Benedict liked. He was a great game player, as long as the games were not too complicated or too shady.

Victor had found Dr. Berger's office address and phone number, then had called and asked what the doctor's office hours were. Upon learning that they began at nine o'clock, Victor had arranged to have his driver downstairs with the limousine at nine.

It was only a short distance from Victor's hotel in Century City to Berger's office in the Wilshire District, but traffic was heavy at that hour. It was almost nine-thirty by the time Dawson arrived. He had made no appointment, and he hoped the doctor's waiting room would not be filled. Victor Dawson did not like to wait.

Victor knew little about Dr. Berger, only that he worked the emergency room and that he had attempted to perform surgery on Dr. Winston. He had no idea of the man's age or his background. However, because of Berger's association with Beverly Hills Hospital, he had expected to find him in a somewhat more pretentious office building.

Dawson had seen offices like this before. They usually were occupied by second-rate general practitioners, older men who, for one reason or another, had never made the grade.

This disturbing fact had barely registered when, as he was waiting for the elevator, he ran into Melissa Baxter. This was even more perplexing to Victor. Of course, the woman could simply have been coming to ask questions about Dr. Winston; she had been a close friend of his. But Victor was suspicious.

Clearly, she was just as surprised to see him. "Good morning, Mr. Dawson," she said, rather flustered. "It's very sad about Dr. Winston, isn't it?"

Out of courtesy, Victor let the elevator door close without getting in. "Good morning," he replied. "Yes, it's very upsetting. I know how close you were to Dr. Winston, and I'm sorry about what happened. He and I didn't see eye to eye, I didn't even particularly like him, but I would not have wanted to see him dead."

Melissa eyed him curiously. "You mean that, don't you?"

"Yes." Victor nodded.

"I'm glad of that." She started to walk down the hall. "I'm sure I'll be seeing you soon," she called over her shoulder.

Victor pressed the elevator button again and watched the woman depart. Beneath her sweet, innocent exterior, Victor thought he understood her. One day there would have to be a confrontation between them, and he didn't look forward to it.

When Victor reached Dr. Berger's office, he had his third surprise of the morning. There were no patients in the waiting room.

As Victor approached the dark-haired young woman at the reception desk, he quickly decided to shift his approach. He had originally intended to be straightforward and direct with Dr. Berger, telling him who he was and what he wanted. But now he decided to question him indirectly, starting off by pretending to be a patient and playing the rest by ear. Dave Berger might not be entirely innocent.

"My name is Dawson," he told the receptionist. "I'd like to see Dr. Berger."

"Have you seen Dr. Berger before?" she asked.

"No, I haven't," Victor responded quickly. "I was

referred by Dr. Winston's office." It was the only reference that Victor could come up with that might make sense.

It satisfied the receptionist. She pulled a form from her desk and went through the usual routine of questions, then told him to have a seat.

Victor barely had time to settle into his chair before the receptionist informed him that the doctor would see him then.

Victor had grown accustomed to seeing doctors who were shrewd, slick young men who made up for their lack of age and experience by impressing their patients with plush offices and modern machinery. Dave Berger struck Victor as being what young doctors just starting out in practice thirty or forty years ago were like.

He seemed open, sincere, and earnest. With such an unpretentious office, Victor assumed he was probably honest, but he couldn't be sure of that until he knew if the man was competent.

There were some troubling items in Berger's files, primary among them the fact that he wasn't fully certified. Victor recalled the paperwork: written boards completed, 1980; oral boards failed, 1980, 1981; third try pending. Victor wasn't sure what boards were, but he knew they were considered important.

"Mr. Dawson," Berger said, greeting him with a pleasant smile. "What seems to be your problem?"

"I've been having some pains in my side," Victor replied. It wasn't exactly a lie. He described chronic symptoms he had had for some time, symptoms that were quite familiar to his doctor back in Chicago. "Do you think it could be appendicitis? That's what's worrying me, since I'm out here on business."

"It could be," Dr. Berger mused, "but it doesn't have to be."

Berger led Victor into an examining room and gave him what he knew was a very extensive examination, complete with blood and urine tests. He then asked pertinent questions about Victor's eating and drinking habits.

When the exam was finished, Berger looked concerned. "How long have you had these symptoms?" he asked.

Victor had answered all the questions the way he had answered them some months ago when he had been examined by his own doctor, but Berger's manner suggested that he could see through his little ruse. So Victor tried to cover up.

"I've had the pain off and on for quite a while, but it wasn't really bad enough to worry about," he lied. "The bad pains started last week, just before I left Chicago. But I've been under a lot of stress out here."

Berger nodded. "How much longer are you going to be in Los Angeles?"

Victor shrugged. "Another two or three days."

"You really ought to go into the hospital for further tests. But you could probably wait until you're home with your own doctor." He paused. "That is, as long as you watch your diet and stay away from alcohol."

He instructed Victor to get dressed and return to his office.

When Victor was again seated across the desk from Berger, he asked, "You think it's my appendix, do you?"

"No, but I can't know for sure without more extensive tests."

"What's your diagnosis?"

Berger sighed. "As I say, I don't think there's any reason for immediate concern, as long as you're careful about your diet. But you should have your doctor check your pancreas."

"Pancreatitis?" Victor asked.

Berger looked surprised. "Yes. That's what I suspect."

Victor Dawson was pleased. The young doctor had

correctly diagnosed his problem much more quickly than his own doctor had. That was enough for him to decide that Berger was competent, despite all that bullshit about having no boards. He now felt he could ask some of the questions he wanted answered.

"I'm grateful to you for seeing me," Victor began. "I would have gone to Dr. Winston, but, of course . . ." He let the sentence hang, watching for Berger's reaction.

"Yes, I know," Berger replied, glancing down at his desk with what Victor took to be embarrassment.

"Were you a close friend of Dr. Winston's?" Victor asked casually.

Berger stared at him for a moment. "I worked for him," he said, "and I suppose he was the best friend I've had in Los Angeles. But I wasn't really close to him. Aside from work, I knew very little about him."

"I understand it was a hit-and-run accident?"

Berger nodded. "Yes, just outside the emergency room at the hospital. I was on duty."

"Did he die instantly?"

Berger looked at him uncomfortably, clearly trying to determine why Victor was so curious. "No," he explained. "As a matter of fact, he died on the operating table."

"I take it he didn't have a chance, though?"

"No, I guess not," Berger replied unconvincingly. Then he forced a smile. "However, I always try to believe there's a chance, as long as the patient is still breathing."

Dr. Berger's expression said a lot; it told Victor much of what he wanted to know. But Victor decided to push further, to see how much the young man would say. "But you think he should have survived, don't you?"

Berger looked confused. "I . . . I'm sure that everything was done for him that could be done." He refused to look at Victor, and there was a crimson flush on his cheeks and brow. A little vein throbbed at his temple.

In the short visit, Victor Dawson felt that he had learned a great many things about Dave Berger. He was a competent doctor; he was an honest man; and he was a man of conscience. Why, then, didn't he have at least the beginnings of a successful practice? And what the hell was all this fuss about a hospital hearing and the business about the boards?

Chapter Thirteen

Something was amiss, but Tony Manchester wasn't sure what it was. He had called Victor Dawson's hotel suite promptly at nine o'clock. Dawson wasn't in. That in itself was not peculiar. What was peculiar was the conversation he had had with Bill Benedict.

It was always annoying to talk to underlings. Secretaries, assistants, and others of secondary importance had a tendency to make everything more complicated than it ought to be. Creating confusion seemed to be their purpose in life.

Tony's secretary had placed the call for him; then she had come back to him to say that Dawson wasn't in, but a Mr. Benedict wanted to speak to him. Since Tony had placed the call, there was no way he could avoid talking to the man.

"Tony," Benedict said briskly as he got on the phone. The familiarity was annoying. "Victor's gone into Beverly Hills to do some shopping, but he asked me to call you to see what your plans were. You beat me to it."

The jocular voice irritated Tony further. "Yes," he said stiffly. "I did want to talk to Dawson. We should be able to move quickly now. I thought perhaps this afternoon we should call a meeting of the board —"

"This afternoon's out for us. Victor suggests tomorrow morning."

"That's impossible," Tony snapped. "Dr. Winston's funeral is tomorrow morning, so it would be in pretty poor taste."

"Does that matter?"

"I'll be going to the funeral," Tony replied coldly, "along with other members of the board, so it's completely out of the question. Perhaps we can set the meeting for tomorrow afternoon."

"That should be satisfactory. If it's not, I'll have Victor call you when he gets in."

The arrogant son of a bitch, Tony thought as he hung up. *He's playing some sort of game.*

And clearly, he was playing it at Victor Dawson's instruction. There was nothing more important right now than getting the deal completed. Tony was sure Dawson could easily arrange to meet that afternoon. He had been pressing matters for weeks, but now he was stalling.

It had to be connected in some way to Dr. Winston's death. Tony suspected that the head of Betco was now going to assume a tough posture; perhaps he intended to try for more advantageous terms now that the major obstacle was out of the way.

Tony was not going to stand for it.

He was still fuming over his talk with Benedict when the call came from the studio. It was Ted Cameron, the director of "The Medicine Men" series. He was having problems with Lina Lathrop, one of the young actresses.

"We've had to make some script changes," Ted said

almost frantically. "The scene wasn't working with her in it. Now she's acting like she's the star of the show. She's got her agent down there, and we're losing valuable time. You've got to handle it."

That was the last thing Tony needed right now, but he agreed to do what he could. With a television series, losing two hours of shooting could be disastrous. As it was, "The Medicine Men" rarely met its budget.

Tony's office was not on the Warner lot, but his company did most of its filming on a soundstage there. His office, in Toluca Lake, was only a few blocks away, so it took him no more than five minutes to drive over to the lot.

Lina Lathrop was a redhead, and she had a temper to go with the color. She was the kind of young actress who would probably succeed in the film industry by sheer force of will, wearing down anyone who stood in her way. Tony respected that; that was how he had succeeded at each stage of his career.

She was standing with her agent, Harvey Sanderson, at the edge of the set. Ted was standing with a group of technicians and actors; when he spotted Tony, he quickly excused himself and crossed the set to greet him.

"I'm sorry to drag you into this," he said, "but she got her agent into it, and he showed up with her contract. I couldn't believe she really had a clause guaranteeing her a minimum of lines."

"Yeah," Tony muttered. "Well, it must have slipped by us. There's no way you can see of giving her what's required?"

"No. This segment just doesn't have room for her character except as a walk-on, with no more than three lines."

"Okay." Tony nodded. "I'll handle it."

When Tony turned to move toward Lina and her agent, he noticed Harvey Sanderson's shrewd dark eyes watching him steadily. He stood where he was and let Tony come to him. That was a sign he intended to stand firm on Lina Lathrop's demands.

"Tony," he said, extending his hand and smiling. "Thanks for coming over to straighten out this matter."

Tony shook Harvey's hand and nodded stiffly but politely to Lina. "You should have called, Harvey," he said. "I'm sure we could have taken care of this matter on the phone. You didn't have to halt production."

"We didn't have a choice. Shooting would have been finished before we came to an understanding. I know you would never want to go back and reshoot an entire episode."

"We can't afford to keep all these people waiting, either," Tony said sourly.

Tony had not yet figured out what sort of game Lina and Harvey were trying to play, but his instinct told him they were up to something more than protesting a minor contractual breach. He knew that Lina Lathrop was out for as much as she could get as quickly as she could get it, but she wasn't yet ready for stardom. She was good, but it would take time, getting the public used to her face.

"Let's see if we can get this over with quickly. What exactly is it you want? Money?"

Harvey looked offended. "We only want what's been agreed upon. We want her scenes back in the script."

"Unfortunately, that's just not possible on this one. So, how can we make it up to you?"

Harvey laughed. "I've heard about the new series you've got in the works. What's it called? 'Gibson's Girls'? There's a part that's perfect for Lina. It's one of the leads."

Tony smiled. Virtually no one knew about "Gibson's Girls" yet, and certainly no one knew that Tony was already considering Lina for one of the leads. It would be very simple to give in now and agree to the request, but Tony didn't like to give the appearance of having been defeated.

"I can't make any commitment on that yet, but I'll be glad to consider her. Right now, the best I can offer is to make up missing lines in a future segment. I think the writers could come up with a story that could center completely around her character. It would be a good test to see if she could hold her own in a starring role."

Lina had said nothing during the conversation, but Tony had been aware of her reactions — an occasional light in her eyes, a shrewd smile threatening to surface, a slight intake of breath. Now Harvey looked at his client to see what she thought of the offer.

Lina smiled and nodded cautiously.

"All right," Harvey said. "I assume you'll write us a letter to that effect?"

"Of course. Now, if you don't mind, we should get back to work."

As they parted, Lina Lathrop finally spoke. "Thank you, Mr. Manchester," was all she said, but there was meaning in the way she said it.

That disturbed Tony. Perhaps she was tougher and more shrewd than he had given her credit for. He had checked her out, as he did with most of the people who worked for him. He knew only that she had worked Vegas for a while, had done some modeling, and had worked for an escort service that was actually a thinly veiled call-girl service. None of that had been particularly unusual for an aspiring young actress.

He had already made plans for her; the "Gibson's Girls" series was only one of several projects. But now, he decided, he'd better have more than a routine check done on her.

Chapter Fourteen

It was a day filled with surprises, but Dave Berger didn't question them. They seemed reasonable consequences after yesterday's tragedy. It bothered him somewhat that he should be profitting by Dr. Winston's death; but, after so many years of bad luck, he was unwilling to deny himself good fortune now.

Dave had spent most of the morning analyzing the proposition put forward by Melissa Baxter and the odd behavior of Victor Dawson. He had forgotten about the charge Andrew Collins was bringing against him, and he had forgotten about filing his own countercharges. However, just after lunch — a tuna fish sandwich and a Pepsi in his office — Dr. Franklin, the head of the hospital committee, called to inform him that the charges had been dropped. That was another surprise. When Dave asked for the reasons, Franklin told him none had been given.

Now, as the day was drawing to a close, there was

another surprise visitor. Dave sat in astonished silence for a few moments after Martina announced, "There's a Miss Shana Winston to see you. She said to tell you she's Dr. Winston's daughter."

The young woman who was shown into Dave's office was a tall, statuesque blonde with sparkling blue eyes. She wore a tasteful, subdued beige suit with a bright silk scarf. She was in her mid- to late twenties, and she was absolutely beautiful. Overwhelmingly beautiful. It took Dave a moment to regain his composure.

"Miss Winston," he said hoarsely. "Please sit down. I want you to know you have my deepest sympathy. Your father was a wonderful man."

"Thank you," she said, sitting in the chair across from the desk, and showing no sign of grief or any other emotion. "From what I've heard about you from my father, I believe you're intelligent and sincere. A dedicated man and doctor. That's why I've come to see you."

"Is there something I can do for you?" Dave asked, flustered and puzzled.

"Possibly," she said, her face still expressionless. "I'd like to know if you have any idea who's responsible for my father's murder."

Dave almost choked. He stared incredulously at her. "Murder?"

"Yes. I'm quite sure of that. But I can't be sure who arranged it."

Clearly, the young woman was overcome with grief and wasn't thinking rationally. Tactfully, Dave didn't tell her that, but tried very gently to dissuade her.

"I can understand how you must feel right now," he said. "But you really shouldn't allow yourself to think such things. Who could possibly have wanted your father's death?"

Shana Winston stared at him calmly, and then a faint smile curved her lips. "I'm not crazy. I'm not paranoid.

There are quite a few people who wanted my father out of the way, and I believe most of those people are relieved now. My father talked to me about the possibility of this sort of accident just last week. He didn't tell me everything that was going on, but he told me enough.''

Tears welled in her eyes, and her voice threatened to crack, but she regained control. "No, Dr. Berger," she said finally, "he was murdered. And whoever is responsible is connected in some way with Beverly Hills Hospital.''

Her words served only to convince Dave that his first impression was right.

"That's impossible," he said as gently as he could. "Everybody at the hospital loved your father. I hope you won't be offended by my saying this, but I think maybe the shock has been too much for you. If you'd like to see a doctor, I could recommend one.''

"A psychiatrist?''

Dave nodded. "Or psychotherapist.''

Suddenly, Shana Winston laughed. "Dr. Berger, I *am* a psychotherapist. And while I admit that doesn't make me immune to serious problems, it does enable me to judge when I need help.''

Dave was immediately embarrassed. "I'm sorry," he said. "But you have to admit you do sound —''

"Hmm?" She paused to take a pack of cigarettes from her purse. "Dr. Berger," she said as she lit one, "what exactly do you know of the events at the hospital these past few weeks?''

"What events?'' Dave asked, mystified.

Shana frowned. "Haven't you heard anything about the possible sale of the hospital to the Betco Corporation?''

"I heard rumors, but that's all. I don't usually listen to rumors unless they come from someone in authority.''

"Have you ever heard of a man named Victor Dawson?''

Dave nodded, astonished. "But what does he have to

do with . . . ?'' He frowned as he stared down at the new file folder with Dawson's name on it, still lying on his desk. He looked up at Shana again. "A man named Victor Dawson came to see me today," he explained. "As a patient. But what does that have to do with the hospital? Or with your father?"

"Victor Dawson is the president and principal shareholder in the Betco Corporation. My father was the only member of the hospital board standing in the way of his getting what he wanted. More than anyone else, he stood to gain by my father's death. I think he was responsible for the 'accident.' "

"That's impossible!" Dave exclaimed. "Dawson is a harmless old man. And a very sick one, besides."

Shana Winston lifted an eyebrow cynically. "That 'harmless old man' is reputed to be one of the most important figures in organized crime in America. My father wouldn't be the first man he's killed."

Dave scowled. She was sounding ridiculous again.

"But what puzzles me," Shana continued, stabbing out her cigarette in the tin ashtray on Dave's desk, "is why he came to see you today."

"You know I can't talk about that," Dave said quickly. "I can only say that he's a sick man, and he needed a doctor. And he said he was referred by your father's office."

"He was surely lying about that. Not only were he and my father enemies, but my father's office has been closed since yesterday morning."

Dave knew that Dawson's behavior had been peculiar. All those questions had struck him as odd at the time. But Dawson was clearly a sick man. In view of what Shana Winston was telling him, he now believed that Dawson had come to him because he wanted a doctor who knew nothing about him.

Shana was slumped in her chair now, studying Dave's face. "I understand that you can't reveal a patient's confidence, but you can tell me about what happened yesterday, can't you? It may be of some help to me.''

Dave told her what he knew about her father's death. He tried to tiptoe around the confrontation with Andrew Collins, but apparently Shana had heard enough of the truth to press him for the details.

"I don't dismiss the possibility that Dr. Collins may also be involved in this," she said. "He and his father-in-law have much to gain by this murder. And I believe Tony Manchester did threaten my father only a few days ago. My father hinted at this, but he didn't tell me how the threat was made or precisely what it was.''

Dave shook his head. "It's still very hard for me to believe that anyone would want to harm Dr. Winston. He was such a kind and good man.''

"You believe that, don't you?" Shana asked gently. "But it isn't true, you know. My father put on a good front, but he was far from being a virtuous man. He took advantage of just about everyone. He certainly took advantage of you; and until about twenty minutes ago, you were one of my suspects.''

"Me?" Dave laughed. "Now I know you're crazy!''

"You don't have any idea how my father took advantage of you, do you?" she asked seriously. "Haven't you ever wondered why your career hasn't gotten off the ground? Haven't you ever questioned the percentage of your emergency room salary that he took for himself? It was in my father's interest to keep you where you were, surviving, but not succeeding.''

A strange feeling was beginning to come over Dave. The more Shana talked, the less he understood. "I don't understand," he said. "How can you talk about your father like this?''

"Because it's the truth. For a great many years, my father and I did not get along. When I began to see what sort of man he was, I lost respect for him. It's only been in the past five or six years that we were beginning to talk to each other again. I understand him now a little better than I used to, but I won't lie about him or pretend that he was better than he was."

Suddenly she got up from her chair. "I don't know yet if what I feel for my father is love, but I do know I don't want to see his murderers get away with what they're doing." She reached into her purse, pulled out a card, and handed it to Dave. "Here's my office number . . . and my home number. If you think of anything that might help me — anything at all — call me."

After she had left, Dave sat his desk, stunned. Could any of the things she had said be true?

What disturbed him the most was what she had said about his own situation. The more he thought about it, the more it seemed possible that Phil Winston *had* used him. He still believed it had been fair to give the senior doctor a percentage of his salary from the emergency room, and he couldn't think of anything that Winston had done actively to keep him down. But if Winston had truly been his friend, if he had wanted to see Dave succeed, he could at least have told him about Melissa Baxter's service. Dave was beginning to see that, if Winston hadn't actually hampered him, it was possible that he hadn't helped him a lot, either.

Chapter Fifteen

By the time Andrew Collins arrived at the studio, Lina Lathrop had already finished work for the day. She was sitting outside the soundstage, talking to a few of the extras.

"Were you waiting long?" Collins asked as he drove up alongside her in the narrow studio street.

"I finished a while ago," she said, "but that's okay. I didn't mind waiting."

For Collins it had been a troubling day, but the moment he saw Lina he forgot his problems. In her presence he could think only of her. It was as if her personality was mesmerizing, and her liveliness infectious. This evening she seemed particularly playful; her eyes glittered with her secret; there was a self-satisfied blush on her cheeks; and she chattered ceaselessly about her possibility for a new job, a starring role in a series.

Collins listened to her with only half an ear. He was waiting for her to reveal what her surprise was.

As he drove her from the studio to her apartment, however, she didn't mention the surprise at all. Instead, she was totally preoccupied with her career.

Lina's apartment was in an elegant, modern apartment complex in Encino. Outside, from the street, all such complexes looked alike: sterile, undistinguished beehives. But once through the iron gates into the courtyard, they were lush private communities with pools and colorful gardens and walkways. Each apartment had its own entrance.

She had once described her decor to him as "Whorehouse Modern." Every room was furnished for lounging, and glittered with mirrors. The focus of the living room was a "conversation pit" of low plush sofas with large throw pillows; the large interior wall of the living room was tiled with mirrors. The bedroom, which was upstairs, featured a king-sized waterbed and a mirrored ceiling. The lighting throughout the apartment was muted and indirect.

When they arrived at the apartment, it was growing dark. Lina ordered Collins to mix a couple of drinks while she went upstairs for a moment. He took this as a sign that she had not forgotten the surprise she had promised him. Expectancy built into elation as he went to the bar to mix Lina's Campari-and-soda and his own Scotch-and-water.

Just being near her excited him. Watching her ascend the stairs, he knew he had to have her, not just for a few weeks or months, but forever. There was something special about her; she was more tantalizing than any other woman he had ever known. Just from the way she walked, with her hips swaying sensuously and head held high and proud, a man knew she was special, and knew that she knew she was special.

Until today, Collins had never considered marriage to Lina as a real possibility. There had been no way that he could break the tie to Alice and to Tony Manchester.

But now he saw a way out. With the Betco sale, the management of the hospital might change. While Tony Manchester would surely gain more power within the Betco organization, he might be eased out of the hospital setup. With Victor Dawson at the head of it all, Collins would no longer be so dependent on Tony's approval.

It would mean cultivating a friendship with Dawson, and that wouldn't be easy, especially since Collins had a reputation of being nothing more than Manchester's yes-man. But Collins had already begun to formulate a plan.

Lina descending the stairs was even better than Lina ascending. She had changed into a russet-silk caftan that gave the impression of revealing, even accentuating, the slightest movement of her body.

"Is this the surprise?" he asked as he gave her the Campari-and-soda.

"This?" She twirled enticingly and then laughed as she took the drink. "Of course not. It's something much better than this. But you'll have to wait a little longer." She snuggled up to him, standing on tiptoes to kiss and nibble his neck. "It's upstairs."

Collins reached around and grasped her right buttock, pulling her into his embrace. Bending his head, he kissed her full, warm mouth, relishing the fragrance and taste of her.

"I don't know if I can wait to get upstairs," he said hoarsely.

"It's worth waiting for," she promised, reaching into his coat pocket to remove his pager and turn it off. "It's something you've never tried, and I know it'll turn you on."

"I don't need anything to turn me on as long as I have you." He ran his hands up through the armholes of the silky caftan to feel her breasts; her nipples hardened at his touch.

"When you were a little boy," she teased, "I'll bet you couldn't wait to open your Christmas present either."

"You're right. I never could. And I never had anything that was wrapped as nicely as you."

"All right, little boy, you can go upstairs now if you want to."

"Alone?" He frowned.

Lina laughed. "Of course not. That wouldn't be any fun, would it?"

She led the way upstairs, giving him hints as they went. "Tonight you're going to make love to me, and then we're going to make love again while watching ourselves make love." She laughed tantalizingly. "And you can even watch yourself watching yourself make love, if you want to."

Collins had no idea what she meant until he walked into the bedroom. Usually lit very softly, tonight it was bright with lights. In the corner was a videotape camera.

"What the hell?" Collins exclaimed apprehensively. "You're not going to take pictures of us, are you?"

"Don't be a party pooper," Lina cooed. "It's exciting, you'll see. A friend loaned it to me, and she said it's terrific to watch yourself. Just relax and forget that it's on."

Reluctantly, Collins gave in and let Lina turn on the camera. As he lay down on the pink satin sheets and allowed Lina to undress him, he was anxiously aware of being watched. But as she began to run her tongue up and down his body, kissing and nibbling him, he began to forget about the camera and to think only of her. He was able to watch what she was doing in the mirror overhead, and seeing her voluptuous body moving over him was incredibly exciting. It was only a matter of moments before he, too, was exploring her with his hands and mouth.

She let him kiss her long and passionately on the

mouth before she pulled away and took his erection in her mouth. Lina could do fantastic things with her mouth and tongue, and she sent him into ecstacy. Meanwhile, his tongue explored her body and worked its way down to the warm folds between her legs. Together, they wordlessly expressed their pleasure and excitement.

Collins was approaching a climax when Lina suddenly pulled away, turned in the bed, and kissed him on the mouth while she positioned herself to take him between her legs. When their lips parted, she lifted herself up slightly on her knees, grabbed his erection in her hand, and then slowly sat down on it.

No other woman had ever felt like Lina. Collins felt that he was being consumed in the soft velvety warmth of her. He groaned uncontrollably as she rode him; his body was being taken within her body, his soul was being taken within her soul. As he looked up into her eyes, he was vaguely aware of seeing their bodies in the mirror above and behind her. She was possessing him, devouring him, and he wanted that, because it meant he was possessing her, devouring her.

They climaxed together. Time stopped, and the only physical reality Collins was aware of was the two full breasts undulating above him, soft and pink, with the nipples straining as if to burst.

Lina lay on top of him for only a few minutes before she got up to see to the videotape camera. Collins had forgotten that they were being taped, and now he felt somewhat embarrassed, but he said nothing. Then Lina turned off the lights and began to play back their lovemaking.

Lina was right — it was exciting. It was also a bit unreal. He hardly recognized the slender naked man on the screen as himself, though the woman clearly was Lina.

Lina lay beside him in the bed as they watched and, as the excitement on the screen began to build, so did hers.

And gradually so did Collins's. They made love again, even more passionately than before. With the actions on the screen and the reflections on the ceiling, Collins felt as if they were floating in space, in a sensual orgiastic space that had no firm foundation below, no sky above.

Hours later, as they lay exhausted in a casual embrace, Collins looked into Lina's eyes and finally voiced what he had been thinking for so long. "I want it to be like this forever. I'm not promising anything yet, but I want to try to divorce Alice. I want us to be married. If we're not, I'm afraid I may lose you."

"Shh!" Lina responded, her eyes darting away from his. "Let's not talk about that now. It'll spoil everything."

Chapter Sixteen

Beverly Hills, November 14 (Five Days Before Boards)

The skies were breathtakingly clear on the morning of Dr. Winston's funeral. It was the kind of day Los Angeleans were proud of, with all the pollution and debris chased away by a night of strong winds, and the warm sun bringing everything into sharp focus. To Melissa Baxter, it made Dr. Winston's death seem even more sordid, and what had been grief and fear before turned now to anger.

She forgot all about her usual caution and humility. When she dressed for the funeral service at the Westwood mortuary, she did not put on one of the simple housedresses that the hospital board members were accustomed to seeing her wear, but chose instead her best black Norell. She chose also to leave her knitting behind, and insisted that her husband accompany her, although Chuck Baxter normally remained in the background. And they drove to the mortuary in the Mercedes, not the Volkswagen. This was Melissa's way of expressing her respect and gratitude to Phil Winston, who had been at least partially responsible for making it possible for her to afford such luxuries.

As she and Chuck left the car in the parking lot, she knew that a number of people were staring at them, but she kept her chin high and did not acknowledge the stares. However, she did take note of those who had chosen to attend the service. Tony Manchester was there, accompanied by Andrew Collins. Indeed, most of the doctors and board members from the hospital had come. Even Dave Berger had managed to get away from his emergency room duties, and was standing just outside the chapel, talking to a young woman whom Melissa assumed was Shana Winston, Dr. Winston's daughter. Melissa had heard a great deal about her from Phil, but she had never met her.

Victor Dawson was noticeably absent, though he had sent his flunky, Bill Benedict, whose flashy manner of dress Melissa considered quite tasteless. She had grown accustomed to the fact that men no longer wore ties, but she didn't think all those gold chains around his neck were appropriate for a funeral. And his manner was even more offensive than his dress. He continued to grin at her long after everyone else had looked away.

Melissa didn't object when the usher seated her near the front of the small, dimly lit chapel, directly behind Dr. Winston's family. She would have preferred to sit near the back, where she could observe the others, but there was only a small group of mourners, and she didn't want to make a scene. The most disturbing fact to her was that she was seated next to Tony Manchester.

The chairman of the hospital board nodded a cordial but sober greeting to her as she sat down. She was still not certain that he was blameless in Phil Winston's death, and she was sure he knew how she felt. The recollection of that threatening phone call hung over them like a pall.

The service was short and simple, and there were no

tears for the deceased. Melissa sensed that of all the people in the room, she had cared most about Phil Winston, and that was a rather desolate thought, for what she felt for Winston was loyalty and gratitude, not love. Melissa had no idea how many relatives Phil Winston had, but she was sure there were more than the five people who sat in the front row.

There were masses of flowers, and Melissa assumed that most were from patients or business associates who felt an obligation to express grief but not to attend the service.

She was grateful when the service was over and she and Chuck walked back out into the sunlight.

Melissa Baxter was not frightened of death. However, a death like this one, which she considered untimely, gave her a queasy, apprehensive feeling. Phil Winston had been a forceful, energetic man. With his force removed from life, there was a kind of vacuum that something or someone would fill. Perhaps it was uncertainty of who or what that would be that was so unsettling.

Melissa and Chuck stopped outside the chapel and waited to introduce themselves to Shana Winston. Tony Manchester and Andrew Collins were directly behind them, and they stopped to wait only a few feet away. Before Melissa had a chance to edge away from them, Tony spoke to her.

"Mrs. Baxter," he said formally, "will you be at the board meeting this afternoon?"

Melissa was caught off guard, and she looked down at the concrete as she replied, "Oh, yes. I'll be there. Two o'clock, isn't it?"

"Yes," said a voice behind her. She turned to see Bill Benedict. "But I doubt if it'll be a long meeting," he added. "There's very little left to discuss."

The lawyer's attitude angered Melissa, and she noticed a flash of anger crease Tony Manchester's face before he spoke.

"There will plenty of time for everyone to speak," he

said smoothly. "I'm sure Betco wouldn't want it to be said that this merger was railroaded through."

Suddenly Shana Winston joined the small group outside the chapel door. "No," she said coldly, "I'm sure everyone wants to keep up appearances, no matter how dirty their linen is."

There was a long moment of uncomfortable silence, finally broken by Tony Manchester. "Miss Winston," he said, with what appeared to be perfect sincerity, "I want you to know I'm deeply sorry about your father's accident."

"Accident?" Her eyes narrowed. "I suppose that's to remain the official explanation. But I want you to know I will never accept it, and I have no intention of letting the murderer get away with it."

Melissa gasped. The ugly word had been spoken, the word she would never have dared utter in front of these men, no matter how much she might have liked to. Melissa knew of some of the problems that had existed between Phil Winston and his daughter, and her sympathy had been with the father. However, she had to grant Shana one thing: She had courage, the same kind of courage her father had had.

Shana moved through the group, as if heading to the parking lot, then turned back and announced, "I've been informed of your board meeting this afternoon. I intend to be there."

No one said anything as Shana Winston turned again and strode to the parking lot, alone and apparently needing no one to console or sustain her through an experience that had to be difficult, no matter what the differences had been between her and her father.

Melissa felt compelled to follow the young woman, although she knew how it would appear. She had always been loyal to Dr. Winston; now she would offer that loyalty to his daughter.

Leaving the group of men, Melissa hurried off after

Shana, calling out in her frail voice, "Miss Winston, just a moment, please."

Shana turned and surveyed Melissa with no sign of recognition.

Melissa was out of breath as she approached the young woman. "I'm Melissa Baxter," she said, "of Maturity Medical Services. Your father and I were friends as well as business associates."

"Oh, yes." Shana seemed to relax a bit. "My father has spoken of you."

"I want you to know that you can call on me anytime if there's anything I can do."

"Thank you, Mrs. Baxter." Shana was polite and respectful, but there was no real warmth in her voice. "I appreciate your offer, but there's really not much anyone can do."

"No, I mean . . ." Melissa stammered. "About your father . . . what you said back there. If I can help, I will."

Shana looked almost as if she might laugh. "Thank you," she said. "Perhaps I will call you."

Melissa sighed and smiled gratefully. "I'll see you at the board meeting."

"Oh, yes," Shana replied. "Of course."

As the young woman turned and walked away, Melissa stood for a moment, watching her go. Only then did she realize that someone was waiting for Shana. Dave Berger was standing beside his car; as Shana approached, he opened the passenger door for her.

Chapter Seventeen

Dave was intrigued by Shana Winston. He had never met a woman quite like her. She was beautiful and intelligent, but she was also strong-willed, decisive, and very, very cool. It was her manner, more than her belief that her father had been murdered, that engaged Dave. Only this morning, when she had approached him before the funeral service, had he realized how much like her father she was — polished, assured, and consciously charming.

To his surprise, she had asked him to have lunch with her. There was no coyness, just the straightforward question: "Will you take me to lunch after this is over? I'd like to know you better."

She had even decided on the place. "I know a cozy little French restaurant in Beverly Hills. It's quiet and relaxed, and the food's good."

She had been driven to the mortuary in a limousine, then had let the driver go, arranging for him to pick her up later at the hospital, confidently assuming Dave would accept her invitation.

Once she was in Dave's car and they were driving away from the mortuary, she seemed to relax. She sighed, shook her soft blond hair as if shaking off a pose, and looked almost vulnerable.

As Dave drove, he couldn't help but glance at her from time to time.

"You're not a native Californian, are you?" she asked, as if aware that she was now playing the game that men and women generally played on first meeting, as if it were more important than the events of recent days.

"No," Dave admitted. "Is it that obvious?"

"Sticks out all over you." Shana laughed. "But that's not necessarily bad. You seem to take even trivial matters seriously — more seriously than native Californians take even serious matters. You've got that East Coast angst, am I right?"

"Right. New Jersey and New York, to be precise. I take it you're a native Californian?"

"Yes. Partly. My parents divorced when I was five. I spent all my life with Father, within a twenty-mile radius of Rodeo Drive. Never out of shopping distance. However, Easter, Christmas vacations, and summers were always with my mother. Deep South — Atlanta. I'm a mix of Beverly Hills and the South . . . with maybe the best and worst of each."

Dave recognized this as a pose. The real Shana Winston was closer to the first one he had met, but he knew — as she probably did — that that woman was just a bit too intimidating. This Shana was meant to make him relax.

And Dave did relax over lunch at Chez Nous. It was the kind of unpretentious place that Dave was familiar with from New York, but would never have believed possible in Beverly Hills. It contained only a dozen small tables and the decor was not elaborate, but the food was excellent, though the menu was limited to one main course per day. Today's dish was *coq au vin*, and it was prepared to perfection.

As he and Shana talked of trivial things, he forgot about the circumstances of their meeting and his recent anxieties. Shana was a delightful woman, and he had the impression that she liked him, too.

Dave found himself feeling inexorably drawn to her. He tried to tell himself that it was ridiculous. They had nothing in common; she could easily do much better, and she probably had more than one suitor. With her looks and intelligence, every eligible male in Beverly Hills must be after her. And she was a psychotherapist. Why would she even bother with Dave Berger? Except as a case study, perhaps. A doctor with one foot on a banana peel and the other on the edge of professional ruin if he made one more false move, or blew his boards again.

Still, Shana's eyes melted his doubts about everything. What incredible beauty and sensitivity and power they had! Her mouth moved with such sensuality that he felt deep stirrings of eroticism he'd nearly forgotten in the past weeks. He fantasized what it would be like to kiss that mouth, feel the softness of her lips, the clean strength of her perfect teeth, the titillation of her tongue. . . . God! He was getting caught up in a wild desire to grab her, right there in the restaurant.

Suddenly, over coffee and chocolate mousse, Shana abruptly reverted to her earlier mood.

"Doctor, I intend to find out who killed my father," she said. "But I don't think I can do it alone. Will you help me?"

Dave was flustered by the suddenness of her question. "Of course," he said. "I'll be glad to do whatever I can. But don't you think that's really a job for the police?"

"I've talked to the police," Shana said, sipping her

coffee. "They refuse to accept that my father's death was anything more than an accident. Run over by a drug addict who was stealing an ambulance."

Dave shrugged uncomfortably. "Then I don't see what you can do. Or how I could possibly help you."

"You work at the hospital," she explained. "I don't. That fact limits what I can observe and learn about. I'll be able to attend board meetings, because I'll inherit my father's stock, but I won't have any power or any rights at the hospital because I'm not an M.D. I can't even vote on any issue of major significance — such as the sale of the hospital to Betco. You're in a better position to hear things from the hospital staff."

"What sort of things?" Dave didn't want to admit to Shana that other members of the staff didn't confide in him.

"I don't know," Shana admitted, "because I still don't know precisely what I'm looking for. Or even *who*. But you could just keep an eye out for anything irregular — particularly anything about Tony Manchester, Andrew Collins, or Victor Dawson."

Dave still couldn't believe that any of them were capable of arranging a murder. He knew very little about Tony Manchester, but he considered him highly respectable. His one meeting with Victor Dawson had given him the impression that the old man was tough and shrewd, but fair. And, as much as he disliked Andrew Collins, Dave refused to believe that he was capable of murder.

"I'll be glad to do what I can," he said finally. "But I really think you're wasting your time and energy."

Suddenly she looked vulnerable again and smiled mischievously. "It won't be a waste of time," she said softly. "If nothing comes of the investigation, we'll at least see a lot of each other."

A charge ran through Dave. Her words boosted his ego, promised an involvement he had already begun to hope for, and confirmed that she was as attracted to him as he was to her. He smiled back at her, but his eyes were serious. "As far as I'm concerned," he said, "we can start to work right now. How about tonight?"

"Maybe," Shana replied.

"Dinner and a movie?"

She shook her head. "Let's just say dinner. At my place. We have a lot to talk about."

Dave gave her a quizzical look.

"You're going to be back in the emergency room this afternoon, aren't you?" she asked.

Dave nodded.

"Then ask around. Try to find out anything that might have been out of the ordinary in the emergency room yesterday. See if you can learn how that ambulance was stolen. I'm sure that drivers don't normally leave the keys in the ignition. Try to find out why Dr. Collins wasn't at the hospital when he was supposed to be on call. Learn anything you can."

Dave was disappointed. Apparently Shana was determined to keep their relationship on a business level. For a few moments, from her words and the look, he had thought there might be some feeling for him. But she kept shifting, so he couldn't be sure where he stood with her.

When he took out his wallet to pay the check, Shana stopped him. "No," she said firmly. "I invited you." She took the check with obvious ease, paid the waiter, and left a sizable tip.

During the drive to Beverly Hills Hospital she was rather withdrawn, and spent most of the time staring out at the traffic. Dave thought she was preparing herself for the board meeting, girding herself to confront the men she suspected of murdering her father. He found himself wishing he could accompany her to help her through the ordeal. This, even though it wasn't his fight, and even though he didn't believe she was right in what she was doing. Shana Winston was getting to him.

As Shana left the car, Dave started to say something but could barely get the words out, for Shana had bent over to say something to him and her full breasts were suddenly revealed as the neckline of her blouse gaped open. She winked and said, "See you at sevenish, David."

"God! What a body!" he whispered to himself. He watched Shana walk toward the waiting limousine, taking in the symmetry of her figure — long lean legs, trim ankles, and hips that rounded into buttocks that evidenced just the right muscular vibration with every step.

He could visualize every bone and muscle and tissue . . . and in one blink went from an anatomical study to a nude fantasy.

Ah, but this is no time to get a hard-on, he told himself.

Chapter Eighteen

The old man had been behaving peculiarly ever since Phil Winston's death, but Bill Benedict attributed it to approaching senility. The only thing that troubled him was that Dawson had become increasingly uncommunicative. As Dawson's lawyer and closest associate, Bill normally knew everything that the old man was contemplating.

For the last few days, Bill could only try to guess at what Dawson wanted of him.

Bill hadn't seen the old man since early that morning in his hotel suite. Then Dawson had seemed listless, almost morose, as he stared out his window toward Beverly Hills, bright and glistening under a strong sun.

"You're not dressed," Bill had observed when he walked into the room. "We haven't much time before the Winston funeral."

"I'm not going," Dawson had responded without turning around. "You should go so that Betco will be represented, but I've decided it would be more tactful for me not to appear."

"Why?" Bill had asked, mystified.

The old man had shrugged. "Just call it intuition." He then fell silent for a long time, finally adding, "You don't have to come back for me before the board meeting. I'll meet you at the hospital."

In a way, Bill had enjoyed having the opportunity to spend time with the various members of the hospital board without appearing only as Dawson's shadow. Dawson wouldn't live forever, and Bill would need to establish an adequate relationship with the important men of Beverly Hills Hospital, as he had already done with various staff members at other Betco enterprises.

After the funeral, Bill had invited Tony Manchester and Andrew Collins to have lunch with him. Tony had refused, saying that he had other plans, but Collins had accepted, and it proved a very interesting lunch.

Bill liked Collins. The two were around the same age, had similar values, and spoke the same language. Of course, Collins had already achieved much of the prestige and influence that Bill was approaching, but that seemed no barrier.

Until now, Bill had seen Collins only at the board meetings and had considered him no more than Tony Manchester's shadow, much as he himself was Victor Dawson's shadow. In that context, Collins had always been rather subdued. However, at lunch, Collins was breezy, outgoing, and very congenial.

"Lunch is on me," Collins announced as they sat down at Le Bistro. "And I insist we have a couple of drinks to celebrate. Or would you prefer a bottle of wine?"

"No," Bill said. "Drinks are fine. But what's the celebration?"

Collins grinned proudly. "As of today, I take over

the emergency room operation at the hospital. Tony told me this morning.''

"Congratulations," Bill said. "But I would have thought that decision would have to be made by the board."

"Oh, it's only an interim appointment," Collins explained. "If it's to become permanent, the board will have to approve it, but possession is nine-tenths of the law, as they say."

"Isn't that position more trouble than it's worth?" Bill asked. It struck him as the sort of thing Collins would consider beneath his dignity, with his emphasis on wealthy, prestigious patients.

Collins shrugged. "It doesn't mean having to work emergency any more than I do now. Mostly, it means managing, hiring, and supervising the staff." After they had placed their order for drinks, Collins added with an intent, confidential air, "I'd like to move more toward management and away from surgery anyway. That's one of the reasons I'm glad we have this chance to talk. I think I have quite a bit to offer Betco."

"Oh?" Bill leaned back in his chair and lit a cigarette. As far as he knew, Victor Dawson had not considered Collins in his plans for the hospital. In fact, the last couple of days, Dawson had given him the impression he didn't think much of Collins. Of course, Bill well knew the old man's attitude toward the younger generation.

"I'm aware that most people think of me as Tony Manchester's son-in-law," Collins began carefully, "but much of the prestige of Beverly Hills Hospital is due to the prestige of my patients. I'm the best surgeon the hospital has, and I'm its best public relations."

Bill was puzzled. What was Collins getting at? "You don't have to sell yourself," he said. "As far as I know, we have no plans to change the staff."

"What I'm trying to say," Collins said, seeming embarrassed at the mild dent to his composure, "is that Tony has held me down. I'm hoping that Betco can separate me from him, consider me on my own merits. I know that Tony will move up to a position of considerable power within Betco. That's why he wants this merger. But I would just as soon not see him as head of the corporation if I can help it."

Bill was beginning to see what Collins was getting at; he was expecting a power struggle within Betco, and was offering his services to Dawson.

They remained silent while their drinks were served, and while Bill decided how to respond. He didn't feel he could be entirely honest with the doctor; certainly he couldn't reveal that Tony Manchester was mistaken about his prospects, should Victor Dawson die or retire.

Bill took a sip of his drink, then said, "It's probably unwise to anticipate trouble, especially trouble that might create problems within your family. Unless, of course, there are problems there already?" He looked questioningly at Collins.

Collins fidgeted. "There are always problems for a man married to the boss's daughter. It just doesn't work to combine home and profession."

Their conversation was interrupted again as the waiter appeared. They quickly looked over their menus, then placed their orders.

When the waiter left, Collins stared down at the tablecloth and said, "Look, I'll be honest with you. My marriage isn't working. The only way out is a divorce, but as long as I work for Tony Manchester, that's out of the question."

"I see," Bill said. "Well, I thought it was made clear that once the merger is completed, Tony Manchester will no longer have control over the hospital."

"I'm aware of the terms of the agreement," Collins said. "But once the agreement is signed, I'm not convinced that Tony is going to want to relinquish his control."

"What are you getting at?" Bill asked. "He's getting a lot of money out of this deal."

"Tony doesn't give a damn about more money," Collins said bitterly. "Power is what he's after, and he'll stop at nothing to get it. I don't know who arranged Phil Winston's accident, but I wouldn't be surprised if it was Tony. And it wouldn't surprise me if he arranged a similar accident for Victor Dawson."

Bill was startled. Dawson himself suspected Tony. And if Dawson's thinking mirrored Collins's, the old man's behavior the past couple of days now made sense. Dawson anticipated an attempt on his life and was probably planning his own move; he refused to confide in Bill because he knew that Bill would advise against any illegal or criminal action.

As this recognition flooded over Bill, he sat silent for a long time, staring at the young doctor across from him. Finally he said, "If what you say is true, perhaps you can be of help to us. Mr. Dawson and I would both be quite appreciative if you could find out precisely what Tony Manchester is planning."

A look of relief and satisfaction crossed Collins's face. Then the waiter arrived with their food, and their conversation drifted to more casual matters. But Bill Benedict was hoping he would have an opportunity to speak to the old man before the board meeting began.

As it turned out, Dawson was late for the meeting. Bill hovered anxiously near the door, hoping to call him aside when he arrived. But as the minutes passed, the board members began to take their seats around the large, highly polished table. When ten more minutes passed, Bill decided to sit down with them.

The old man arrived at a quarter past the hour, red-faced and blustering, with a look that Bill Benedict could interpret only as anger.

Chapter Nineteen

The boardroom was filled with tension. The external signs varied with the individuals around the table, some unable to contain a kind of elation or anticipation, others fearful and apprehensive.

Melissa Baxter sat in her usual seat at the back of the room, where she would be less noticeable and could watch the reactions of the others. After the funeral, she had returned home, changed to a simple housedress, and picked up her knitting. Now, out of self-protection, she resumed her efforts to blend into the background. Her survival depended on it.

She had arrived early, selected a seat, and had begun to knit. She always appeared to be concentrating on her work, oblivious to everything around her. But knitting required very little concentration. Her real efforts were directed toward the words and actions of the board members. She watched everything out of the corners of her eyes.

She took note of the fact that Tony Manchester was one of the first to arrive. He gave her and the others present a hearty but brief greeting, in his usual smooth, polished manner. However, beneath his actor's exterior, he was having difficulty keeping in check a boyish excitement, a pride in having bested his associates, in having won. Until now, he had managed to submerge his pleasure in order to express shock and grief for Phil Winston; now it took all his effort to contain himself.

Andrew Collins arrived only a few minutes later in the company of Bill Benedict. Collins, too, seemed happier than Melissa had seen him in some time, but his elation wasn't quite the same as Tony Manchester's. It seemed as if a heavy weight had been removed from his shoulders. That intrigued Melissa. It could have been because Winston's body had been cremated and now there could be no trace of any mistake he might have made in surgery. Or it might have something to do with the fact that he and Bill Benedict had come in together, though she couldn't even guess at what they had been discussing. She had never noticed the two young men engaged even in casual conversation before.

Strangely, it was the young lawyer who now seemed anxious and preoccupied. He had always seemed relaxed and casual before, almost ludicrously so, in the face of tense, bitter arguments of earlier negotiations. This afternoon, he hovered by the door, his body tensing every time the door opened. Melissa realized he was waiting for Victor Dawson, but she couldn't fathom his behavior.

Finally, when he realized that people were staring at him, Bill Benedict took a seat at the table, reserving the seat beside him for his boss.

Then the room fell into a strained silence as Shana Winston arrived. Her brief show of anger after the funeral had carried with it a threat. Those who had witnessed the scene were waiting now to see what she would say or do; those who had not were perplexed at learning who she was and why she was present. Here Melissa had quite an advantage; she knew more about Shana than anyone else in the room.

Shana was the only child of a bad marriage that had ended in a bitter divorce. Of course, Melissa knew that there were two sides to every divorce, but the fact that Shana's mother had not attended the funeral seemed to confirm much of Phil's side of the story. Angela Winston had done everything possible to turn Shana against her father. By the time Shana was in her teens, her mother's campaign had been successful. Only in recent years had Shana and her father begun to communicate again, and then it was always difficult for them. But even Phil had noticed how much his daughter was like him.

She swept into the board meeting, still wearing the beautifully tailored black gabardine suit and cream satin blouse she had worn to the funeral, her shoulder-length blond hair shimmering. She didn't speak at all, but nodded a firm greeting to Tony Manchester, then found her way to a seat at the opposite end of the table from the chairman. She had brought with her a small zippered leather case, from which she removed several folders and spread them out on the table in front of her.

She then sat silently and expectantly on the edge of her chair and stared down the table at Tony.

It seemed an eternity before Victor Dawson arrived. When he finally made his entrance, Melissa found his manner the most puzzling of all.

Victor Dawson seemed to be seething. He strode into the room with hasty, impatient steps, his head lowered, his brows fiercely pinched at the bridge of his nose, his face flushed. His jaws were clenched so tightly that his small mouth seemed almost to disappear.

His only greeting to Tony Manchester and the board was, "I'm sorry I'm late. It was unavoidable."

Tony Manchester's call to order was less than robust. His strong, well-trained voice broke the tension almost hesitantly, as he skirted the business at hand — the business with which everyone was most concerned — in order to speak of Phil Winston.

"I'm sure everyone joins with me in mourning the passing of an important member of the board. Phil Winston was not only a valued associate, he was one of the founders of Beverly Hills Hospital. I don't think it would be inaccurate to say that this facility could not have been built without him. In recent years, he and I have had numerous disagreements, but I never ceased to respect him, or to value the important contribution he made at the time this hospital was financed. It was his guarantee to fill one-third of the beds that enabled us to secure the loans necessary to start construction."

Melissa Baxter knew that these words were true, but they made her uncomfortable. It seemed out of place for Tony Manchester to be speaking them now. If Tony meant what he way saying, he — and everyone else at the table — had owed a degree of loyalty to Dr. Winston. The more Tony spoke in praise of Winston, the more Melissa considered him capable of arranging the murder.

Apparently Shana Winston was thinking along the same lines. Melissa could see the anger rising in the young woman's face.

"Mr. Manchester," Shana interrupted Tony icily, "I think we all realize what my father meant to you and to the staff of the hospital. However, we're here to conduct business, not offer a memorial."

For a moment, Tony seemed stunned. Melissa expected him to reply heatedly, but he said gently, "Of course, Miss Winston."

From across the room, Melissa noticed a slight grin on Victor Dawson's lips; it relaxed his clenched jaw a fraction.

It took Tony Manchester a few seconds to regain his composure and bring the meeting around to business. "When Tuesday's meeting was canceled," he said haltingly, "the questions of the sale of the hospital to the Betco Corporation had not yet been settled, though there was virtually full agreement on all points. Today, I hope we can clarify whatever points remain in doubt and bring the question to a vote."

"Mr. Manchester." Shana broke in again. "There's no need to hedge around the truth. Everyone at this table knows why the sale had not yet gone through. Everyone also knows that my father's death has resolved that problem for you and Mr. Dawson."

Tony Manchester smiled stiffly but managed to keep his voice in control as he said, "Miss Winston, you're out of order." But an angry flush was spreading over his face. "You're not even a member of this board. It is only by our generosity that you've been allowed to sit in on this meeting."

Shana's eyes flashed, and she arched her back, as if she was about to leap to her feet. "You know as well as I do," she said shrilly, "that the only reason I'm not a member of this board is that there hasn't yet been time to enter my father's will into probate. If you wish me to take this matter to court, I will do so."

"Tony," Victor Dawson interrupted, smiling, "I suggest you allow the young lady to speak."

The chairman glanced around the table. "Are there any objections?"

No one spoke. Most members of the board stared down at the table.

"All right, Miss Winston," he said irritably. "You may speak, but please keep your remarks brief."

Shana rose to her feet as Tony Manchester sat down. Her suit jacket was now unbuttoned, and it was obvious she had a bosom that commanded attention when she moved. Except for the slight shuffling of chairs, there was total silence in the room. Expectancy hung in the air as heavily as the smoke of cigars and cigarettes that formed a layer just beneath the fluorescent lights.

"I am not here to prevent this merger from taking place," she began. "I realize I have no authority to prevent it. I want only one thing — justice for my father. I want to see my father's murderer pay for his crime."

"Miss Winston," Tony Manchester said evenly, "in your grief, it may be difficult for you to realize the truth, but your father's death was an accident."

Shana remained calm. "I'm sure you and others at this meeting would like everyone to believe it was an accident. But I don't doubt that everyone suspects the truth, even if they don't say so. The fact that this meeting is being held here today confirms that fact. My father was killed in order to make this merger possible. If there is anyone here with any conscience or sense of justice at all, I want to ask you to vote to delay this merger. If there is anyone who knows anything about who was responsible for my father's death, I want to ask you to help me. I will respect your confidence and reveal no names."

She surveyed the group, as if looking for some sign of sympathy or hope, then continued. "My father was no saint. I would be the first to acknowledge that. But I take the manner of his death as an affront to human dignity, and I am angry. I hope that there's at least one person in this distinguished group capable of feeling as I do." She pinned them all with her unblinking gaze, then sat down.

There was a moment of silence. Then Tony Manchester began to rise, but his movement was interrupted by Victor Dawson.

"Mr. Chairman," he said formally, "may I be permitted a word?"

"Of course," Tony said, surprised but obviously relieved.

Dawson directed a strangely sympathetic look at Shana Winston before he began. "I have been concerned about some of the same matters as Miss Winston," he said. "It has distressed me that this merger may take place under a cloud of suspicion and rumor. That will benefit neither Betco nor the hospital. In fact, when I learned of Dr. Winston's death, I considered withdrawing our offer."

Dawson glanced toward the head of the table and saw Tony Manchester's scowl, then continued. "However, after careful consideration, I realize that would be foolish. Ultimately, good can still come of our association, and ultimately the timing of this board's decision will make no difference. There will be a cloud, no matter when the papers are signed. As far as I'm concerned, the sooner that's done, the better. I don't want us to run roughshod over Miss Winston, though. If anyone does know anything, I urge you to give her your help. It would be hypocritical of me to say I liked or respected Dr. Winston. But I acknowledge the contribution he made to Beverly Hills Hospital, and I suggest that Betco and this board agree on a suitable memorial to him. Perhaps it would be appropriate to rename a wing or a floor in his honor. Perhaps Miss Winston might have some suggestion. It would, I think, be a terrible mistake to ignore the man or his manner of death." Again he looked up at Tony Manchester. "That's all I have to say."

Melissa Baxter was awed by the way the crafty old man had turned around the entire mood of the meeting. Melissa knew it was a shrewd maneuver, but she couldn't help wondering if he truly meant at least some of what he had said.

The only person who looked uncomfortable after the speech was Tony Manchester. Of course, Melissa realized this might stem from the fact that he didn't quite know how to follow Dawson's words, but she also felt there might be more than that.

Very pleased with herself, she stopped knitting and spread her handiwork out in her lap, checking to make sure she had made no mistakes.

Chapter Twenty

Andrew Collins was delighted by the turn the board meeting had taken, chiefly because it had upset his father-in-law. It was rare that Tony Manchester failed to get his way, rare that cracks appeared in the fine veneer and he was revealed as human and vulnerable.

After his lunch with Bill Benedict, Collins was feeling much better about his prospects, and he took the events of the meeting as further encouragement. After Victor Dawson took charge of that difficult and embarrassing situation and resolved it smoothly, Collins knew he had aligned himself with the winning side. Dawson wasn't much to look at, but he knew how to take charge and make quick decisions.

Winston's daughter was taken completely by surprise by Dawson's suggestion. After her little speech, there was no way she could refuse the offer of a memorial to her father, and she accepted the suggestion that the emergency room be officially renamed the Philip Winston Emergency Care Center.

After that, the doctors on the board who constituted the general partnership felt they had disposed of their obligation to Shana Winston and to her father. They voted unanimously in favor of the sale to Betco. The necessary documents would be ready for signing within twenty-four hours. It would take longer than that to transfer stocks and readjust the power structure. But Tony Manchester was now a lame-duck officer, relatively powerless over Collins.

After the meeting was adjourned and the board members were chatting among themselves, Collins rose and moved swiftly to catch Victor Dawson before he and Bill Benedict left. Several other board members had surrounded Dawson to speak to him briefly and shake his hand. Collins waited patiently for the excitement to subside, then found his opening.

"Mr. Dawson," Collins said, extending his hand, "Tony and I would like you and Bill join us for a celebration dinner tomorrow evening."

Dawson was reserved but friendly as he took Collins's hand and shook it. "Thank you," he said, "but as soon as the papers are signed, I'd like to get a plane home to Chicago."

"Surely you can stay over just one more evening," Collins pressed. "My wife has been wanting to meet you, and I promised her you would come to dinner."

Suddenly Dawson seemed more interested. "Well," he said, "I wouldn't want to let Mrs. Collins down. I used to enjoy hearing her sing. I'll have Bill check into late flights."

Tony had stepped into the group in time to catch the subject of conversation. Collins hadn't mentioned his idea to his father-in-law, but by Tony's expression it was clear that he approved.

"You won't regret it," Tony said, smiling. "Alice is even a better cook than she is a singer."

Collins wanted to say more to Victor Dawson; but

once Tony had joined the group, he fell silent, and eventually he moved on to join a group of doctors who were comparing gas mileage statistics on their leased automobiles, though he paid the conversation scant attention.

Collins wasn't sure how much of their luncheon conversation the lawyer would pass along to his boss. He wanted an opportunity to speak to Dawson himself, but as time passed, it seemed less and less likely that the opportunity would come that day. After the vote, the board members were unusually relaxed — possibly relieved — and seemed eager to leave.

Collins glanced at his watch. It was almost four o'clock, and he had a lot to do in the emergency room before the day was over. The memo announcing that he would be taking over supervision of the ER had been issued shortly after noon. He didn't want to give the staff time for gossip and conjecture before he appeared and took a firm hand.

Most important, he had to take care of Dave Berger.

He thought about Lina as he went downstairs to the emergency room, and he caught himself humming happily in the elevator. It would be only a matter of weeks before they could enjoy each other completely without having to sneak around, snatching their moments between other obligations.

He felt a new confidence and assurance as he entered his new office — the office that had been Phil Winston's. He decided to do something to improve the sterility of the space. If everything worked out as he expected, he would be able to manage the emergency room from his other office in the executive wing, getting an assistant to take care of most of the work in the ER.

What he disliked most about this office was that it was next to the nurses' station. Of course, that was where it should be for the sake of efficiency, but he disliked being so accessible to the nurses. It would be particularly annoying when Emily was the supervisor on duty, as she was now.

The glimmer in Emily's eye as she caught sight of Collins told him that the memo announcing his appointment already had been widely discussed. Her former coziness became the intimacy of a sycophant. Clearly, she recognized the need to get on the good side of her new boss.

"Well, Dr. Collins," she said warmly, "congratulations, and welcome to the lunatic asylum."

Collins didn't return her smile. "This isn't a mental hospital," he replied coolly. "Our patients are physically ill. I realize you're referring to the slipshod and chaotic way Dr. Winston ran things here, but I want it to be understood at the outset that I intend to run things differently. This is an emergency room, and the staff is here to do a job, not to socialize and have a good time. We want fully qualified people, with *boards* in their practiced field of specialty, whether it is emergency room medicine, family practice, or even general surgery! Anyone who doesn't accept that isn't needed here." It delighted him to see her face fall and the color drain from her cheeks. "Do you understand?" he asked.

"Yes, sir," she said meekly.

"Good. Now, find Dr. Berger and tell him I want to see him in my office."

"Yes, sir." And then, as if trying to soften his attitude again, she added, "I think there's something you ought to know before —"

"I want to see Dr. Berger *now*, if you don't mind."

"Yes, sir," she said, and marched off down the hallway.

Collins watched her with considerable satisfaction. He knew that a greatly exaggerated account of their confrontation would reach every member of the emergency room staff within fifteen minutes. If that didn't put them on their best behavior, he had a few other tricks in mind. Whatever it took, Collins was going to have the emergency room working at top efficiency within a matter of weeks. Phil Winston had been far too lax with the staff, striving more for a friendly atmosphere and for personal loyalty than for rules and regulations. But Collins knew that figures were what impressed corporations like Betco, and he intended to show Victor Dawson some very impressive ones.

Collins didn't give Emily's attempt at a warning a second thought, until he opened the door to claim possession of Phil Winston's office.

Shana Winston was sitting at her father's desk — now Collins's desk — riffling through a stack of papers. The office was a shambles, with files scattered about, and drawers opened, their contents piled on the floor.

"What the hell is this!" Collins exclaimed.

Shana Winston glanced up. "Oh, Dr. Collins," she said coolly, then returned to her work. "I'll be out of here in a few minutes."

"A few minutes? You'll get out right now! You have no right to be here!"

She glanced up at him again, her pretty face hard as stone. This time her gaze remained steady as she said, "I have every right to remove my father's personal belongings before you take over."

Collins took her presence as an affront, an obstruction to his newly acquired power and freedom. He tried to keep his rage under control as he said, "Everything in this office is the property of Beverly Hills Hospital."

"Apparently you haven't read my father's contract. The only things in this office that belong to the hospital are certain records."

Collins realized that she was probably right. He had already planned to use the Winston contract to his own advantage — to nullify staff contracts and renegotiate them. That she was taking advantage of that same clause only made him angrier.

"It's not for you to decide what does and does not belong to the hospital," he said primly. "But there's no question that the space you're occupying is mine, and you're obstructing the management of this facility. If necessary, I'll call the police to have you removed."

Collins saw her hesitate. She knew he was right, but she stood her ground.

Suddenly there was a knock at the door. Then Emily Harris walked in, with Dave Berger behind her. The interruption caused Shana Winston's resistance to soften.

"All right," she said. "I'll go. For now. But when I return, it will be with a court order." She slammed her briefcase shut, grabbed her purse, and marched from the room, leaving Emily and Dave to stare after her.

It wasn't the way Collins had intended to greet Berger. He had wanted to be seated behind the desk, in full control of the situation, keeping Berger at a disadvantage from the time he walked into the room until he walked out. But Collins was rattled by the confrontation with Shana Winston; it made him feel that he was as much an intruder in this office as Berger was.

He had intended to give Berger his notice with an air of power and dignity. Instead, he said abruptly, "Pack your things. You're out."

Berger stood there staring at him. "What?" he asked, more confused than stunned.

"You're fired," Collins said, almost peevishly. "Canned. Your association with Beverly Hills Hospital's emergency room is terminated as of this moment."

"But my contract has over a year to go," Berger said. "You can't fire me without some grounds."

"Perhaps you haven't read the fine print." Collins smiled, regaining his confidence and his air of authority. "Your contract isn't with Beverly Hills Hospital, but with Phil Winston. It's automatically terminated by his death. All of the ER staff contracts are. However, we'll be negotiating new contracts with the rest. Yours is the only one we wish to terminate.''

The message finally got through to Berger. "I see," he said. "And you don't want me to finish my shift today.'' He stared at Collins without expression.

However, that wasn't the reaction Collins had hoped for or expected. There was no anger or outrage or wounded pride; if anything, there seemed to be a sense of relief, as if Collins had done Berger a favor.

"No," Collins said. "You can leave immediately.''

Then Berger smiled broadly. "With pleasure," he said. "Thank you. I'll see you at the board meeting of the medical staff.''

"You bet you will," Collins chimed, trying to sound confident and unconcerned.

Chapter Twenty-one

It had never occurred to Dave that he might feel good about being fired; but then, it had never occurred to him that he might be fired. His first reaction had been stunned disbelief, or that he had not heard the words correctly. Then, very briefly, rage and resentment swept through him as he realized that Collins was doing this out of spitefulness. But before Dave could open his mouth to respond to the action, a wave of relief swept over him and put out the fire.

He was still amazed at his reaction as he left the office and went to collect his personal belongings. There were several nurses gathered in the hallway, as if expecting him to tell them what had taken place, but he didn't even stop. He was as eager to get out of the place as a prisoner was to get out of jail. In fact, that was an apt comparison, he thought; he felt like a condemned man whose sentence had been lifted.

It took him only a few minutes to toss his few possessions into a paper bag and vacate the small cubicle the hospital called an office. Again, there were curious looks as he made his way to the emergency room exit, but he didn't stop for the nurses and orderlies who now seemed to know what had happened, if the grim looks on their faces were any indication. He knew they were all wondering if they might be next, anxious to know if this was the beginning of one of those personnel purges that followed corporate mergers.

That sort of thing might yet come to Beverly Hills Hospital, Dave realized, but his firing had nothing to do with business.

He was almost out the door when someone called out, "Dr. Berger, just a moment."

He didn't want to stop. It was a woman's voice, and he assumed it was Emily or one of the other nurses. He was pushing open the swinging door when the voice called, "David." This time he turned.

It was Shana Winston. She was slightly out of breath and wearing a frown. "I waited for you to come out," she said. "I wanted to talk to you." Then she looked at his paper bag and at the exit door. "What happened?"

Dave lifted the bag. "I've been sacked."

"I was afraid it might be something like that. I'm sorry," she said, sounding like a little girl. "It never occurred to me that I might get you into trouble."

"This has nothing to do with you," Dave said. "And anyway, I'm glad it happened." He looked around and saw Emily Harris staring at him from the nurses' station. "But if it's okay with you, I'd rather not stay around here right now. Can I buy you a drink?"

"No," she said. "I'll buy you one. My place? We had a date tonight, remember?"

Shana's place was a showplace of the starkly modern, a monument to chrome and glass. But it wasn't so cold and sterile, possibly because her color scheme emphasized a deep chocolate brown, which was complemented by other earth tones. One wall of her living room was given over to bookcases; the others bore fine paintings and lithographs.

The bathroom, he noted with a laugh, was done in pink and purple, from the towels to the wallpaper to the shaggy throw rugs — even the toilet paper.

By contrast, her bar was small and the selection was limited. To simplify Shana's bartending, Dave requested wine. He was actually less interested in the drink than he was in this woman who had suddenly walked into his life.

"You like the color scheme of my bathroom?" she teased.

"Pink and purple?" Dave shrugged.

"That's the rural South in me. Small-town girl; I take after my mother. She lived most of her life on a farm."

Shana set two delicate crystal flutes of white wine on the glass-toped coffee table in front of the sofa. Then she slipped off her suit jacket almost provocatively, sat down next to Dave, kicked her shoes off, and tucked her legs beneath her.

"I guess that's why my mother and father never made it. Too different. He was a big-city boy, from the North, and she liked her quiet Southern nights."

She saw Dave eyeing a wedding picture of her parents on the table beside the sofa.

"Taken at the church," Shana said. "My favorite shot of them. Look how happy my mother looks." She paused. "My mother was Southern Baptist, and Daddy was Catholic. 'Grandma never liked him,' my mother always said, 'but at least he wasn't Jewish.' "

"What's wrong with being Jewish?" Dave asked slowly. "I'm Jewish."

"Don't be offended. I know that. My mother lived on a farm. She thought Jews all had horns and worked in pawnshops and hid their money in pillowcases!"

"Have you ever been to a synagogue?" Dave asked. "To see a Jewish service?"

"You mean a Jewish church? Yes, once."

"Would you like to go this Friday night? There's a nice one on Wilshire Boulevard in Westwood."

"Well . . ."

"It'll be good for me to check in for a prayer before my boards," Dave said. "Might help."

"Okay," she agreed. Then suddenly she asked seriously, "So, what . . . will you do now?"

She shifted her position on the sofa, her skirt now well up on her thighs. Dave swallowed and tried to avert his gaze. He failed, and cleared his throat. Shana smoothed down her skirt but not much, and stared at Dave, waiting for a reply.

Dave shrugged. "I haven't had much time to think about it. And there may not be any hurry. I do have those Medicare patients from Melissa Baxter."

Shana scowled at this, but gave Dave no indication of why she found this distasteful. She said only, "Yes, I know."

"It may talk a while to find out if I can survive on that alone," he added.

"You can survive very well on it, if that's what you want."

Dave looked curiously at her. There was something she didn't want to say but was trying to communicate by innuendo. He started to ask her what it was, but she cut him off.

"Can you still practice surgery at the hospital? Or did that privilege go with the job?"

"No, it's separate. That would have to be taken away by a vote of the surgery committee, and Collins would have to provide something more than a personal grudge there." Then he added, frowning slightly, "Or at least I think he would. And the meeting of the surgery committee and the executive board of the hospital is still ahead — my biggest problem.''

Shana took a sip of her wine. "You know," she said pensively, ''I'm going to have to sell my father's practice as soon as the will is probated. I don't suppose you would be interested in it.''

She didn't put it as a question, but Dave knew she intended it as one, and he was embarrassed. "I don't know," he said. "I doubt if I could afford it at the moment."

To Dave's relief, she suddenly changed the subject. "Tell me," she said brightly, "why did you become a doctor?"

Dave shifted in his seat, took a sip of wine, and looked into Shana's eyes. She looked back at him warmly.

"You'll laugh," he said honestly, "but I really wanted to help people. Ever since I was a kid, I thought being a doctor was the finest thing a person could do. I guess maybe it was from seeing too many 'Dr. Kildare' shows."

"I am laughing," Shana said. "I had suspected that was the reason, and actually I admire you for it. There aren't many like you anymore, but there ought to be. My reasons for going into psychotherapy weren't as noble as that; I just wanted to solve my own problems. But now that I've solved them, I've come around to your way — I want to help others."

Dave shook his head. "And I've come to the conclusion that you can't help others unless you can make money."

Shana sighed and reached for the bottle of wine to refill their glasses. "And that's what everybody else is out for," she said. "It's a vicious circle. The almighty dollar is like power. And dollars corrupt."

"Yeah," Dave said bitterly. "But these past few months, I've begun to realize there isn't any other way."

"You mustn't let yourself think that way," she said softly, gently, then reached out and took his hand. "I like you, Dr. Berger, and I wouldn't like to see you change."

Her blue eyes were soft and misty, and her blond hair seemed to shimmer in the subdued light. Dave sensed a vulnerability about Shana Winston, almost a frailty, a deeper, more human beauty beyond the obviously physical.

He was trembling as he lifted her hand to his lips and kissed it. Then he pulled her toward him and kissed her lips, gently at first, but as she responded, he embraced her more passionately, her breasts crushed against him. Soft, yet firm, and warm. It was a long kiss, filled with promise. Dave wanted to carry it further, and moved his hand to Shana's open blouse, but she pulled away.

"It's getting late," she said. "I'd better see what sort of dinner I can put together so we don't have to go out."

The more time Dave spent with her, the more he realized what an amazing woman Shana was. She was constantly changing, slipping from flirtatious to prim and tough, from soft and passionate to domestic. This last was the most surprising. A line from something, he thought from a song, crossed his mind: *And what's more, she can cook.*

She was still wearing the elegantly tailored black suit and cream satin blouse she had worn to the funeral. Perhaps that was why she looked so out of place in the kitchen, with the small, neat apron tied around her. She was certainly no stranger to a kitchen. She clearly knew her way around, moving decisively from refrigerator to cabinet to stove, reaching for utensils with practiced efficiency.

Dave studied her every move, absorbing and recording every curve and line of her body. It was all he could do to keep from embracing her, devouring her, from making love to her right on the kitchen floor.

The sexual fantasies in Dave's mind, the wine, the smell of the food, and the pure joy of the moment were an exquisite tonic. He closed his eyes and reveled in it.

While they were eating, Shana suddenly returned to the subject of the hospital. "I suppose this new development will make it difficult for you to help me out with my investigation," she said casually. "Since you're no longer working the emergency room, people would think it odd if you hung around there, asking questions."

"Oh," Dave said, "I forgot to tell you. After my meeting with Dr. Collins, it slipped my mind. I did question a couple of people this afternoon — Dr. Nino and the nurse, Emily Harris."

Shana set down her fork and stared anxiously at him. "Did you find out anything?"

"Very little more than I already knew, or suspected," Dave admitted. "When Collins went into surgery, he was completely unprepared for the kind of case he was taking on. According to Dr. Nino, Collins thought your father had had a heart attack. That means Collins didn't get the message on his service, as he claimed — that is, unless Emily Harris is lying about the kind of message she left."

Shana frowned. "Dr. Nino was in surgery with Dr. Collins?" she asked.

"He was the only one available to assist, besides me. And Collins was so angry, he kicked me out before I could even brief him on the case."

"Did Nino tell you anything after the surgery itself?" Shana pressed.

"Yeah," Dave said somberly, "though it wasn't much. He was kept so busy clearing out the blood, he couldn't see precisely what Collins was doing. All he knows is that Collins closed awfully fast.''

"Was my father dead by that time?"

"No. He died while they were closing."

Shana scowled. "I don't know that much about surgery, but it doesn't sound right to me."

She looked at Dave, but he offered no comment. She shoved her plate away.

"Dr. Collins would do whatever Tony Manchester told him," she said, thinking aloud. "And, after what happened at the board meeting this afternoon, I'm inclined to think Manchester is the one responsible. But of course he could still be acting on Dawson's orders."

"If that was true," Dave said doubtfully, "why wouldn't Collins have had some idea of what had happened to your father before he arrived in surgery?"

"It could be an act," Shana offered. "He could have been pretending to be surprised."

"I don't know. But there's one other thing that doesn't fit in."

"What?" Shana asked sharply.

"It may not be important," Dave said carefully. "Probably just some of Emily Harris's gossip. But she swears that Collins's wife had no idea where he was two nights ago. She claimed he was supposed to be spending the night in his office. Emily tried his office and found no sign he had been there. Emily thinks Collins spent the night out with a woman. That's something Tony Manchester wouldn't be too happy about."

Chapter Twenty-two

Melissa Baxter arrived at Dave's office just ahead of the truck. She was more then usually flustered, out of breath and flushed, as Martina showed her in. Her hair was in disarray and she had even forgotten to bring her knitting bag with her.

"This is the worst part of my job," she said wearily, "transferring medical records. I wish there were some easy way — microfilm or something. Or if they could be kept in some central location."

She collapsed in the chair in front of Dave's desk. "The driver will be up in a minute," she said. "You'll have to tell him where you want them."

The driver was an ill-tempered man with a potbelly that suggested he would rather be drinking beer than delivering file boxes. When he arrived, Dave met him in the waiting room and told him to start piling the boxes in the receptionist's office.

The man guffawed. "Impossible. There's too many of them."

"Well, put what you can in there," Dave said, annoyed. "The rest can go in my office."

The man was swearing to himself as he left.

When he was gone, Melissa said, "He's right, you know. There are too many of them for this office of yours. They're going to be in your way until you can find a new place."

"After what happened yesterday, it may be a while before I can afford a new place."

Melissa started. "What do you mean? What does this have to do with the board's decision?"

"Nothing. I guess you haven't heard that Andrew Collins fired me from the emergency room."

"Oh, my God!" Melissa paled. "I've been so busy sorting and packing files, I guess . . ." Her voice drifted off. "But what about your patients in the hospital?" she asked, horrified.

Dave smiled. "Don't worry. I can still practice at the hospital. That shouldn't affect my patients at all. And we'll have the other matter between Dr. Collins and me out in the open at the hearing of the surgery board, including exactly what happened on the morning of Dr. Winston's death."

Melissa looked skeptical and unhappy. "I hope the board meeting vindicates you. It would be terrible for my subscribers if they were refused admission when they went in for surgery."

"I've already thought of that problem," he assured her, "and I'm planning to apply for surgical privileges at two other facilities, just in case."

Melissa still looked doubtful. "Even so, it would be a terrible inconvenience for some of my subscribers. Their trust is important."

She said nothing more about it, but Dave could tell she was worrying about what his change of status might mean for her own business, and he realized how dependent he was on her now. Without the files that were now being moved into his office, he would be completely out of business. If she chose to take those patients to another doctor, he would have to close his office.

He knew that as a safeguard he would still have to build his own independent practice, in case she ever decided to take back what she had so generously given.

He couldn't blame Melissa Baxter for his precarious position; he understood her needs. Instead, he found himself blaming Andrew Collins, and he finally began to grow angry about being fired. At first he had been glad to be released from what he had considered a profitless obligation, but there was more to his firing than that. Behind it was an implication that he was medically incompetent, and that implication would be picked up immediately by others. Just as it had been by Melissa Baxter.

He was sure Collins would attempt to have the surgery committee remove his privileges when the board met, and this interference could become a major point in his argument. After all, Collins could point out that Dave had been fired from the emergency room staff for incompetence.

Dave knew now how he would have to fight. As much as he detested the games the doctors like Collins played, he would have to play them for his own survival. Collins had turned on Dave to cover his own mistake, whatever it was. Possibly, as Shana Winston suspected, he was covering up a murder. Learning what had happened to Phil Winston was no longer just a matter of helping Shana get her revenge; it was a matter of his own professional survival.

And the one person who had witnessed Phil Winston's "accident" was sitting across Dave's desk from him.

"Mrs. Baxter," he said a bit too suddenly, "you said

some very odd things on the morning we met. Do you remember?''

She looked cautiously at Dave. ''No,'' she said softly, ''but of course I was very upset that morning.''

''When I told you that Collins had taken charge of surgery, you said you weren't sure Dr. Winston would survive. Why?''

Melissa stared down into her lap, where her hands were clasped, at a loss for something to do without her knitting. ''I was very upset,'' she repeated.

''Do you believe that what happened was an accident?'' Dave pressed.

She looked up at him then, her jaw firm, her eyes steady. ''The police believe it was an accident.''

''But Shana Winston doesn't believe it was, and I don't believe you do either.''

She started at Dave for a long moment. ''No, I don't think it was. But I have no proof, and I can't afford to make trouble. I know I offered Shana my help, and I would like to help her in any way I can, but unless it can be proved, I'd rather not get involved.''

''You don't have to be involved,'' Dave assured her. ''Just tell us anything you know.''

''I don't really know anything,'' she said nervously. ''I just suspect.''

''Do you suspect Andrew Collins?''

''I'll put it this way. I wouldn't be surprised if he was involved.''

Suddenly the deliveryman and his helper wheeled in a stack of boxes. They stopped their dolly next to Dave's desk and began to throw the carton haphazardly onto the floor.

''My God!'' Dave muttered.

''I told you there were a lot,'' Melissa said softly.

When the men left to reload their dolly, Dave turned back to Melissa. ''Who do you think is responsible for the accident? Tony Manchester? Victor Dawson?''

"It's just a suspicion," she said flatly, "but I think it was Tony Manchester."

Dave nodded. "That's what Shana thinks. Do you have any reason for suspecting him?"

She twisted her fingers as if knitting them together. "It's because of the phone call," she said hesitantly. "Dr. Winston wouldn't have gone to the hospital that early if it hadn't been for the phone call."

Dave leaned forward, perching on the edge of his chair. "What phone call?"

"I was meeting Dr. Winston at the hospital that morning at Tony Manchester's insistence. He had phoned me the night before to insist that I do so, threatening me if I didn't manage to change Dr. Winston's mind concerning the vote on the merger."

Dave was stunned. This was more than a suspicion. "Did you tell this to the police?" he asked.

Melissa hesitated. "No. It would have served no purpose."

Dave wanted to ask what kind of threat Tony had made, but they were interrupted again by the deliverymen. By the time the men left, Melissa seemed determined to change the subject.

"I appreciate what you and Shana are trying to do," she said. "But it's really no use trying. People more poweful and more important than you have tried to prove things against Victor Dawson, and they've failed. He and Tony Manchester haven't survived for so many years by being careless."

"Why do you think Victor Dawson is behind this?" Dave asked.

Melissa shrugged. "He has a reputation for such things. It goes all the way back to the forties, and the government's been trying to pin something on him since the fifties. He seems to be linked to organized crime — the Mafia, or whatever you call it."

Dave smiled wryly. "That seems hard to believe.

From the little time I spent with him, I liked the man.''

''I wouldn't know,'' Melissa said abruptly. ''But I understand these people aren't like they're portrayed in the movies. They simply operate according to their own laws.''

Dave had met Victor Dawson with no prejudices whatever. He wondered what he would have thought of the man if he had known then what he knew now.

He could get no further information out of Melissa Baxter, so he turned his attention to the growing stacks of boxes in his office. Only after the deliverymen had finished their work did he realize how much space the files would take. He would have to find new office space immediately. And he would have to find someone to assist Martina.

Dave sat back and surveyed the boxes. He felt torn. What would all the other general surgeons say if he became a primary-care physician? Would he be less accepted in the community if he didn't act like a ''pure surgeon''?

Dave thought about Dr. Stein and the other surgeons who took on GP work.

''Wake me up to see a sore throat anytime,'' Stein often said. ''It's easy. After all, I trained as a doctor. I do a culture, give a shot of penicillin, and the patient gets better. Piece of cake. I earn my sixty dollars that way, rather than on some poor-ass Medi-Cal consult.''

But Dave also knew how the other, more established surgeons would react.

''What's the matter, Dr. Berger? Can't you get enough work in your own specialty? Haven't you got enough referral sources?''

He would be accused of demeaning himself and the entire general surgical staff of Beverly Hills Hospital by lowering himself to do GP work.

Dave knew that Collins and the others didn't really care whether he did GP work. The bottom line was financial, because any case Dave took was a case out of their mouths. They might even get him off the Wilshire corridor. Whether it was for not having passed his boards yet, or for his GP work, they would attack whatever vulnerable area they could find.

Dave still felt a cold panic when he thought back to Andrew Collins and his first associate, Dick Klein.

There was really no limit to the hospital games! After working with Collins as a junior associate on a fixed salary for two years, Klein had asked for a larger percentage of the business and surgeries he brought into the practice. Collins hesitated. He didn't want to make Klein a full partner. When Klein finally demanded more money and a better position, Collins responded.

Klein, a hard-working, naïve young surgeon, went skiing for the weekend. When he returned, he found that Collins had locked him out of his office — actually changed the locks and keys. Klein was through as a partner and associate of Andrew Collins.

Klein tried to open his own office down the street from Beverly Hills Hospital, but with no consulting business and few emergency room cases, he and his family were eventually forced to relocate to the East Coast.

Dave tapped his fingers on his desk. He wouldn't be caught like Dick Klein. He wouldn't stand by and watch a Dr. Collins or a Dr. Stein and the others destroy him and his practice. He would take Melissa Baxter's offer. He would do whatever was necessary, even GP work, to survive.

Chapter Twenty-three

The signing of the agreement was a big moment for Tony Manchester. It was the final step before the crowning achievement of his career. That would come when Victor Dawson retired or died, and Tony could step up to be head of the entire Betco Corporation and be one of the most powerful businessmen in America. It was a long climb for a character actor.

Sometimes even he couldn't believe that he had done it. There had been a great many big gambles along the way, and this latest was the biggest of all. He was giving up control of Beverly Hills Hospital in the hope of gaining even more power eventually.

Power was a strange thing; Tony had never really understood it until he had obtained it. At first he had thought it was merely freedom he had wanted — economic freedom. But then he had begun to realize there was no such thing as economic freedom; there was only economic power. To have any kind of freedom for himself, he had to have power over others, and not just a little either.

Sometimes he wondered if the sort of freedom he sought was even possible. What he had wanted was to be free of dependence on others. After burying two wives, both of whom he had loved deeply, he had determined never to suffer such pain again.

To himself, he acknowledged that he had grown cold and perhaps ruthless. There was now only one area of his life in which he was vulnerable — his daughter. He knew that Alice was miserable in her life with Andrew Collins, and so far he had been powerless to help her. He had been too dependent on Collins for maintaining his control over the board of Beverly Hills Hospital. Soon, he hoped, that would change.

It took more than ten minutes to sign all the copies of the agreement between Beverly Hills Hospital and Betco. Each of the general partners of the hospital had to sign along with Tony, and there was a great deal of passing of pens and papers. The agreement was witnessed by the lawyers for both sides, and photographs were to be taken to go with the news release that had been prepared.

When it was finished, Tony felt a moment of apprehension, a sensation of speeding downhill on a roller coaster. It wasn't exactly fear, but the knowledge that now there was no turning back, whatever the consequences.

There had been no promise that Tony would succeed Dawson as president of Betco, but with his combined stock, it was understood that he would become vice-president, and he was certainly the logical choice for Dawson's successor.

But there had been something in Dawson's behavior the past few days that had bothered Tony. Rather than bringing the two old friends together, the Winston matter seemed to have driven a wedge between them.

Tony tried to believe that the old man's ill will was not directed against him personally. It was possible that Dawson was worried about his health and was taking out his frustration on those around him. Dawson certainly didn't look well, and his appearance seemed to deteriorate more each day.

Today he looked particularly bad. His dark eyes seemed swollen with pain, his leathery skin was sallow, and his hands shook as he signed the agreement for Betco.

Tony would never have brought up the subject of another man's health; it was impolite and impolitic. But Bill Benedict brought it up.

It was after the signing, when they were all standing around, congratulating one another and posing for the photographer. Tony had just finished posing with Dawson and the two lawyers. Collins had been standing off to the side, watching the photo session. When it was over, Collins joined the group.

"Collins," Bill Benedict said brightly, extending his hand, "there's something I meant to tell you yesterday after you invited us to dinner. Victor is rather limited in what he can eat these days. His doctor has him on a special diet of —"

But Dawson broke in angrily and said to Collins, "Don't listen to him. He doesn't know what he's talking about. I can eat whatever your wife serves."

Collins looked confused and embarrassed. Not knowing how to respond, he looked foolishly from one man to the other.

That was when Tony said, "If there's anything particular you have to watch, I'm sure Alice could adjust her menu." He smiled. "I know a doctor's wife doesn't like to go against doctor's orders."

"It's nothing that serious," Dawson said, flashing an angry look at Benedict. "I'm not sick, just trying to lose a little weight. It won't do any harm to go off it for one night."

"But I've got my orders," Benedict said firmly. "I'm not supposed to let you —"

"That's enough! I know what I can and can't do!" Then he turned to Tony and Collins with a laugh. "He's going to make you think you just sold your hospital to an invalid. And nothing's further from the truth."

The look he turned on Tony then was one of defiance, as a defeated soldier might give an enemy when faced with a choice between surrender and death. It was such a cold look that Tony shivered. He had the impression he was supposed to take that look personally, which he did, though he had no idea what he had done to deserve Dawson's enmity.

Tony was resentful and angry but did his best to hide it. Smiling pleasantly, he said, "I don't think anyone here doubts that we've made a good deal. We're very pleased to be a part of the Betco Corporation, and we're aware that Betco is synonymous with Victor Dawson." Then he stared straight into Dawson's eyes. "We're counting on your good health."

Dawson glowered at him but said nothing, then turned away to join a group of the doctors.

"Is something wrong with him?" Collins asked. "Something serious?" Until now, Tony hadn't noticed the anxious, almost frightened look on his son-in-law's face.

Bill Benedict replied nervously, "I'm afraid I've already said more than I should. Forget it."

Whatever effect Benedict expected his answer to have, it didn't make anyone forget the question of Victor Dawson's health. The young lawyer had already acquired a reputation for bluntness, but even he should have been capable of more subtlety than that. Now everyone present was wondering just how long Victor Dawson would be overseeing the new administration of the hospital.

Immersed in thought, Tony barely heard Collins say,

"If there are certain foods he should stay away from, I'd be glad to call my wife and ask her to make adjustments. He wouldn't have to know."

"No, we'd better leave it alone," Benedict replied. "He would be sure to suspect that we'd interfered. With the mood he's in, that would be worse than having him go off his diet. It really isn't anything that serious."

Chapter Twenty-four

The vultures were already hovering, and he wasn't even dead yet. Victor had expected it, but it made him angry that they were all so predictable. He had no idea how he might have behaved if he had been in their shoes, waiting for someone else to die, but he didn't think he would have made his eagerness quite so obvious as Tony Manchester had done, or even Andrew Collins and Bill Benedict, for that matter.

He had to squelch the urge to get rid of all of them, reminding himself that any replacements he might find would probably be even worse. Individually, none of them meant anything to Victor; he hated them all. The only thing that was important to him was the success of Betco, and especially the success of Beverly Hills Hospital, now that the merger was complete. The merger completed, he wanted to get the first plane to Chicago and go straight home. But he would need the cooperation of Manchester and Collins for at least a few more months, so he would have to keep up the appearance of friendship. It would have been too obvious of him to turn down the invitation. Just as it was obvious to him that Collins had issued the invitation on the spur of the moment. After all, Victor had been in town for several weeks, and there had been plenty of time to plan ahead.

Victor couldn't be sure what sort of game Collins was playing, but he didn't need to know. Of them all, he trusted Collins least. He was an opportunist, a chameleon, changing with the moment. Benedict had reported to Victor on his lunch with Collins, detailing the conversation with the satisfaction of a back-fence gossip, and he had been disappointed when Victor had not responded with enthusiasm.

At times, Victor was dismayed by the young lawyer. Benedict could be positively brilliant in business, displaying shrewdness and fine judgment; but he could also be an utter fool, completely gullible and startlingly crude, as he had been this afternoon. At such times, Victor wondered if it had been wise to place so much faith in him.

Benedict had certainly used poor judgment at the hospital this afternoon. Even the most insensitive fool would have known better than to give Tony Manchester the impression that Dawson's health was failing.

In the limousine on the way back to the hotel, Benedict apologized for his gaffe in his own bungling way, and that angered Victor even more than the mistake he had made.

"I didn't realize it would create such a problem," Benedict said honestly. "I only wanted to avoid a more serious problem. Before we left Chicago, you told me yourself how important it was to keep you from going off your diet. And the doctor did give me detailed instructions —"

"I'm not a child," Victor said curtly. "And I've got

as good a memory as you have. If I'd wanted you to say something to Collins and Manchester, I would have told you. Remember, you're working *for* me, not against me."

One thing had to be said for Bill Benedict: He didn't grovel like the others did when Victor reminded them who was boss. Benedict stood his ground. "They're not stupid," he said. "They would have suspected something was wrong if you attended the dinner and ate nothing."

"They would have suspected," Victor said. "They wouldn't have known for a fact."

"So you're on a diet." Benedict shrugged. "So are half the people in the country. It's fashionable."

It was possible that Benedict was right, but Dawson was unwilling to admit it to him. In order to convince Manchester and Collins that nothing was wrong, he and Benedict would have had to discuss the matter beforehand and agree on an approach. Benedict was still wrong to have sprung it so suddenly.

Victor glowered across the seat at him. "It's too late to do anything about it now," he said. There were more important matters to be taken care of: messages to be forwarded to the office in Chicago, arrangements to be made for a meeting with the Betco board as soon as they returned, and personnel records to be reviewed. After the long stalemate, there was now much to be done.

By the time they reached the hotel, Victor had given Benedict all his instructions for the afternoon, so he excused himself to go to his room for a rest. All this talk of his health seemed to have increased the pain in his side. It took a great effort for him to behave normally and maintain his strong, forceful manner. Benedict appeared to notice but said nothing.

The strain of the past week had taken its toll, but Victor did not accept that until he walked into his bedroom and closed the door. Only then, alone and with his goal accomplished, did he give in to his pain. It overwhelmed him. His hands shook uncontrollably as he untied his tie and loosened his collar. He managed to remove his suit jacket; but when he sat down on the edge of the bed to bend over and remove his shoes, the pain was too severe for him even to reach them.

He felt as if his belly were going to split open. He collapsed back onto the bed, clutching his arms around his belly as if that would keep him whole and drive out the pain. But, if anything, it seemed to worsen. He crawled up the bed, writhing in silent agony, then buried his face in the pillows for fear that he might have to cry out. He shuddered, caught between his determination to fight and his desperate need to relax.

Gradually he was able to relax, and the pain subsided a little, but his clothes had become damp and uncomfortable from perspiration, and the pillow felt hot and sweaty. However, he didn't want to move to undress and crawl between the sheets for fear the pain would increase again.

He drifted into an uncomfortable, fitful semisleep.

When the phone awakened him, he had no idea how long he had lain there. The shadows in the hotel room had gone very dark, so he guessed it was about five o'clock. He didn't answer the phone, but waited to see if Benedict would pick it up. The pain had subsided but had not ceased, and he preferred not to speak to anyone unless he had to.

The phone stopped in the middle of the third ring, and Victor relaxed, waiting to see if Benedict would call him.

After a moment the bedroom door eased open a few inches and Benedict peered into the room, a dark shadow lit from behind.

"Victor," he whispered, "are you awake?"

"Yes," he replied, his voice cracking from sleep. "Is it important?"

"It's your daughter," Benedict said, still speaking softly. "Shall I tell her you're asleep?"

His daughter! As far as he knew, none of his children knew where he was. Of course, when Margot needed money, she could be amazingly resourceful in tracking him down, and he naturally assumed she was the daughter who was calling.

But he asked, "Which daughter? Margot?"

"No," Benedict replied, opening the door fully and stepping into the room. "It's Phyllis. That's why I thought I should ask."

That was enough to awaken Victor fully. He hadn't heard from Phyllis since last Christmas. Since she had taken the trouble to find out where he was, he knew it was important.

"I'll talk to her," he said to Benedict. "But give me a moment."

He sat up slowly and reached out gingerly to switch on the bedside lamp next to the phone. After taking a moment to adjust to the light and to sitting up, he picked up the receiver.

"Hi!" The voice at the other end was still familiar, though Victor had not heard it often in the past few years. It always recalled the little Phyllis, the impish one who delighted in playing one-upmanship with her father. As a child, her favorite game had been Chinese checkers, and she hadn't been satisfied until she had mastered it sufficiently to beat Victor eight times out of ten. When she had grown into her teens, however, they had grown apart. She had become a hippie, and afterward she had joined a commune, disappearing from Victor's life almost completely.

"To what do I owe this honor?" he asked as cheerfully as he could.

"I didn't expect you to remember," Phyllis said playfully, "so I thought I would call to remind you it's my birthday. I thought you might want to wish me a happy birthday."

"I forgot completely." Victor had to smile. "But of course I always have, haven't I? Happy birthday. Are you doing anything to celebrate?"

"At my age?" She laughed. "I can't admit my age to anyone but you."

Victor realized he didn't even remember how old she was. *Twenty-six? Twenty-seven? My God! No, she was much older than that. Thirty?*

"No," she said, "I'm just going to spend the evening alone in my apartment, maybe read a little, maybe watch television."

"Your apartment? Aren't you in that commune in Arizona anymore?"

"No," she said, serious now. "I left there three months ago. I'm in San Francisco. I've got a job and I'm going back to school part-time. It may take me six years, but I'm going to get my master's."

This pleased Victor, but he didn't say so. He merely asked, "Would you like some money so you won't have to work?"

"Thanks, Dad, but it's important to me to do it by myself. Anyway, I enjoy the work I'm doing."

"What sort of job is it?"

She laughed nervously. "It's just an ordinary book-keeping job, but it's kind of nice for a change."

Phyllis had been an economics major in college and had been at the top of her class until she began her flirtation with Marxism. She was capable of far more than bookkeeping, but Victor tactfully didn't say so. It was pleasure enough for him to know that she had moved back out into the world. Also, since it was her birthday, and since he didn't feel well, he didn't want to start an argument.

"Why did you leave that place in Arizona?"

There was a moment of silence at the other end. Then

Phyllis laughed. "Well, Dad, I have to admit that you won that one. It just didn't work. I guess you were right about people needing a power structure. We all finally called it quits in August."

"I'm sorry you're spending your birthday alone," Victor said, to change the subject. "Do you have friends in San Francisco?"

"Oh, sure, but I wanted to spend the day alone. It's the big three-oh, and you know what I used to say about that."

Victor did. Her whole generation used to say it: *You can't trust anyone over thirty.*

Suddenly he was struck by a fierce pain in his side, and he dropped the phone as he doubled over, clutching at his belly. He knew Phyllis was saying something; he could hear the crackling sound coming from the receiver lying beside him on the bed. He told himself that he had to endure the pain long enough to finish the conversation without her suspecting anything was wrong.

He forced himself to pick up the receiver and put it to his ear again.

"Hello?" she was saying anxiously. "Dad, are you there?"

"Yes," he managed.

"Is something wrong?"

"No, but I'm going to have to go soon. I have an appointment."

"You sound funny, Dad," she said warily. "Are you sick or something?"

"I was just reaching for a pad and pencil. I want to be sure to get your new address and phone number."

He had a pad and pencil on the bedside table, and he took down the information as she gave it to him.

And then he said, "I've got to go now. Thanks for calling so I could wish you a happy birthday."

"Sure." She laughed. "I'll do it again next year."

Victor hung up, then doubled up again on the bed. He

knew he would somehow have to find the stamina to get up and shower and change to go to the dinner party.

The longer the pain stayed, the angrier he became. And finally, when he could delay no longer, it was his anger that enabled him to get up and go to the shower.

Chapter Twenty-five

Andrew had given her very short notice to plan the dinner party, but Alice was pleased nonetheless. It always pleased her to be included in his life, no matter what the inconvenience for her. All the anxiety, the scurrying around shopping, and making plans since yesterday were preferable to the endless weeks of sitting at home alone, watching television and wondering where her husband was.

She wanted to make the evening a success for both her husband's sake and her father's. She was preparing the finest dishes in her repertoire, centering the dinner around a beef Wellington and concluding with rich, creamy chocolate mousse. She had restocked the brandies and liqueurs in the bar and hunted down the finest wines to accompany the meal.

Victor Dawson would simply have to be impressed, and Andrew would have to be grateful. The success of the evening might bring her and Andrew close again.

The most difficult problem had been to find suitable dinner partners for the three single men. Of course, there were plenty of unattached women in Beverly Hills, but finding the right ones for two men she had never met required great effort, especially on such short notice. After going through her address book several times, she finally settled on Angela Driscoll, the widow of a successful film producer, and her daughter, Heather, who was a student at UCLA. For her father, Alice invited her old standby — and his — Danielle Dore, a well-known press agent.

She arranged to have Tony and the women guests arrive before Dawson and Benedict so that there would be a festive atmosphere in progress. Just in case the party proved to be so successful that everyone lingered long after dinner, she managed to get a new, unreleased film from the studio and a projectionist to show it.

Alice had no problem selecting something to wear. During all the time that Andrew had been leaving her to her own devices, she had done a great deal of shopping on Rodeo Drive. Her closet was filled with unworn clothes, among them a long at-home gown she had been wanting to wear for some time. It was pale blue, matching her eyes exactly, backless, and practically frontless as well, softly draped like something from classical Greece or Rome. She knew she looked glamorously seductive in it. If it did nothing to improve her marriage, there was something seriously wrong.

The evening began well, even though Alice picked up an air of tension between Andrew and her father. It was not that there seemed to be a strain between them; rather, they both seemed preoccupied with some concern that neither was willing to voice. Or perhaps it was separate concerns; she couldn't be sure. Both were making an effort to hide their feelings, and of course Tony was doing it more successfully, because he had more practice at being inscrutable. Only Alice, who knew their every mood intimately, could perceive that there was something beneath the surface.

Tony seemed anxious, apprehensive, almost frightened. He was more subdued than usual. Andrew was unnaturally elated, laughing and talking with the women and drinking more than was appropriate for the occasion.

Alice assumed their concerns were connected with Victor Dawson, because their moods became more extreme with his arrival.

Victor Dawson was not what Alice had expected. Despite his girth, he was a little old man, almost frail in appearance. He was not the personification of evil that the newspapers had described, nor was he the image of ruthless power that Tony and Andrew had led her to expect. She found him quiet and charming. And there was something about his eyes that she liked instantly. There was intelligence in them, but also something sympathetic — a suggestion that he had endured pain silently, as she had.

When she greeted him at the door, his face broke into a warm smile, and he took her hand, lifted it to his lips, and kissed it, saying, "I'm very glad to meet you at last, so I can tell you how much I've missed you. They're not making voices like yours anymore."

She sensed that he was sincere, and she was gratified. She laughed and blushed slightly as she replied, "I think it's more that they aren't writing songs for voices like mine anymore."

Bill Benedict was also a surprise, though not a particularly pleasant one. The look he gave her when they met was a little too familiar. It was the sort of hungry, sexual leer that suggested that they skip the formalities and hop right into bed. Certain kinds of men gave her that look all the time; Alice despised them.

However, she tried to be as nice to Benedict as she was to her other guests. The problem was that it only encouraged him, and she had to look for ways to avoid him.

At first, she was stuck with him. After she made the necessary introductions, Andrew led Victor Dawson to the bar, leaving her to escort the young lawyer. She tried to signal to Andrew to take him off her hands, but he was so intent on being charming to the guest of honor that he didn't see her look.

Nor did he see that Bill Benedict had slipped his arm around her waist and was holding her much too tightly.

"I agree with Victor." Benedict cooed in her ear. "You're the kind of woman who was meant to be shared. How does Andrew manage to keep you all to himself?"

Alice felt like slapping his face, but she forced herself to give him a stiff, formal smile and said flatly, "It isn't difficult; it's just something called love."

She didn't like the smug, knowing look that crept over Benedict's face. Somehow he seemed to know that things were not as they should be between her and her husband, and that angered her more.

To her relief, they reached the bar before anything more could be said, and Andrew called out, "What will you have to drink, Bill? Victor?"

When Benedict pulled away from her to say, "Scotch-and-soda," she managed to move over to stand next to Victor Dawson, hoping Benedict wouldn't follow.

There was a strange look on Dawson's face, a look almost of pain caught unaware, and Alice wondered what Andrew had said to him. However, as soon as the old man saw Alice beside him, the look disappeared and he smiled warmly and said, "You know, you look even lovelier than you did ten years ago, when I caught your act in Vegas. Do you have some secret formula?"

Alice laughed. "I suppose growing up has something to do with it. I was still a kid then, you know."

"Victor?" Andrew interrupted. "What'll you have to drink?"

"Scotch-and-soda will be fine."

Alice noticed a strange look pass between Bill Benedict and Dawson, and wondered what it meant. Did it have something to do with the drink? With her? Or possibly with Andrew?

She quickly realized that it was the drink. Dawson took his Scotch and downed it in one swallow, then handed the glass back to Andrew for a refill. The look on Benedict's face delighted her, but she was worried about what significance this had for her guest of honor.

If he got drunk, there might be problems ahead.

Just to make sure, once Dawson had his second drink in his hand, she guided him over to rejoin the ladies, so that he had no chance to repeat his gesture of defiance.

Chapter Twenty-six

The pain had not lessened by the time Victor arrived at the Collins home with Bill Benedict, but with great effort he had managed to cover it up. He knew that Benedict suspected his condition because he had again brought up the subject of being careful about eating and drinking tonight. However, Victor had silenced him angrily, saying that if he didn't leave the subject alone, he would have the driver take Benedict back to the hotel.

Benedict said no more, but it became clear that he was not going to mind his own business while they were standing at the Collinses' bar. Victor had asked for a Scotch-and-soda, intending just to carry it around for appearance's sake. But when he saw the look from Benedict, he downed the drink to remind the son of a bitch who was boss.

It had been a long time since he had had a drink, and it felt good. It seemed to numb the pain, so he decided it would do no harm to drink for one evening; if anything, it might help.

Victor liked his hostess. He meant every compliment he gave her. She was beautiful, intelligent, cultured — much too good, in fact, for a man like Andrew Collins. Benedict had told him about the Collinses' marital situation, and Dawson couldn't imagine why any man could want more than what Alice Collins offered. He thought even less of Collins after meeting his wife.

Collins had been trying to ingratiate himself with Victor ever since he had walked in the door, but Victor was having none of it. He was pleased when Alice took his arm and guided him back into the room to join the other guests.

Both Collins and Benedict followed uneasily, each watching Victor jealously as he sat on the sofa between Angela and Danielle. The two young men hovered on the edge of the group, waiting, Bill to remind him to be careful of what he ate and drank, Collins looking for any opportunity to have a conversation with him.

Vultures. No, Victor thought suddenly, that was not quite accurate. They were more like hounds yapping at his heels. The hounds of hell. He had been pursued by such creatures for as long as he could remember, but until now they had never gotten so close, never made him so aware of their pursuit.

Tony Manchester, another hound, but a quiet one at the moment, sat across from him, listening to Danielle tell a funny anecdote about a famous actress whose luggage had been lost on a publicity tour.

Victor felt safe seated between the two mature, attractive women who couldn't possibly want more from him than the pleasure of his company for the evening. He allowed himself to relax and feel comfortable, laughing at the story along with the others.

When he finished his drink, he gave his glass to Alice for a refill. He noticed Bill Benedict follow her to the bar and speak to her, and he wondered if the lawyer was advising her to make it a light one. But when he accepted the drink and took a sip, it tasted no different from the last.

The alcohol didn't eliminate the pain in his side, but it dulled it and helped him to relax.

Victor was actually feeling pretty good by the time they went in to dinner. The formal dining room glowed with soft candlelight and the table fairly glittered with silver and crystal. Seated between his beautiful young hostess and Angela Driscoll, he was lulled into the illusion that he was still young and vigorous, attractive as much for his wit and charm and masculinity as for his power.

Bill Benedict sat across the table from him, constantly watchful, but Victor ignored him. He intended to enjoy himself. He had almost forgotten how wonderful rich food could taste, and he ate everything that was put before him, complimenting Alice on each dish.

He knew that he was eating too much, even without the reminder from Benedict, but he was like a man enjoying his first meal after months of starvation. In fact, his senses had been starved, and the joy of sensual pleasure welled up in him, almost bringing tears to his eyes. He could feel again; he was still alive.

No matter how much wine he drank, the glass at his hand seemed always to be full. As the evening progressed, the attractive widow to his left appeared younger and more beautiful, less and less a masterpiece of the beautician's art. He ceased calling her Mrs. Driscoll, preferring the more familiar Angela.

Angela had green eyes. Before, he had been aware that their color was intensified by green eyeshadow, but now he saw only the beauty of the eyes themselves; they were the sea on a bright, sunny day. The waves of her honey-colored hair were soft and lush, now appearing to fall naturally, not the carefully calculated arrangement made possible by chemicals and rollers.

She talked with enthusiasm of her art collection,

which she had begun with her husband, referring lovingly to each piece as if it were one of her children. The names Matisse and Utrillo and Gauguin issued from her lips like a caress.

"To me," she said warmly, "no other group of painters has been able to evoke such feeling as the Impressionists. Harry never really understood my passion for them. He saw art primarily as an investment, and the Impressionists were already expensive when we began collecting. I let him buy the Pop, as long as he let me indulge myself as well."

Victor had had little time for such things as art, so he could only comment, "Your collection must be very valuable."

"Yes, I suppose it is," she replied. "But I don't really like to think of it in those terms. Actually, when Harry died, I sold the Pollocks and Warhols and Oldenburgs in order to buy more of my favorites, and I would have made more money if I had waited. But love is much more important than money, don't you agree?"

Victor agreed automatically, out of courtesy, though it was a question he hadn't thought about in many years, if ever. Love, the kind Angela was speaking of, had not been a part of his life in a long time.

Angela was a very seductive woman, and Victor allowed himself to be seduced after the company retired to the living room. She accepted a crème de menthe, and he a brandy and a cigar, even though Bill Benedict came over to him finally and said, "Victor, don't you think you've had enough?"

Victor slurred his words deliberately. "Until he's dead and lying in his grave, a man's never had enough."

Then he followed Angela Driscoll through the large sliding-glass doors onto the balcony. The air outside was cool and he could smell the lush foliage. The view of the city lights from the hilltop was breathtaking.

Angela sighed at the sight. "It's strange that no artist has ever been able to capture the beauty of a city at night. I wonder why."

Victor had no answer, so he didn't respond. Instead, he took a puff on his cigar and blew the fragrant smoke out into the garden.

"I suppose it could be that the light isn't natural," she mused. "Van Gogh was able to paint a starry country night."

Again Victor took a puff on his cigar, but this time the smoke caught in the back of his throat, and he broke into a fit of coughing. He took a sip of brandy, hoping it would clear his throat, but it did not. The coughing became uncontrollable. His eyes filmed over, and the distant view of the lights seemed to swirl and flicker, becoming frighteningly surreal.

Suddenly an excruciating pain ripped across his side, catching him completely off guard. He dropped his cigar and glass and clutched at his belly, emitting a cry that was a combination of a groan and a scream. His legs crumpled beneath him and he fell against the wrought-iron railing, then collapsed onto the cement floor. The pain was more severe than any he had ever experienced. His defense weakened by alcohol, he couldn't pretend any more. There was only the pain.

Angela screamed and bent over him, her hands clutching his. Within moments the others were there, hovering over him, the vultures, the hounds.

He knew it was Andrew Collins who felt for his wrist and checked his pulse, then ripped at his tie and shirt, frantically trying to form a diagnosis. He knew Collins assumed it was his heart, and that angered Victor. He didn't want to be at the mercy of any of them.

Bill Benedict's voice seemed to come from far away. "It's his pancreas. He's not supposed to eat and drink like this."

Victor's anger doubled in intensity.

"Dr. Berger," he managed to say hoarsely. "Call Dr. Berger. He knows the problem."

"Relax," Collins said firmly. "Leave everything to me." Then he turned to someone and said, "Call for an ambulance. We've got to get him to the hospital."

Since Collins was the only doctor present, Victor said nothing more. Once they got him to the hospital, he was sure he would get his own way.

Chapter Twenty-seven

At the sight of Victor Dawson lying on his patio Andrew Collins panicked. He could see all his hopes and plans disappearing. They had been as fragile as a single human life, and they could be snuffed out in a single moment.

He couldn't allow Victor Dawson to die — not before he, Andrew, regained his freedom.

He had no idea what was wrong with the old man until Bill Benedict explained, "He's been suffering from pancreatitis for some time. He came out here against the advice of his doctor. When he insisted, the doctor charged me with keeping him on his diet — no liquor, no smoking, no rich foods. But there's no way I can control him."

While waiting for the ambulance, Andrew gave Dawson a shot of Demerol to ease the pain and help him relax. He would have no idea of the old man's condition or his chances until he could get him to the hospital and give him a proper examination.

It puzzled him that Dawson was asking for Dave Berger. As far as he knew, there had been no connection between the two. He considered the possibility that the old man was delirious and somehow connecting this with the Phil Winston case. Perhaps, out of a sense of guilt, he viewed his condition as retribution for causing Winston's death.

No matter what the reason, Collins had no intention of turning this patient over to a surgeon without boards. Victor Dawson was going to get the best medical care Andrew could provide. *Andrew's* life might depend on it.

Benedict rode to the hospital in the ambulance with Collins, having given instructions to the limousine driver to follow. Tony stayed behind with Alice and the guests, having asked Andrew to call with a report as soon as he knew anything. Andrew was thankful for that; it was a relief to know that his father-in-law would not be looking over his shoulder. He didn't know what Tony was thinking at the moment, but he could guess. Tony did not look greatly upset about what had happened.

Strangley, neither did Bill Benedict.

After his initial expression of concern, which was actually more a defense of his inability to keep Dawson on his diet, the Betco lawyer settled into a self-satisfied smugness, almost as if he was pleased that his warning had come true.

By the time they reached the hospital, Dawson was resting easily due to the Demerol. In the bright lights of the emergency room, he awakened and began to insist that he was all right.

"I'm the doctor," Andrew said sternly. "Let me determine that."

"You're not my doctor."

"No," Andrew admitted, "but there may not be time to have your doctor fly out from Chicago."

"I have a doctor in Los Angeles. Dr. Berger."

Andrew stared at him. Dawson wasn't delirious. Was it possible that Dave Berger had been a part of the old man's scheme to get rid of Winston? If so, that would explain why Dawson had been so cold to Andrew, who had come in and taken over the Winston surgery.

Andrew's voice was tight as he said, "Well, I'm sure if your condition is serious you'll want to be looked after by a good, qualified surgeon."

Dawson glowered at him. "Yes," he said, "that's why I want Berger."

Andrew stiffened. "Dr. Berger is no longer associated with Beverly Hills Hospital. And, as far as I know, he doesn't have privileges at any other hospital. And he isn't even board-certified!"

Dawson's dark eyes narrowed. "If you want to keep your privileges at this hospital," he said venomously, "you'll get him here immediately, and you'll restore his privileges!"

Andrew was confused and frightened. He couldn't understand Dawson's attitude, and he needed time to think. "I'll do what I can," he said, and left the examining room.

Bill Benedict was waiting in the hall. "What's his condition?" he asked anxiously as he saw Andrew coming out.

"I don't know yet. I haven't examined him." He took Benedict by the arm and guided him down the hall to his office. Once they were assured of privacy, he continued, "Bill, I'm going to ask you to level with him. What's Victor's connection with Dave Berger?"

Benedict's brow furrowed. "None as far as I know."

"Well, there has to be some connection," Andrew said hotly. "He refused to allow me to attend him. Insists that Berger is his doctor in Los Angeles."

Benedict looked blank. "Well, maybe you should call Berger and ask him."

"No. Berger and I aren't on very good terms. I fired

him yesterday." He began to pace around the room.

"Okay." Bill shrugged. "Then I'll call him."

Andrew stopped pacing. "I want to keep that son of a bitch out of this. You must know how important it is to me to keep Victor Dawson alive right now. If he goes, I'm back under Tony Manchester's thumb again."

Oddly, Benedict smiled. "Don't worry about that right now," he said. "It doesn't look like we have any other choice but to call Berger."

"All right, but *you* call him." He gestured to his desk. "You can use my phone."

Andrew stood at his office window, pretending to look out, but actually he was listening carefully as Benedict called information and got Berger's service number, then called it and said, "My name is Benedict. I work for Mr. Victor Dawson, who says he's a patient of Dr. Berger's. Mr. Dawson is in the emergency room at Beverly Hills Hospital and needs Dr. Berger's attention immediately. Please have him call me." Then he read off the number from Andrew's phone and hung up.

Turning to Andrew, he said, "She'll page him immediately. He should call us back any moment."

Two minutes later the phone rang. Andrew gestured at his desk and said, "You take it."

From Benedict's manner, it was obviously Dave Berger on the line. Again Benedict explained who he was, then said, "I'm familiar with Mr. Dawson's medical record through Dr. Weinberg, back in Chicago. I wasn't aware that he'd seen a doctor here in Los Angeles, but he's asking for you. . . ." He glanced meaningfully at Andrew. "Oh, you have examined him? As recently as that? Hmm. Yes, well, could you come to the hospital now . . . ?" Pause. "Very good. Thank you." He hung up.

He looked at Andrew and scowled.

"Apparently Victor went to see Berger on Tuesday,

complaining of acute pains in his side." Then he shook his head, obviously worried. "He said nothing about it to me."

"Why the hell would he pick Berger, of all doctors?" Andrew exploded.

"Yes." Benedict nodded. "And why would he pick Tuesday morning, of all days?"

Andrew began to pace again, muttering, "Berger's a nobody, a nothing. He was just an ER flunky, with virtually no real experience. He's not even board-certified. The only reason he could possibly have to be connected with Dawson is Phil Winston's death."

Benedict gave Andrew the strangest look then. "You're right," he said very softly. "That could be the reason."

"If Dawson's in as bad shape as I think he is, he may require surgery, and Berger just doesn't have the experience for that," Andrew said. Then he walked over and sat down at his desk, burying his face in his hands and massaging his forehead as if that would help him to think. Finally he looked up at Benedict and said slowly, "You've got to convince Dawson to agree to surgery with someone else — if it comes to surgery." He knew he was defeated — "He doesn't have to have me as his surgeon if he doesn't want to, but it's got to be somebody better than Berger."

Benedict smiled. "You don't know Dawson. Once he gets his mind made up, nobody can change it. He can be an obstinate, spiteful old man when he wants to be." He shrugged, then laughed. "If Berger's the doctor he wants, why should we stand in his way? Maybe Berger is what he deserves."

"How can you say that?" Andrew was incredulous. "That's like saying he deserves to die."

Benedict chuckled. "I know."

Andrew stared at the lawyer, stunned. His meaning was clear.

"Look," Andrew said, trying to back up a bit, "I realize that Victor Dawson isn't an easy man to work for, but he's got to be better than Tony Manchester. You can't imagine what you'll be letting yourself in for."

"I won't be working for Tony Manchester," Benedict said smugly. "And neither will you."

"What do you mean? That was the reason Tony went for this deal."

"Yeah, but it wasn't Dawson's reason. He's made other plans."

"Who?" The word was hardly more than a whisper.

"Who else?" Benedict smiled. "You're talking to the next president of Betco right now."

Andrew felt dizzy. "How?" he asked.

"Dawson isn't very happy with the way his kids have turned out. He doesn't want to see them destroy what he's built, so he's set up a trust to be managed and controlled by me. It's as simple as that." He gave Andrew a moment to let that register, then continued: "I can use a man like you here at the hospital. But first we have to get rid of Dawson. If this Berger is as incompetent as you say he is — no boards or whatever the shit that means — that seems the best way. Let the old man have what he's asking for."

Chapter Twenty-eight

Why me? Dave wondered. Victor Dawson could have his pick of any doctor in Los Angeles — doctors with established reputations and proven records of success. It made no sense for Dawson to have called on him at a time like this.

Since he had learned who Dawson was, Dave had assumed the man's reason for coming to see him on Tuesday was merely to find out what Dave knew about Winston's death, possibly to make sure his tracks were covered. But Dawson's complaint had been a legitimate one; he couldn't have faked his physical condition.

The questions not only puzzled Dave, they frightened him. Words from old gangster movies kept running through his mind — words like *patsy* and *fall guy*. He was sure that he had been used to cover for Collins in the Winston case. Was Dave now to be used as a scapegoat for something bigger?

Or had Dawson actually asked for him?

Dave drove fast to Beverly Hills Hospital, but he thought even faster. He didn't like being paranoid; he preferred to keep his own needs out of the practice of medicine, to think only of the needs of the patient. But the past few days had taught him that this wasn't always possible. In the real world, nothing was sacred — not even the practice of medicine. A doctor had to think of himself first, the patient second.

Despite his new resolution, Dave's natural inclinations took over the moment he walked into the examining room and saw Victor Dawson.

The old man was obviously in pain, and a doctor's first duty was to alleviate it, whatever the consequences. The fact that Dawson was conscious answered one question for him: It was clear that he had specifically requested Dave.

Bill Benedict followed him into the examining room and lingered. Dave had no idea who he was or what his relationship was to Dawson, but his presence made him nervous and finally he asked him to leave. Benedict didn't obey until Dawson himself said, "Do what the doctor says."

Dawson's eyes were dulled with pain, but he watched Dave intently as he began the examination. He didn't speak except to answer Dave's questions with simple yes or no.

"Does it hurt here?" Dave asked, pressing into the large roll of fat at Dawson's waist.

Victor winced and nodded.

Dave sniffed near Dawson's face. "You've been drinking, haven't you?" he said.

This time Dawson looked embarrassed when he nodded.

Tests and X rays confirmed Dave's suspicions: Dawson would have to have surgery, the sooner the better. Without it, his chances of living out the week were minimal; with it, his chances were only slightly better. Again, the fear returned to gnaw at him: If Dawson didn't survive, could Dave expect to?

The only safe thing to do would be to refuse to handle the case, but something in Dave would not allow him to do this. Perhaps it was ego, a desire to prove himself; perhaps it was that he couldn't live with himself as a coward — boards or no boards.

He could, however, be honest with Victor Dawson, in the hope that he would receive honesty in return.

Armed with X rays and test results, Dave returned to the examining room. To his surprise, Dawson wasn't lying on the table but was sitting up, his feet dangling. This was not a sign that the patient was feeling better; on the contrary, he knew that Dawson's condition was worse. Dave had seen the reaction before — the kind of patient who knew only one way of fighting: actively and defiantly.

Dawson was clutching his side so tightly that his fingers were digging into the roll of fat, making the veins on his hands stand out. Beads of perspiration stood out like tiny blisters on his greasy forehead.

Dave sat on the small stool beside the table and looked up into the dark eyes. "Mr. Dawson," he said, "the outlook is not good. You need surgery."

The eyes did not flinch. "What are my chances?"

With another patient, Dave might have hedged. Now he had to rely on the hard facts. "Virtually nonexistant without surgery," he said. "Roughly sixty–forty with. That's sixty-forty against."

Dawson's manner did not change. He kept his eyes on Dave and nodded. "When?" he asked.

"I would suggest immediately. The longer we wait, the less the chances."

"Can you perform the surgery?"

If Dave was going to back out, now was his chance;

the door had been opened for him. He promptly shut it.

"I can," he said, "but only if you and I are completely honest with each other."

Something approximating a smile flickered on Dawson's ravaged face. "I see," he said. "You know."

"No," Dave corrected, "I don't know anything about what's going on in the hospital. But I've heard things, and I've seen things that don't seem to be quite what they should be."

"What do you want to know?" Dawson asked.

"Why me?"

"I like you."

"Is that the only reason?"

For the first time, Dawson's eyes darted away from Dave's. "And I trust you."

"Our trust has to be mutual," Dave said. "And it seems very suspicious that you would seek out a young, untried doctor when this city is filled with some of the best in the world."

"I can't explain that," Dawson said, returning his gaze to Dave, "except to say that I use my intuition to judge what a man is and what he's capable of. To most successful doctors, success is very important, sometimes more important than their patients' health. When you meet them, you can literally see them asking: 'What have I got to gain or lose?' I didn't see that in you. Even now, when you're asking the question, your eyes are telling me it doesn't really matter. Am I right?"

Dave nodded.

"Do you have any more questions?" Dawson asked.

Dave got up from his stool. "I have, but I don't have to have an answer now."

"You want to know if I'm responsible for Phil Winston's death, don't you?" Dawson asked softly. Then, before Dave could say anything, he said, "I'm not. But I think I know who is, and I'd like to live long enough to straighten things out." He tried to smile. "If you think you can help me."

Dave smiled warmly. "I'll do my very best." He moved toward the door. "I'll go arrange to have you checked into the hospital right now."

"You can have Bill Benedict take care of all the paper work," Dawson said. "He has power of attorney. But before you go, I have some questions for you."

Dave had already opened the door, but he closed it and walked back into the room. "Sure, go ahead and ask."

"If I get through surgery, how long will I have?"

"That's hard to say. The surgery is the easiest part. The first few days after surgery are the most difficult. If you survive them, you should have a few more good years." He paused, then added, "As long as you're careful about what you eat and drink."

"Fair enough," Dawson said, as if they were making a business deal. "How many people will be in surgery with you?"

The question surprised Dave. He counted on his fingers as he spoke. "I'll have to have a doctor to assist, the anesthesiologist, and two nurses. That's four, in addition to myself."

"The other doctor won't be Collins, will it?"

"Not likely. Collins and I aren't on the best of terms."

"That might not matter to him," Dawson said. "But I don't want Collins. Do you understand?"

Dave nodded.

Again Dawson looked away from Dave. There was no way to know whether it was pain or embarrassment. Dawson was almost mumbling when he said, "Also, I understand that patients sometimes talk when they're under anesthetic. Is that true?"

"Yes, but they rarely say anything intelligible, and we don't take it seriously."

"Can you instruct the others to keep it to themselves?" he pleaded. "And would you tell me what I said when it's over?"

"Sure. Don't worry about it. Confidentiality is part of the doctor's job."

"Thank you," Dawson said simply. "There's one last thing." He lifted his arm and gestured toward the clothes rack across the room. "There's a small scrap of paper in the right pocket of my coat. It's got my daughter Phyllis's phone number on it. Would you call her and tell her what's happened? Without telling Bill Benedict?"

"Of course."

Three hours later, Victor Dawson had been prepared for surgery and was wheeled into the operating room. Dave had gotten Dr. Nino to assist and Dr. Warner as anesthesiologist. To his surprise, Bill Benedict had suggested that Collins assist, but the lawyer seemed to understand when Dave told him that Dawson had expressly *not* wanted Collins there.

As Dave went over the preoperative X rays with Dr. Nino, he said, "Chest looks fine. Abdominal series only, that's sentinel loop in the left upper quadrant. No obstruction, a slight ileus. And the amylase is three times normal. And there," Dave said, "there, the calcifications on the abdominal series. Classic for chronic pancreatitis."

Nino agreed. "I think you're right. The patient has a chronic pancreatitis — and much, much more!"

"He was warned by his doctor in Chicago about his diet and drinking," Dave said. "I think he just stirred up an acute attack, and it could just do him in."

Dave watched as Dawson was wheeled past. His fourth unit of plasmanate had been hung. "How many units have we got on him?" Dave asked the scrub nurse.

"He's typed and cross-matched for six, Dr. Berger, and we have four more on the way."

"Good. That should do it."

Dave and Nino scrubbed, then went into the OR as

Dawson was being put to sleep. Under the anesthetic, Dawson did speak, but what he said wasn't unusual. Several times he cried out, "Mama, Mama, don't leave me!" Reverting to childhood was a typical reaction.

Once Dawson's body was draped and painted with betadine solution, he should have become anonymous to Dave; but he didn't. Dawson was too important a patient, and this was a big surgery.

Dave knew his limitations. He likened the inert form on the operating table to an automobile in need of repair. He was not the manufacturer but simply the mechanic. Dave's actions were mechanical, decisive, and skillful. It took only two swift incisions to open Dawson's abdominal cavity, neatly exposing the colorful layers of skin and fat, with Dr. Nino retracting and the nurses handing Dave his instruments.

Dave explored the inside of the cavity. "Liver is slightly enlarged," he noted, "with a little fatty infiltrate . . . years of drinking."

"More than a little," Nino said. "That's a damned sick liver."

Gradually, the surgeon's gloved hands explored farther. A swollen, nasty-looking pale yellow organ, just under the stomach greeted them. "God, it's hard as a rock," Dave said. "Pancreatitis, acute and chronic! And he's sure got a hell of an attack now."

"Tough decision," Nino said. "We could either drain it and get out, or we could try to remove the pancreas, or at least most of it. God! The mortality would be approaching fifty percent or more. A tough operation, especially in the middle of the night."

"We could resect two-thirds," Dave said, thinking aloud. "No, better to drain and get out."

Dave knew he was in a tough spot. This was one of the hardest operations for a general surgeon to handle. Acute pancreatitis, superimposed on chronic pancreatitis and years of abuse. And Dave would be held responsible. He thought back to the lecture on pancreatitis in Chicago: "There's gonna be one night, gentlemen, when you all get in there over your heads, and find yourself eyeball to eyeball with a swollen, tender pancreas, and you're going to be wondering whether to drain it or get out. I'd hate to be in your shoes, it's a tough decision, but a mature surgeon, a surgeon who has the skill and ability to be a board-certified surgeon, would know how to handle it."

Dave stared deep into Dawson's abdominal cavity as he and Nino suddenly grew silent. Should he resect the pancreas? It would probably kill Dawson. Yes, it would, and yet to drain and get out . . . Either way, Dave knew he was in trouble. He thought of the complications that could arise — further pancreatitis, leaks of anastamosis, infection, pulmonary complications, pneumonia, bowel obstruction.

Dave's hands were shaking.

He looked at Nino and said, "I think we should remove the dead tissues, clean it up, drain, and get out. That's Dawson's only chance."

Nino stared at him for a long moment, as did the scrub nurses. Then the doctors proceeded to remove the dead, inflamed pancreatic tissues, place large sump drains and penrose drains around the oozing swollen pancreas, and close.

Victor Dawson's operation was over.

Chapter Twenty-nine

Beverly Hills, Friday, November 16 (Three Days Before Boards)

Victor Dawson was aware of the passage of time. There had been some change in his body, some movement from one place to another, but his mind couldn't comprehend it at first.

As Victor awoke, he had no idea where he was. His first impression was that he was in a hotel room. He had been in a great many first-class hotels in his life, with much the same sort of furnishings, but he did not recognize this one. At the windows were heavy swagged drapes in a soft cool green, held back over delicate Austrian curtains. At their top was a gilt rococo cornice. The gilt Louis XV chairs and loveseat were covered in tapestry featuring the same green. The floor was carpeted, and there were French lamps on gilt occasional tables. On the wall opposite his bed was a large, ornately carved piece of furniture that looked like an armoire, but which he suspected had been converted to house a television set or possibly a bar.

Victor thought he was in a hospital room. He must be. The IV bottle attached to his arm, the smell of disinfectant, and the stiff pain in his side confirmed that.

Slowly, the pieces of memory began to fit together and make sense. He recalled the tour he had taken of Beverly Hills Hospital some time ago; he had been startled then at the fact that the VIP floor did not resemble a hospital. The individual rooms were actually suites, intended to make high-paying customers more comfortable and less aware that they were in a medical facility.

Victor was grateful to be alone; he didn't care what his surroundings looked like. What mattered to him was competence, not appearance.

There was no one in the room with him, but one of the doors — apparently the one into the other part of the suite — was ajar. He was confident that if he called out, someone would come — either Bill Benedict or a nurse — but he was glad to have a few moments to adjust and get his bearings before seeing anyone.

He tried to move, to change his position, but found it too painful. He couldn't see the stitched incision, but it felt as if his entire body had been cut open.

He lay there thinking for a while, then dozed off again. When he awakened the second time, a nurse was bustling around the bed. She was not the old-fashioned starched sort of nurse, but Victor was grateful that she at least dressed in the traditional white.

"Oh," she said brightly, "you're awake. Just in time for me to take your temperature and check your pulse," which she proceeded to do.

It was difficult to talk with the thermometer in his mouth, but Victor managed to ask, "Where is Dr. Berger?"

"Don't talk," the nurse said. "Dr. Berger will be in to see you in a few minutes."

Suddenly Bill Benedict's anxious face appeared in the doorway; apparently he'd heard Victor's voice. He hesitated a moment, then slipped quietly into the room. He said nothing, but there was a tired, almost frightened look about him. He had obviously spent the night on the sofa in the other part of the suite, and had clearly slept little. There were dark circles under his bloodshot eyes, and he'd had no opportunity to shave or even comb his hair. He was wearing the suit he had worn to the Collins party the night before, and it was more than a little wrinkled.

The nurse didn't even notice Benedict until she had taken Victor's pulse. "You can talk to him when I'm finished," she said briskly, "but only for a moment. And don't excite him in any way."

When she left, Benedict asked cautiously, "How are you feeling?" Victor thought there was a note of disappointment in his voice.

"As well as can be expected, I suppose," Victor replied. "I don't know how I'm supposed to feel."

The young lawyer attempted to smile. "That was pretty stupid — what you did last night."

Victor merely grunted. He didn't say that he had had some help, that Benedict should have known better than to have behaved like a jailer. He should have known that Victor would take it as a dare.

"Don't worry about the business," Benedict continued. "I've got everything under control."

"I'm sure you have," Victor mumbled.

It was the kind of barb that Victor frequently made, enjoying the way the insensitive Benedict let it slip by unnoticed or unacknowledged. But this time it seemed to make him extremely uncomfortable. He remained standing, shuffling from one foot to the other, staring at Dawson.

Dawson did not recognize this Bill Benedict. For a moment, he wondered whether it was the lawyer who seemed different, or was it that he himself had never before looked at his subordinate in this way?

Finally, Benedict asked, "Is there anything I can do for you? Anything I can get you?"

"No. Just leave me alone."

But Benedict did not leave. He lingered, as if wanting to say something more. Victor found it annoying but said nothing; instead, he studied the young man.

When the hall door opened and Dr. Berger slipped in, Benedict suddenly became his usual self — brash and arrogant. "Well, our boy's awake," he said. "I'll leave you alone with him." Then he walked into the other part of the suite, again leaving the door ajar behind him.

Though Victor noticed this, Dr. Berger did not. With a smile, he moved to the bedside. "I told you mine was the easy part," he said. "Now you've got the hard part. How do you feel?"

"I don't feel like getting up and dancing. Everything hurts — even breathing."

"That pain will pass after a few days."

Victor grunted his understanding and acceptance, then asked, "Doctor, would you mind closing that door for me?"

Berger turned, saw the open door, and moved to close it.

As Berger returned to the bedside, he said, "The surgery went very well. With the proper rest and diet and medication, you shouldn't have any problems at all."

"What did I say when I was out?" Victor asked anxiously.

"Nothing of any consequence. You called out for your mother. You asked her not to leave you."

Victor studied him suspiciously. "And that was all?"

Dr. Berger nodded. "That was all."

"Did you call my daughter?" Victor asked.

"Yes. She said she would try to come down to see you this weekend."

Victor grunted his satisfaction. "Have you had any interference from Collins or Manchester?"

"No," Berger replied. "Just before surgery, Mr. Benedict suggested that I have Collins assist, but when I refused, he said nothing more about it."

Victor frowned. "Benedict suggested it?"

Berger nodded.

Victor was not completely surprised by that, but he was annoyed that he hadn't anticipated it, and he wondered if there were other things he hadn't anticipated.

He looked thoughtfully at Dave Berger. Victor knew that he had not been entirely fair to the young doctor. Berger was skilled, honest, dedicated, and idealistic, but he was also naïve and far too trusting. When it was a question of survival, Berger was the only kind of doctor Victor wanted to take care of him; Victor was like any other patient, concerned only about himself.

Victor knew that if he died, Berger would be in trouble, but just how much trouble he wasn't sure. Victor could leave written instructions for Bill Benedict to protect the doctor, but now he wasn't sure Benedict would obey.

This younger generation confused Victor. They were all so changeable. It appeared that he had misjudged his daughter Phyllis, too. And how many others?

Victor Dawson had always kept his thoughts to himself, at least for the past fifty years. But now, strangely, he had the urge to talk, to tell Dave Berger everything. But he checked that urge, telling himself it was a sign of weakness in the face of death.

Instead, he said simply, "You can't trust Dr. Collins. The less you have to do with that man, the better off you'll be."

Berger grinned at him. "I've already figured out that much myself. For some reason, he seems to have it in for me."

"That's because you have something he doesn't have," Victor said, but he didn't tell Dave what it was. "If he can't have it, he doesn't want anyone else to have it either."

Victor was feeling drowsy again. His eyes were beginning to close. He was asleep before the doctor left the room.

Chapter Thirty

One of Dave's professors in med school had likened the practice of medicine to a battlefield: "It's war and it's hell. And a doctor has to have a suit of armor to survive — a suit of white armor."

Dave, like most of the other students, had laughed. But now he was beginning to see that the professor was right. He had became almost constantly aware of the need to survive, pushing aside his desire to help and to cure. But Dave was uncomfortable with these thoughts; if survival was all there was to life, there could be no such thing as human dignity, or even self-respect.

It was the Victor Dawson case, more than anything else, that made Dave feel this way. Dawson himself was not a threat, but a morbid sense of fear and destruction seemed to surround him.

And then, again today, Dawson had implied that Andrew Collins posed a serious threat to Dave. Dave was aware that Collins hated him, but he wondered if there was more to it than he had suspected.

Was the old man trying to tell him something? That Collins was behind Phil Winston's death? That Collins would kill Dawson as well? That he would kill Dave if Dave got in his way?

Dave hadn't seen Shana Winston since he had received the emergency call about Dawson. In fact, since the evening at her apartment, he had spoken to her only once on the phone. With his dismissal from the emergency room and the pressure of finding a new office, he had had very little free time.

However, after leaving Dawson's suite, he called her and made a date for lunch, suggesting that they meet at a small sandwich shop several blocks from the hospital.

It was a noisy place, but the service was quick and no one there knew them. They managed to get a large corner booth where they would have some privacy.

Shana had come directly from her office. She was dressed in a conservative gray-and-blue pants outfit, with her hair tied up in a gray scarf. Her manner was as restrained as her appearance, and Dave couldn't help feeling that the intimacy of their evening together had been a figment of his imagination. Certainly there was nothing intimate in her manner now. If anything, she seemed brusque and impatient with him.

"What have you learned that you couldn't tell me on the phone?" she asked after they had ordered.

Dave told her about last night and this morning, emphasizing that Dawson had denied having anything to do with her father's death and had issued vague warnings about Andrew Collins. She listened quietly until he had finished the story.

Then she frowned. "I can see how you would be puzzled by why he would come to you. It puzzles me, too. But I don't think it tells us anything more than we already knew or suspected."

"It confirms that Dawson had nothing to do with your father's death," Dave said.

Shana gave him a patient smile. "No, not really. The fact that he denies any involvement doesn't mean anything. He could lie as easily as anyone else."

"I suppose so." Dave nodded. "But I believe him."

The look she gave him could only be described as disparaging. But she said, "I don't think anyone can be trusted. I've been trying to learn everything I can about Collins and Manchester. From what I have learned, I don't think either of them would take it on himself to have my father killed. They've both done some pretty dirty things before, but almost always on someone else's orders. Collins does Manchester's dirty work, and Manchester does Dawson's. No matter what you say, it always comes right back to him."

"Perhaps. But then there would be no reason for Dawson to be afraid of Collins. Or for him to warn me about him."

Shana's laugh was without mirth. "Remember the old adage, 'There's no honor among thieves.' "

That was hardly a satisfactory argument, but Dave didn't say so. There was something she wasn't saying, and he had begun to suspect that it had little to do with Victor Dawson, Andrew Collins and Dave Berger.
and more to do with Shana Winston and Dave Berger.

They finished their lunch quickly, with fifteen minutes to spare before they had to return to work. In the hope that a quieter atmosphere might relax Shana, Dave suggested they take a walk.

Shana looked at her watch and said reluctantly, "Okay, but it'll have to be a short one. I have a patient coming in."

Dave guided her to a small park in a residential area off Wilshire, where they sat on a bench. But Shana's manner didn't change; she remained cool and distant.

"What's wrong?" he asked.

"Nothing," she said, but her false smile told him otherwise.

Dave took her hand. "Try again. You're not very convincing."

"It's a long story, and there isn't time for it now."

"It's us, isn't it?" Dave prodded. "The other night."

"Yes and no. I enjoyed the other night, and I like you." Suddenly her face softened. "But I don't love you, and I think I've misled you into thinking I do."

"I believe only what I'm told, and you never said anything about love."

"Not to you," she acknowledged, "but I have to myself. I've told myself that I could love you. I've tried to persuade myself." She sighed heavily and looked at her watch. "I told you I had worked out all my emotional problems, and I thought I had. I thought I knew what kind of man I wanted to love. I told myself I wanted a man who was everything my father was not, and you fit that formula perfectly. You're kind and gentle, and you're idealistic and good. Too good."

Dave frowned. "You can't work out formulas for love. If one could, the world's problems would have been solved centuries ago."

"I know, but with me it's a bit more complicated than that. I'm not sure even I understand it. But I did want to love you."

"Give it time," Dave suggested. "Don't push yourself. I don't know if I love you either. I don't think I even know you yet. I'm fascinated by you, but that's not love."

She looked at her watch again. "I'd better start walking back to my car. I really do have an appointment."

Dave walked back with her, relieved that the air had been somewhat cleared, and wishing that he could do or say something to relieve her anxiety. He knew she was trying to work out something in her head, and he wanted to help, if only by listening.

"I'm your friend," he said quietly. "I don't know what you expect from a friend, but you only have to try me."

"Thanks," she said, squeezing his arm affectionately. "I think maybe I expect too much. It all goes back to my problems with my father. I certainly expected too much of him. I expected him to be totally the opposite of what he was, but now I'm beginning to realize there were some things about him I liked. They were qualities that couldn't have existed if he were different. If he were like you, for instance."

"Thanks," Dave said wryly.

Shana blushed. "I knew you'd misunderstand. That's why I didn't want to say anything. You're wonderful, you really are, and I shouldn't expect you to be any different." She was silent for a moment, then added, "That's my problem — I expect things of people, and I know I shouldn't."

They walked the rest of the way in silence.

When they reached Shana's car, she said, "I think we should forget about our investigation."

Dave looked at her, puzzled. "Why?"

She looked away uncomfortably. "Because it's really no use. Because they're bigger than we are, and much more ruthless."

"You're saying that because of me, aren't you?" Dave asked, staring at her. "Because you think I'm weak and gullible?"

She shook her head, and her eyes met his. "You're not weak," she said. "Not at all. But you aren't able to function from a position of strength. You have so many other stresses on you, I'm surprised you haven't cracked up already. What with your surgery boards, and the hospital board meeting." She smiled. "That's not a phrase a therapist should use, but you know what I mean. You don't need my problems on top of your own."

"At this point, your problems can't really be separated from mine. I would have been drawn into this with or without you."

"Perhaps," she admitted. "But it was my father who brought you to Los Angeles in the first place. If something should happen to you, I couldn't stand the guilt."

"Then I'll have to make sure nothing does happen to me," he said, and kissed her gently on the cheek.

Chapter Thirty-one

"I really don't think he should be disturbed," Bill Benedict said smugly. "The doctor says he must be kept quiet and allowed to rest."

Normally, Tony would have understood and accepted this, but there was something about the lawyer's manner that suggested it was not precisely the truth. Benedict seemed to be testing him, challenging him to defy his order. It was the typical attitude of an underling suddenly thrust into a position of authority — arrogant but empty.

"Has the doctor specifically ordered no visitors at all?" he asked. "Or is that your interpretation of his order?"

Benedict backed down a step. "He's asked that we keep visitors to a minimum," he said smoothly, looking away. "Only family and close friends."

Tony's voice became threatening as he said, "Dawson and I have been close friends since before you were born." He paused. "I would like to see him."

Benedict stepped aside and gestured to the door. "Then keep it short, and don't say anything to upset him."

Tony approached the half-opened door and cautiously peered in to see if Dawson was awake. At first he seemed to be sleeping, but then his eyes opened and he looked straight at Tony. He did not invite him to enter; in fact, he gave no sign even of recognition. But neither did he say or do anything to suggest that Tony should go away. He simply stared at him vacantly.

Tony moved quietly into the room and shut the door behind him.

The light in the room was soft and yellow, accentuating Dawson's sallow complexion, giving him the look of a wax figure. He seemed barely alive. Tony knew enough about medicine to know that much of the effect stemmed from the combination of physical shock — from the surgery itself — and the drugs necessary to keep the patient resting with a minimum of pain. But it was still unsettling to see Victor Dawson like this; he had always seemed invincible.

Tony was almost as surprised by his own reaction as he was by Dawson's appearance. A strange mixture of emotions flooded over him, but the strongest was fear.

To Tony, Victor Dawson had been a symbol of power and freedom, a man who had all the things Tony had worked so long to achieve. He had tried to construct this moment in his mind numerous times, anticipating the day when Dawson would pass on, or be forced by ill health to retire, making room for Tony to replace him. He had expected to feel elation, the purest and most complete sense of freedom possible. But that was not at all what he felt.

What he was most aware of was a sense of frailty, an ultimate powerlessness at the heart of human power, a terribly confining loneliness in which there was only despair.

There was only one bunch of flowers in the room, and Tony suspected it was the one he had ordered. The cabinet that housed the television set was open, and the television was on — tuned to one of the daytime game shows — but the sound was not. There was absolute silence in the dimly lit room.

Tony's voice shook slightly as he asked, "How are you feeling?"

Dawson did not answer immediately, giving Tony the impression he hadn't heard, though he continued to stare at him, his eyes unwavering. "All right, I suppose," he said finally. "The doctor tells me I'm going to survive."

"Alice was very upset when she learned you were on a special diet," Tony said gently. "She feels responsible for what happened."

"Assure her it was no one's fault but my own," Dawson said regretfully. "I was being a foolish old man."

"Is there anything I can do for you?"

Dawson ignored the question.

Tony was ill at ease, standing in the middle of the room like an intruder. Although Dawson had not asked him to sit down, Tony pulled up one of the gilt armchairs and sat where Dawson could see him without having to turn.

"Alice is a lovely young woman," Dawson said suddenly with surprising strength. "She's turned out all right."

"Yes. It hasn't been easy for her."

Dawson looked at him quizzically.

"Growing up without a mother, I mean," Tony explained. "She hasn't had all the advantages I would have liked her to have."

"Maybe that's why she turned out so well. If I had it to do over again, I don't think I would have done so much for my own. They've turned out to be a sorry lot.'' He paused, then added, ''Except Phyllis. She may be able to get herself together one of these days.''

Victor Dawson rarely talked about his family, and it embarrassed Tony to hear him speak of his children this way.

''I made it too easy for them,'' Dawson said. ''Anything they wanted I handed them on a platter. I made it so they could be anything, do anything they wanted. And they haven't done a damned thing.''

''Maybe you're being a little hard on them,'' Tony said softly, remembering the instruction not to get him excited. ''They're still young.''

''Not that young,'' Dawson snapped. ''No, with few exceptions, that generation isn't worth the clothes we've put on their backs. They're weak, self-centered, and lazy. They've got loud mouths and little brains, and they think they can change the world by doing nothing but making noise.''

Dawson's voice had been gradually getting louder. Now the door opened and Bill Benedict stepped inside, saying, ''Tony, I think you'd better leave. You're getting him much too excited.''

Tony started to reply, but Dawson didn't give him a chance. ''Mind your own business,'' he snapped at the lawyer. ''And get the hell out of here or you'll find yourself out of a job!''

Benedict withdrew, closing the door behind him.

''And that one!'' Dawson spat venomously. ''I'm beginning to think he's like all the rest.''

''He's right, though, '' Tony said. ''I'm not supposed to get you excited.''

Dawson eyed him curiously, then seemed to relax somewhat.

''Alice is too good for that son-in-law of yours,'' he said quietly. ''Why doesn't she get rid of him?''

Tony squirmed in his chair, then said, ''She loves him, I guess. Despite his faults.''

Dawson seemed to ignore this response. ''Sure, I

know he's useful to you," he said. "But you don't really need him anymore, do you?"

"Andrew is good at his work," Tony said evasively. "He's a fine surgeon."

"That doesn't make him a good man," Victor snapped.

He was getting excited again, and Tony felt he had to distract Dawson to get him to calm down. If they kept on like this, there was likely to be a fight. In fact, it seemed to Tony that Dawson was trying to pick one.

He grasped at the first thing that came into his head. "Have your children been notified that you're in the hospital?"

"There's no point," Dawson said, "unless they have to cart me out of this place through the wrong door." He paused, then said abruptly, "Tony, would you do me a favor and turn that damned television off? It's beginning to drive me crazy."

The tension broke. It was with a sense of relief that Tony obeyed and returned to his seat. When he looked at Dawson's face again, the expression of anger and frustration was gone, replaced by something of the old confident, mischievous smile.

There was even a note of strength in Dawson's voice as he asked, "Tony, what kind of game are you and Collins playing?"

"Game?" Tony asked, confused. "I don't know what you mean."

"I'm talking about Dr. Winston. Why did you have to get rid of him that way?"

Tony stared at him, his mouth gaping. "I didn't get rid of him," he said. "I only followed your orders."

Dawson scowled. "What orders?"

Tony's mind was racing, trying to find its way out of confusion. "The order to have him arrive early at the hospital. To set him up for the accident."

"Bullshit!" Dawson spat. "I gave you no such order."

Tony felt his anger rising. "But Benedict called me on

Sunday," he said, his voice strained. "He gave me your instructions."

Slowly Dawson's frown lifted, releasing his dark eyes from their folds. "Benedict called you?" he asked. "You swear to it?"

Now Tony frowned. "You mean you didn't tell him to?"

"No," Dawson said with a weary sigh. "I've been a stupid, foolish old man."

Chapter Thirty-two

It was likely that Bill Benedict had been listening at the door. Victor had said very little, but it was enough for the young lawyer to suspect he now knew everything, and that was enough to be dangerous.

This wasn't the first time a trusted employee had attempted to betray Victor. However, in the past, he had been able to smell the treachery and had managed to move quickly to outwit his foes. They disappeared quietly and were never heard from again.

Victor knew he was slipping. Perhaps he was getting too old. Or perhaps Bill Benedict was simply far more subtle than Victor had ever given him credit for. Certainly Benedict was shrewd; perhaps that brash, clumsy exterior was a deception, carefully calculated, and Victor had fallen for it — hook, line, and sinker.

Benedict had known what effect his warnings last night would have on Victor. He had wanted Victor to react in defiance and spite, because the doctor had told him quite clearly what the result would be. Benedict had been prodding Victor to kill himself; if he had succeeded, it would have been much neater than committing murder.

The entire plan was clear to Victor now. It had probably been in the works ever since he had set up the trust with Benedict in control. The lawyer had simply been waiting for the right opportunity, an occasion when Victor would be far from the doctor who knew his medical history. He hadn't wanted to act before the hospital merger was completed, but he had grown impatient with the stalemate caused by Phil Winston. He had arranged Winston's death, confident that Victor would assume Tony Manchester was responsible.

Victor recognized Benedict's weaknesses — impatience and overconfidence. Under normal circumstances, Victor could have used those weaknesses to his own advantage, allowing Benedict to trap himself. But these were not normal circumstances. Victor was trapped in this room, in this bed, unable to move without help, unable even to use the telephone without help.

Now that Victor knew the truth, he was sure that Benedict would have to act quickly, perhaps hastily. Somehow, Victor would have to move surely and with more speed. But how? And to meet what sort of action?

So far, Benedict had been playing a coward's game, avoiding any direct action or confrontation that would risk discovery. Whatever he did, Victor's death would have to seem natural, accidental, or caused by medical error. And he would get someone else to perform the act.

Probably Andrew Collins.

For that reason, Victor didn't know just how far he could trust Tony Manchester.

Tony sat in the chair beside Dawson's bed, perhaps even more stunned by the revelation than Victor was.

"I've done you a very grave injustice," Victor said.

Tony seemed not to hear. "But why?" he asked, staring down at his hands. "Why would Benedict take it upon himself to do something like this?"

"Power," Victor said, "and money." He sighed painfully. "You see, I've set it up so that he'll control Betco when I'm gone."

Tony lifted his gaze. His eyes met Victor's with disbelief. His mouth opened as if to ask a question, but no words came out.

Victor answered the look. "I didn't trust you," he said. "And I wanted to give the corporation a fresh start. It's been handicapped by its image since the very beginning. It wanted to set it free from all those old associations, clean up all the dirt."

Tony still did not speak, but hurt and anger were all over his face.

"I couldn't tell you," Victor said almost apologetically. "You understand that, don't you?"

Obviously, he did not. The hurt look remained. "We've been through a lot together," Tony said weakly, "and I thought we had always been honest with each other."

"I'm sorry," Victor said softly. "But the important question is: What do we do now? They can't afford to let either of us survive."

Tony's expression changed slowly to one of perplexity. *"They?"*

"Benedict and Collins," Victor whispered, hoping not to be overheard in the next room.

"What does Andrew have to do with this?" Tony kept his voice low.

Before he could answer, Victor saw that Tony was beginning to answer his own question. "They've become very friendly the past few days," Victor said.

"I could take care of Andrew," Tony said, frowning. "But I would need some time."

"I don't think there is much time." He nodded

toward his helpless body. "Not for me, anyway."

"There's always the police."

Victor grimaced. "That would be fitting, wouldn't it? After all these years." He shook his head. "No. More than anything else, I've wanted to put an end to talk of Betco's supposed connections with crime and violence."

"Then I don't see what we can do," Tony said, staring at the door to the other half of the suite.

"Do you have a pencil and paper?" Victor asked.

Tony reached into the inside pocket of his suit jacket and pulled out a small leather-bound pad and a gold pen. He handed them to Victor. Then, seeing Victor trying to open the pad with his left arm, hampered by the IV, he sat down on the bed, opened the pad, and held it while Victor painfully and shakily wrote down his instructions.

It took a long time, and Victor had to pause every few minutes to rest his hand. Each time, he commented on his pain and discomfort, more to keep the silence from becoming suspicious than to obtain sympathy.

When he had finished, Tony read the instructions, nodding his understanding and agreement.

However, when he had finished reading, he said, "I don't think I should leave you here alone. Perhaps I should have one of the nurses come in to stay with you."

Victor shook his head. "I should be all right for the next few hours. It's later on, when everything is quiet that may be difficult."

Chapter Thirty-three

"No." Andrew was adamant. "I won't do it! I can't."

His voice trembled as he spoke. He understood clearly the dilemma he faced. He had bent, twisted, and skirted ethics for years, but there was no way he could rationalize the act Bill Benedict was suggesting. It was murder, clearly and unequivocally. If he was caught, that would be the end of everything.

At the same time, all would be lost if he didn't play ball with Benedict.

Obviously Benedict realized that. An arrogant smile creased his face as he gazed steadily at Andrew. "Sure you can," he said. "You're a doctor. You would know how to make it look like an accident." He shrugged. "Too much of a medication. Or too little."

Andrew shook his head. "It's too risky," he said, as much to himself as to Benedict.

"There's a greater risk if you don't," Benedict pressed. "If we give Dawson time to act, we're both going to be out in the cold. Or up shit's creek without a paddle.''

Andrew was gripped by a sense of unreality. The opulent sitting room seemed to spin around him. Victor Dawson was only a few feet away, on the other side of a closed door — close enough for him to hear them discussing the prospect of his death.

Andrew turned away from Benedict's determined gaze to stare out the window at Beverly Hills. Muted lights were beginning to come on behind windows that were sheltered by neatly manicured trees and shrubs.

"But if Tony knows," he said, still gazing out the window, "as you say he does, then we're still up the creek.''

"Screw Tony," Benedict said harshly. "It would be his word against ours. And we would have the power on our side.''

"There's Berger to think about, too," Andrew said. "He would be sure to suspect." He turned away from the window to face Benedict. "He might even be able to prove that something was wrong.''

Benedict was still confident. "You said yourself that Berger was incompetent. No boards, remember? If it showed up that something was wrong, he could easily be blamed for it. He's the doctor in charge, and you aren't. You've got an unimpeachable reputation, and from what I've heard, Berger hasn't.''

Unwittingly, Andrew found himself nodding in agreement. Benedict had thought it all out carefully, and it did seem the logical solution. Perhaps the only solution. If only it weren't for the fact that it involved murder, a murder that Andrew would have to perform. . . .

Benedict pressed his advantage. "It would be easy to convince people that Berger was careless or made a mistake," he suggested. "As soon as the old man is dead, you get in there and accuse him of malpractice or negligence. Don't even give him a chance to suspect you of anything.''

"It might work," Andrew said reluctantly, "except for one thing. The nurses would be sure to see me entering and leaving the room. They're all busybodies. They'd be bound to make a connection. I can't take that chance."

Benedict's eyes narrowed but remained steady on Andrew. "Then what do you suggest we do? Sit on our asses and wait for the axe to fall?"

"I don't know," Andrew admitted. "But I'm not going to put my head under the axe knowingly."

Benedict stared at him for a long moment. Then suddenly the tension in his neck and shoulders relaxed and he smiled. He sat down on the sofa and leaned back casually. "There's always the possibility that we may be worrying for nothing. Fate could very easily take care of the problem for us. You never know. People die of natural causes all the time."

The change in Benedict's manner was obviously intended to calm Andrew, but it made Andrew even more guarded and suspicious. "What are you getting at?" he asked nervously.

Benedict flashed him that arrogant smile. "I'm sure you could think of any number of ways Dawson might die simply by letting nature take its course." He made the statement seem like a question.

"Perhaps," Andrew said cautiously.

"I'm curious to know what might happen to a man in Dawson's condition." He paused for a moment. "Assuming medical technology isn't infallible, of course."

Andrew knew what he meant. Benedict wanted Andrew to tell him how a safe murder could be committed. The lawyer was staying in the hospital suite day and night; he could take care of Dawson without any suspicion being directed toward him. Andrew was relieved that Benedict was no longer suggesting he kill Dawson, but this latest suggestion was an even greater challenge to Andrew's conscience. If he simply told Benedict how Dawson could be killed, Andrew wouldn't be guilty of murder, in a legal sense, but he would know what he had done; and he had to ask himself if he could live with that knowledge.

He looked out the window again at Beverly Hills, where night had settled in. It was quite a while before he turned to face Benedict.

"Victor Dawson is entirely dependent on the plasma that's being fed to him intravenously," he said mechanically. "Without that plasma, his own enzymes would literally devour him. The nurses are required to check his intravenous regularly, to make sure the plasma level is sufficient. I'm sure he himself has also been advised to keep an eye on it and to notify them if it begins to run low. If something were to happen to the plasma and he were unable to notify the nurses' station, it would be extremely unfortunate."

Benedict didn't hide his satisfaction. "You mean" — he grinned — "if the bottle should break?"

"No. The bottle's made of a sturdy plastic. It couldn't break. But it might be attached improperly so that it would leak, or it might be set incorrectly and drain out too rapidly. Or the nurse might not have recorded accurately the last time it was replaced."

Benedict was clearly excited now. "And of course," he offered, "Dawson might be asleep and not even notice that it had run out."

Andrew nodded.

"That's good to know." Benedict faked a frown. "I should be careful to look in on him tonight while he's sleeping. I ought to look at that bottle just in case a nurse has slipped up somehow."

Andrew was surprised at how good he felt as he left the hospital that night. He walked across the parking lot feeling a lot better than he had in a very long time, and he actually caught himself humming. It was as if an enormous load had been lifted from his shoulders, taking all his worries and anxieties with it. Everything he wanted now seemed within his grasp.

His thoughts were of Lina as he sped out of the parking lot. Hope and anticipation soared within him. Soon Lina would be his completely, and his life would be perfect in every way.

Andrew had not yet talked to Lina of marriage; he wasn't a man to make promises he couldn't fulfill. But tonight he would tell her; he was confident about the future. He would propose to her, and they would celebrate.

As he drove along Santa Monica Boulevard, toward the freeway, Andrew realized he hadn't spoken to Lina today, even though they had vaguely discussed spending the evening together. One of the ground rules for their relationship was that neither would appear unannounced at the other's home or place of work.

Andrew pulled into a gas station to use the phone. He didn't particularly like the new open public phones. The old booths with doors offered a bit of privacy and shut out the traffic noise. But he couldn't be choosy.

He dialed Lina's number. Normally she picked it up on the second ring, but this time there was no answer. Finally, after the fifth ring, her service answered.

His immediate reaction was simply to hang up. He didn't like leaving his name with a stranger. But he was disturbed by the fact that Lina wasn't at home waiting for his call.

"Yes," he told the service operator. "This is Dr. Collins calling. Did Miss Lathrop leave a message for me?"

"Dr. Collins?" she asked in that nasal voice so peculiar to operators. "Just a moment and I'll check." He was placed on hold for a bit longer than a moment before she came back to say, "Yes, Miss Lathrop said to tell you she would be out of town for a few days."

"A few days?" Andrew was startled. "How many days? Did she say?"

"No, she didn't. The message was 'a few days.' "

"Is it business or personal?" Andrew asked irritably.

"I don't know," the woman replied just as irritably. "If you wish to leave a message, perhaps she'll call in."

Andrew was trying to decide what sort of message to leave.

There was a clicking sound at the other end and the woman said, "Please hold. I have another call." Then there was a long silence.

Andrew slammed down the phone and stormed back to his car.

Chapter Thirty-four

Victor Dawson was not in a deep sleep. He lingered on the edge of wakefulness, as if giving in to full sleep might prevent him from ever awakening again. It was not a restful state. It held neither the assurance of reality nor the comfort of dreams. In the dim light the nurses left on during the night, his mind played tricks on him.

Time after time he opened his eyes and scanned the room. He sensed that he wasn't alone. One moment, he was sitting drowsily in front of the TV in the den of the house he had owned years before, waiting for Phyllis to come home from a date. Another moment, he was sleeping on a plane to Havana, apprehensive that the man sitting across the aisle was a federal agent about to slap a subpoena in his hands. At yet another, he was in a hotel room in Las Vegas, waiting for one of his men to arrive to tell him that an adversary had finally submitted to pressure and the casino deal could be concluded.

Each time he would jerk awake, frustrated to find

that the person awaited was not there, and increasingly annoyed with himself as time and place adjusted and he realized where he was.

He berated himself for being so foolish, reminding himself that he was in a hospital, that he was expecting no one, and that he had to sleep in order to recover.

But he was expecting someone. Not someone who expected to be expected, and not anyone specific. Just someone. Victor knew that Bill Benedict would make his move tonight, one way or another. If Benedict was as shrewd as Victor thought, he would not make the move himself. It would be a nurse or a doctor, or an orderly — someone who couldn't possibly be connected with a suspicious death. A big man, a powerful man, never did the dirty work himself.

That was the way Victor had always operated, the way he had survived. He had never been the executioner; he had always been the judge. His hands were clean, and his conscience was clear.

He drifted into semisleep again. He wanted desperately to rest.

He had no idea how long he had slept, when he again awakened with that odd sense of apprehension, again feeling that someone had come into the room. This time he was certain that a door had opened and closed, but he could see no one in the light or in the shadows. He could hear no sound of movement.

He waited for a moment, watching and listening, and then, cursing himself audibly, forced his eyes to close.

When they opened again, he was sure that it wasn't simply his imagination; there was someone in the room with him. Victor was certain that there had been some sound, some movement. Something in the room had altered, but he couldn't immediately determine what it was.

Then he saw it.

The intravenous bottle was swinging on its pole — and it was empty! There was none of the precious life-sustaining plasma at all.

Victor reached for the buzzer to call the nurses' station.

It was not there.

He groped frantically around the edge of the bed, desperately searching for the small plastic box, for the cord that held it. It had been there earlier in the evening. Someone had obviously taken it away, just as someone had obviously emptied the IV bottle.

But the buzzer could not have been removed completely without cutting the wire. Certain that it would be somewhere just beyond his reach, Victor tried to raise himself to look over the right side of the bed.

The pain that ripped through his belly was excruciating, and he cried out weakly, then gasped. Because of the pain, he had to move slowly and carefully, inching his way toward the edge of the bed. Finally, when he was able to look over the edge, he spotted the buzzer, right where he expected it to be — lying about a foot from the bed, on the carpeted floor.

In his strained, half-sitting, half-lying position, he stared at the buzzer for a long moment, contemplating what to do. Unless a nurse should just happen to come in — which he was certain would not happen — reaching the buzzer was his only chance for survival. The pain was unbearable now, even without moving, but he told himself that he had to endure it. Somehow he had to get out of bed and onto the floor. If he succeeded in reaching the buzzer, it would be only a matter of moments before help arrived. If he did not succeed, the pain would soon be over anyway.

His hand trembling, he removed the IV needle taped to his arm. Then, feeling as if he were ripping out his insides, he twisted his legs around to set his feet on the floor. The intense pain blotted out all his other senses.

His eyes were blinded, and his ears roared with static, destroying his sense of balance. Unable to control his body, Victor fell to the floor.

He lay there, gasping, until he had calmed himself and regained control. Then he searched around himself for the buzzer. It lay only a few inches away. Straining, he extended his hand to grasp it.

Suddenly a figure stepped out of the shadows, and a foot came forward to kick the buzzer just beyond Victor's grasp.

Victor looked up into the smiling face of Bill Benedict.

He knew instantly that he had no chance for survival. He withdrew his hand. The most he could hope for now was to die with a certain amount of dignity, though that would be difficult while lying helpless on the floor.

"I overestimated you," Victor said, his voice an almost inaudible croak. "You won't get very far, managing things this way."

For a brief moment, doubt and uncertainty flickered across the lawyer's face. Then the confident smile returned. "I don't think you're in a position to give advice anymore," Benedict said. "I'm in control now."

It took great effort for Dawson to smile, but he managed, though weakly. "You won't be for very long," he said. "I give you no more than twelve hours after I'm gone."

Again the lawyer looked uncertain. "You're bluffing," he said angrily. "No one will ever know what happened."

"Perhaps," Dawson acknowledged. "But you don't have it in you to succeed. You're just as weak, just as clumsy as the rest of your generation. You don't know how to manage anything. Your being here right now proves that."

A pain cut through Victor at that moment, more

powerful than any he had known before, a pain so severe he could not fight it. He could only give in to it.

He said nothing more. There was nothing more worth saying.

Chapter Thirty-five

No one had called Dave Berger. He didn't realize anything was wrong until he arrived at the nurses' station and asked for the file on Victor Dawson, preparing to make his early morning visit to his patient.

"I'm sorry, Dr. Berger," the nurse said. "Dawson's records have been appropriated by the surgery committee."

Dave was stunned. "What do you mean 'appropriated'? Why should the surgery committee want my records?"

The nurse looked at him oddly, then shrugged. "I'm sure you would know that better than I. I only follow orders."

Something in her manner told Dave what had happened. He rushed down the hall toward Dawson's room. "Just a moment, Dr. Berger," the nurse called after him. "Wait." But Dave didn't stop.

He was stopped at the door of Dawson's room by a big, beefy orderly who blocked his way.

"What's going on here?" Dave demanded. "I'm Dawson's doctor. I've got a right to see him."

"There's nobody in this room," the orderly said curtly, "and I've got orders to keep everybody out."

"Where's the patient who was in that room?" Dave demanded.

The orderly shrugged. "You could try pathology."

"He's dead? Why wasn't I notified?"

Again the orderly shrugged. "Ask at the nurses' station. I don't know nothing."

The nurse at the nurses' station told him little more, only that Victor Dawson had been discovered dead in his room shortly after four in the morning, and that the chief of surgery had questions about the cause of death.

Victor Dawson was dead. . . . It still didn't register fully with Dave. What registered was that there was some question about the cause of death. Dave knew immediately that Andrew Collins was behind that question, and he was determined that Collins would answer it for him.

He went directly to Collins's office and demanded to see him.

"He's not in," the secretary said icily, "and I don't know what time he'll be back. He's at a surgery committee meeting."

"A surgery committee meeting? At this time of morning?"

"It was an emergency," the secretary replied. "Called suddenly, before I arrived at work. That's all I know."

Dave had never had the distinction of being invited to a surgery committee meeting. But, invited or not, he intended to attend this one.

He was slightly intimidated by the elegance of the executive wing, but his indignation carried him down the carpeted hall to the boardroom.

He didn't bother to knock on the closed door, but burst into the room, then stood staring at the group around the table, suddenly realizing he hadn't even considered what he would say to them.

They were stunned by the intrusion and stared back at him. Dave didn't know all the doctors in the room, though he had had some dealings with most of them. None of them could be called his friend.

It was Collins, ashen and frightened, who spoke first, rising to demand, "What do you think you're doing here? You have no right to barge in here."

Dave quickly found his tongue. "Where is Victor Dawson? And why was I not called? He's my patient."

"This committee has taken charge of your patient," Collins snapped. "And your rights in this hospital have been suspended because of gross incompetence."

If Collins had not been on the opposite side of the table, Dave would have punched him. Instead, he started to shout back a countercharge, and was stopped by the chief of surgery.

"That's not quite true, Andrew." Dr. Franklin's voice was mild but forceful. "Dr. Berger's privileges have been temporarily suspended, pending the outcome of this committee's investigation of charges of malfeasance."

"Brought by whom?" Dave demanded. "Collins?"

"It doesn't matter who brought the charges," Dr. Franklin replied. "This committee will be entirely fair in its investigation, and you'll have ample time to answer all charges. All we know at the moment is that a patient has died in this hospital under suspicious circumstances. And a very important patient, at that."

"What kind of suspicious circumstances? So far, nobody will even tell me that."

Collins broke in, and Berger saw real terror in his eyes. "You'll find that out when you get the charges in writing."

"Just a moment, Andrew," Dr. Franklin said evenly. "I think Dr. Berger is entitled to a full explanation."

"He isn't part of this committee," Collins said shrilly. "He wasn't invited here. He should get the charges in the customary manner."

"This meeting hasn't taken place in a normal way," Dave argued. "If you can make an exception for it, you can make an exception for me."

Dr. Franklin cut off another retort from Collins with a wave of his hand. "Dr. Berger," he said, "this committee is concerned about the manner and the cause of your patient's death. It occurred last night sometime between three and four in the morning. His body was found on the floor beside his bed. His IV needle had been removed from his arm, and his IV bottle was empty. His hand was stretched out on the floor as if reaching for the buzzer to signal the nurses' station for help."

Dave frowned. "But how does that indicate malfeasance on my part? I last saw Dawson somewhere around six last night. And no one called me to indicate any problem existed."

"You're lying, Berger!" Collins shouted.

"Let me handle this, Andrew," Dr. Franklin said, then turned back to Dave. "According to the patient's chart, you visited Victor Dawson at three-fifteen this morning. And that has been confirmed for us by Dawson's lawyer, Bill Benedict."

"That's preposterous!" Dave exploded. "I left the hospital at seven last night and didn't return until half an hour ago. What would I be doing here in the middle of the night?"

"That's what we'd like to know," Collins said with an evil smile.

"What was the cause of death?" Dave demanded.

"We don't have the pathologist's report yet," Dr. Franklin said. "But, if the patient's records are correct, he should have had another four hours before the IV bottle had to be replaced."

Dave looked accusingly at Collins. He felt confident that Victor Dawson had been entirely honest with him, but there were obviously things that Dawson hadn't known. Andrew Collins and Bill Benedict were playing the game by another set of rules, and they clearly intended Dave to be their patsy. They had been setting him up for this all along.

"How long will I have to answer charges of malfeasance?" he asked Franklin.

"As long as you need. Within reason. A week, two weeks."

"Fine," Dave said with assurance. "I shouldn't need longer than that." He turned to leave.

Actually, he wasn't as confident as he sounded. He wasn't sure he would be able to prove anything, but he had decided in that moment as he stared at Andrew Collins that his only weapon was to bluff, to buy himself time to prove they were framing him.

Chapter Thirty-six

It disturbed Melissa Baxter to do what she was about to do. She liked Dave Berger and had considerable respect for him, but she had no choice. She had to think of her patients. They came first, before any other feelings or loyalties she had. If what her sources told her was true, and she had no doubt that it was — her sources being very reliable — Dr. Berger could no longer admit patients to Beverly Hills Hospital. In fact, he now had no affiliation with any hospital at all. For some of Melissa's patients, who were in very frail health, that could spell disaster.

When she finally reached him by phone, Dr. Berger had tried to avoid meeting her that day. "I'm going to be terribly busy," he had said, the strain evident in his voice. "Can't it wait until tomorrow?"

"I'm afraid not," she had said. "I know what's happened at the hospital, and I must see you immediately."

He was just leaving the hospital and would meet her

at his office in fifteen minutes. If she wasn't on time, he couldn't promise he would wait for her.

His abruptness had made it easier for her.

The boxes of patients' files were still stacked haphazardly around his small office. Since his office wasn't officially open that day, he hadn't bothered to turn on all the lights, giving the place more than the usual desolate appearance. Seated behind his desk, Dave Berger looked small and forlorn, a totally defeated man.

Melissa carried her knitting bag with her, as usual, but she didn't work at it. Instead, she sat apprehensively on the edge of the chair across the desk from the doctor, her knitting in her lap.

"Dr. Berger, I know you're upset about what's happened," she began. "I am, too. It places me in a very difficult position."

Puzzled, Dave frowned. "How so?"

"My patients," she reminded him. "They can't afford to be without the services of a hospital, even for one day." She paused, watching his face for some sign of understanding. "What do you propose we do about them?"

"I'm sorry," Dave said falteringly. "I'm afraid I haven't even had time to think about that. I was only given word of the suspension less than an hour ago."

"You don't have an affiliation with any other hospital, do you?"

"No, but I suppose I could get one."

"That would take at least a week, perhaps two, wouldn't it?" Melissa asked, already knowing the answer.

"Yes." Dave nodded, beginning to realize what she was getting at. A look of dread passed across his face. He was down, and he was waiting to be kicked.

"I have an obligation to my patients," Melissa said, refusing to look at him. "I have to be able to provide them with whatever care they need. I don't want to do this, but I have to take them from you and reassign them to doctors who can care for them."

"I understand entirely," Dave said glumly. "I assume you'll send another truck for the files?"

Melissa began to pick at her knitting. "I wish it could be otherwise. I wish there were something you or I could do to avoid this." She paused, then looked at him. "If it's any comfort, I know you're not guilty."

"Thank you, Mrs. Baxter," he said without thinking. Then he stopped and stared at her. "What do you mean?"

She picked up her needles and absently began to knit. "I mean," she said, "I know you weren't at the hospital at three in the morning."

"How do you now that?" Dave demanded.

Melissa shrugged and blushed. "I can't say, but I have my sources. I try to keep up with everything that goes on at the hospital." She squirmed. "For the sake of my patients, of course."

Dave broke into a wide grin. "I might have known," he said. "Do you happen to know who was in Victor Dawson's room around three in the morning?"

"Well . . . yes, I know, but you can't ask me to prove anything, if that's what you're getting at. I know who was in and out of that room all evening." She paused, looked at her knitting, then looked back at Dave. "You left at about seven-fifteen, just like you told the surgery committee. That was about fifteen minutes before the nurse checked in on Mr. Dawson. Dr. Collins was in between eight and eight-thirty. That lawyer, Benedict, left shortly after that — the first time he was out of the hospital suite all day.

"While he was gone, Tony Manchester came back," she continued. "He had been in earlier. This time he went directly into Mr. Dawson's room, not through the sitting-room door, and he had a man with him. I'm sorry, but I don't know who the man was. He was a stranger to . . ." — she hestiated — ". . . to the person who gave me the information. But he was a rather conservative type, like an accountant or a lawyer, and he carried a briefcase. They stayed less than half an hour. Shortly after they left, Bill Benedict returned, looking rather annoyed about something."

She surveyed the stitches she had made while talking. "Except for the nurses who checked on the patient at ten and at one," she said softly, "that was it — all the visitors he had."

"I don't understand," Dave said, puzzled. "Who went into Dawson's room between three and four?"

"No one," Melissa explained. "Don't you see? The only person who could be responsible for Dawson's death is the lawyer, Benedict, who was right there in the suite with him."

Dave scowled. "But that's conjecture, not proof."

"I told you you couldn't ask me to prove it. And don't you dare say anything about this to the board or to the police, because I'll have to deny it. If I revealed my contacts, they'd never tell me anything again."

Dave fell silent for a moment, staring down at the notes he had made on a piece of paper on his desk. "One thing puzzles me," he said. "Why did Tony Manchester come back to see Dawson a second time? And why did he bring the stranger with him?"

Melissa shook her head. "That I don't know. My sources can't read minds. Perhaps you could ask Tony Manchester."

She had made the suggestion facetiously, but Dave nodded. "I might just do that," he said. "No harm in asking, is there?"

"Dr. Berger." Melissa hesitated. She wasn't sure how much to confide in this young man. Normally she wouldn't have revealed as much about herself and her ways as she already had but she felt she owed Dave something, perhaps for Phil Winston's sake. "I wouldn't rock the boat if I were you. I've found the only way to survive in today's world is to be as unobtrusive as possible. If you commit yourself too openly to anything, you leave yourself open for someone to knock you down.''

Dave looked thoughtful. ''You may be right. And I can see how it works for you. But it hasn't worked for me. For two years I tried simply to be good at my work — I didn't try to be noticed, just to be good — and it got me nowhere. For the past week, I've been stumbling around in the dark, still trying to be a good doctor, and I've just about destroyed myself. I've been backed into a corner, and I have only two choices. I can give in and accept total defeat — the loss of everything I've ever worked for and believed in — or I can fight back, stick my neck out, and take chances.'' He smiled kindly. ''No. But I appreciate your advice. I'm going to Tony Manchester, and I'm going to do whatever's necessary to protect my right to be a doctor — ethical or unethical.''

Melissa picked up her knitting and stood up. ''When can I arrange to pick up the files?'' she asked.

''Whenever you want. Just let me know. I'll arrange to have someone here.''

''I'll call as soon as I know when I can get a truck.''

He opened the door for her. ''One other thing,'' he said suddenly. ''Your witness doesn't happen to know how Dawson's medical record was altered to indicate that I was in Dawson's room at three in the morning?'' He raised an eyebrow and smiled wryly. ''By some miraculous chance?''

''Why, yes . . . as a matter of fact.'' She paused, then said significantly, ''It hadn't been altered at the time Dr. Collins picked it up to take it to the surgery committee.''

Chapter Thirty-seven

Phyllis Dawson read through the document again, and was just as bewildered as she'd been the first time.

Tony Manchester was aware of some of Phyllis's background, having heard Victor talk about her on numerous occasions, but her appearance had surprised him. She was not unattractive, as he had expected, though she did not seem to want to make the best of her looks. Perhaps it was a holdover from her time in the commune.

Phyllis had her father's dark, intense, intelligent eyes, a bit small for her face, but winning nevertheless. Her long dark hair was straight and worn in a neat bun at the back of her neck. She wore a loose-fitting khaki pants outfit, consisting of trousers and bush jacket, with a large leather shoulder bag. It did not fully disguise the fact that she had a trim, well-endowed body. She wore only light makeup and no jewelry.

At Victor Dawson's request, Tony had called Phyllis

and arranged to meet her plane. Victor had wanted her to receive the news of his death as gently as possible, and it was important that everything be explained to her immediately. Tony had given her the news in the car on the way in from the airport. Phyllis had remained quiet and had shed no tears.

Now, as she reread the letter her father had signed, the tears began to flow down her cheeks. "If he knew what was going to happen," she said softly, "why didn't he ask me to come sooner?"

"He didn't want to get you involved," Tony said sympathetically.

"What difference could that make?" she challenged, offended at being treated as a helpless child. "I'm involved now."

"But it would have been much more dangerous for you to have gotten involved sooner. And there really wasn't time. We only discovered what was happening last night."

"Surely there was something that could have been done," Phyllis protested. "It must have been horrible for him lying there alone in that hospital room, just waiting to die."

"Yes," Tony acknowledged. "We could have had someone sitting watch day and night, but that would only have prolonged the wait for him. And he knew he couldn't live much longer anyway. He would have been an invalid for the rest of his life. And I'm sure you have an idea of what your father thought about that."

"He would have hated it," she said, and her tears stopped.

"At this point," Tony said, "there's only one thing you can do to help your father, and that's to do as he requested. Are you willing?"

"Yes."

"You accept that the letter and the notarized document are from your father?"

"Of course. I recognize his handwriting, and it's exactly the sort of thing my father would do. I know how he felt about the younger generation, particularly his own children, and I know he thought more of Betco than of any human being. I'll do as he asked, and I'll leave everything else to you." She hesitated, then added, "I'm afraid I don't know very much about business — not at this level — but I'm willing to learn."

"That's all that's necessary at the moment," Tony assured her. "When the board meets, if you vote your shares with mine, we can control Betco. I can manage the corporation while you're learning the ropes. The only problem we may have is if Benedict goes to court to challenge this will. It was prepared quickly and signed under circumstances filled with loopholes. We can only hope he'll decide not to press his luck too far."

Phyllis was still in Tony's office at Beverly Hills Hospital when Tony's secretary buzzed him on the intercom and said, "Dr. Berger is here to see you. He doesn't have an appointment, but he says it's very important."

"Dr. Berger?" Tony asked, surprised. "Dr. Dave Berger?" After his secretary confirmed this, he hesitated, then said, "Ask him to wait, I'll be with him shortly."

But Phyllis asked suddenly, "Is this the Dr. Berger who performed surgery on my father?"

Tony nodded.

"I'd like to meet him, if you don't mind."

He buzzed his secretary back and said, "Show Dr. Berger in now."

The tension was obvious as Dave Berger entered the room. Both men were strained, uncertain of how the meeting would unfold. Tony knew very little about the young doctor, and he assumed Berger knew as little about him. Each knew the other only by reputation.

Tony was uneasy about the purpose of Dave's visit,

and worried about what he might say in front of Phyllis Dawson.

To head off a potentially difficult conversation, Tony took charge and introduced Victor's daughter before asking Dave to sit down.

Phyllis offered her hand and said pleasantly, "I want to thank you, Dr. Berger, for doing everything possible to try to help my father." She paused, withdrew her hand, and smiled. "I know you did everything a doctor could possibly do."

Dave's smile was brief. "Thank you, Miss Dawson. I wish others felt the same way."

Phyllis eyed him warily. "What do you mean?"

Dave hesitated, glancing uneasily at Tony. "It seems that I'm being blamed for your father's death. That's what I've come to talk to Mr. Manchester about."

Phyllis frowned and looked at Tony. "I don't understand. Why is he being blamed? And who's blaming him?"

Tony tried not to appear flustered. "It's just a small misunderstanding," he explained. "The surgery committee is investigating your father's death, and Dr. Berger has been suspended until it's resolved. When it's all over, I'm sure he'll be cleared." He turned to Dave and added, "If you don't mind, Dr. Berger, we can discuss this later."

"No," Phyllis said firmly. "Since I'm now going to be involved in the management of this hospital, as well as other Betco enterprises, I'd like to know everything that's going on — especially where it relates to my father."

It was foolish, really, for Tony to want to protect Andrew Collins at this point, but he and Andrew had been associated in people's minds for so long that he hesitated to bring the truth into the open for fear he would be incriminated. So far, he had Phyllis Dawson's confidence, but would she continue to trust him if she knew the entire story?

While he hesitated, Dave Berger stepped into the breach.

"There were a few suspicious circumstances surrounding your father's death," Dave said softly. "I don't know if you're aware of them."

"Yes, I'm aware that there seems to have been tampering with his IV." She paused. "And, for some reason, he was unable to signal for help."

"Yes." Dave's voice was bitter. "Well, the hospital needs a scapegoat, and it seems I'm it."

Tony laughed nervously. As they both stared at him, he said quickly, "That's not quite accurate. It's only the guilty party who's trying to do that." He smiled. "I assure you, when it's all straightened out, the hospital will be entirely fair. Your reputation and your standing here will be intact."

"Maybe," Dave said grimly, "but twenty-four hours from now I won't have a practice." They stared at him, not understanding, so he explained, "I'm a surgeon. My patients can't stick with me if I can't perform in a hospital."

"Melissa Baxter?" Tony asked suddenly.

Dave nodded.

"I'm sorry," Tony said sincerely. "We'll find some way to make it up to you."

"I don't want charity. I just want the truth to come out the next time I meet with the surgery committee." He paused, giving Tony a hard, cold look. "I know who killed Victor Dawson. I know who entered his room last night, and I know what time they went in and went out. I know you were there right after I was, Mr. Manchester. I know Andrew Collins came in after that. And I know you came back later, bringing another man with you, but I don't know who that man was. Except for the nurse, and Bill Benedict, you and this man were the last to enter Dawson's suite before he died."

Tony frowned. "If you're suggesting that we killed Dawson, you're wrong."

"No. I know you didn't. But I feel you and this man might know something that would help me to prove who did."

Tony considered for a moment before answering, "The man was a lawyer. Victor wanted to make some changes in his will. That was all." He paused. "If you know who was in that room, then you must have a witness. I would think that would be sufficient to clear you."

Frustration and anger competed for control of Dave's face. He rose to his feet agitatedly. "I should have known better than to come here. You'd do anything to protect that damned son-in-law of yours. You're probably the one who put him up to this in the first place."

"What do you mean?" Phyllis broke in. She looked suspiciously at Tony, then back at Dave. "Are you suggesting —"

But Tony interrupted before she could voice her suspicions. "I don't care what happens to Andrew Collins," he said harshly. "He's dug his own grave, as far as I'm concerned. I'll do nothing to protect him, from you or from anybody else."

"What exactly does Andrew Collins have to do with this?" Phyllis asked.

"Truthfully," Tony said with disgust, "I don't know. But nothing would surprise me. I do know that he and Benedict have been more than friendly these past few days."

Phyllis turned to Dave. "What *does* he have to do with it?"

"Everything, as far as I'm concerned," Dave said hotly. "He altered the patient records to indicate that I was in Victor Dawson's room at the time of his death."

"What?" Tony was genuinely startled. He rose to his feet, his eyes boring into Dave's. "Can you prove this?"

Dave didn't respond immediately. Then his shoulders slumped and he sat down again and sighed. "No, I can't prove that any more than I can prove who entered and left Dawson's room last night. There was a witness to all of it. One of the nurses, I think. But she *or* he — wants to remain anonymous. According to this witness, it was Collins who took Dawson's records to the surgery committee, and those records hadn't yet been altered at the time he took them."

"I see," Tony said. "Well, there's only one person who is authorized to release patient records — the head floor nurse." He paused. "All you have to do to get your proof, Dr. Berger, is to find out who was head floor nurse on the night shift."

Dave frowned. "If I prove this," he said, "Collins's reputation won't be worth much."

"I told you, I don't give a damn about Collins."

Chapter Thirty-eight

Dave felt the thick carpet outside the boardroom give slightly under his feet as he approached the special Saturday meeting. The geometric wallpaper contrasted sharply with the ornate French furniture and heightened his uneasiness.

The doctors were taking seats around a long polished table as the surgery board assembled. The fluorescent lights gave Dave the eerie feeling that everything in the room was underwater.

As Dave entered the room, he saw Andrew Collins at the head of the table, serious and preoccupied, and Emily Harris, the emergency room nurse, sitting next to him. Collins gave Dave a brief nod as he took his seat. Dave looked around the table. Dr. Stein was looking straight ahead.

Nobody said hello. He got only blank stares or nods. Dave was definitely not state of the art — not here anyway.

Dave looked around and saw Niles Kelly, who looked away. Sandra Coyle tried to give him a smile of reassurance, but he could only think of the gallbladder patient she had referred to him, then had sent elsewhere.

They had him locked up cold. Dave thought ahead to tomorrow, when he'd fly up to Palo Alto for the boards. He needed confidence. He also needed a pat on the back, some reassurance. He certainly wasn't going to get it here.

Andrew Collins brought the meeting to order.

"We are here to discuss Dr. David Berger," he said matter-of-factly. "There are two cases on the books: one, Victor Dawson; and two, Dr. Philip Winston."

Dave saw Dr. Coyle and Dr. Curtis shift uneasily as Collins continued.

What were they really doing here? Dave wondered. These were war games, games played through committees. The bottom line was finance. Every surgery Dave did was a surgery out of Collins's pocket. God . . . what greed. Collins didn't need Dave's cases. Collins was doing just fine; he had Tony Manchester, he had movie people, he had everything.

Collins stood up at the head of the table. "To begin with, the Victor Dawson case. A very important patient has been operated on in this hospital, and he has died. Supposedly, he had the very best care the hospital had to offer; yet, he is dead. The purpose of this meeting is to find out what happened, if there was any problem with the surgery . . . or with the surgeon involved. We have had other problems with this surgeon. . . ."

"Yes," said Dr. Stein.

Collins continued: "A partially trained surgeon is always an awkward situation to deal with in a hospital."

Dave had heard enough. He jumped up. "I'm fully trained!" he shouted.

He saw clearly what Collins was doing. He was setting him up for the kill, bringing up the Victor Dawson case first in order to minimize and draw attention away from himself on the Winston case!

"I did four years and a chief residency in general surgery. I have passed the written and I am taking oral boards this week."

"It is not true that you have failed the orals twice before?"

Dave swallowed hard. "That's true. However, I'm considered board-eligible by the boards now, and I don't think that ought to be a factor."

Collins looked around the room. Dave could tell by the faces of the surgeons in the room that not many agreed. The board certificate was necessary to survive in the politics of modern medicine.

Collins continued: "It has come to this committee's attention that David Berger is not a board-certified surgeon. We must think first of the safety of the patients in our hospital and of the reputation of our hospital itself."

"Perhaps major surgery is too much for Dr. Berger," Dr. Stein put in. "Perhaps we should monitor him more closely before he passes, and *if* he passes, his boards."

"If he doesn't pass his boards this time," Collins said, "there will be no problem. Having failed the oral exam three times, Berger will have to go back to his residency for additional training. Judgment — the very thing that the oral boards are meant to test, the very thing that Dave has failed twice — is the big question here. Granted, the patient had a bad pancreas. The question is: Was Berger right in operating on the patient at all, and was the correct operation performed?"

Dave broke in. "May I present the case so that we can all get the picture?"

"Well, I don't . . ." But the others overruled and Collins sat down.

Dave rose to his feet. "The patient, Victor Dawson, a fifty-eight year-old white male, first came to my office seeking a private physician. I examined him and felt his diagnosis was a chronic pancreatitis. I counseled him on what diet to follow and not to smoke, and gave the same precautions that his doctor in Chicago had given him."

"We know the history of the case, Berger," Collins said. "Let's get on with it."

"Dr. Nino assisted me at the surgery, and we found an acute smoldering pancreas with half the pancreas actually eaten away."

"What was the pathology report?" Collins asked.

The pathologist stood up and circled the slides on the board. "Acute necrotic pancreatitis. Here's a slide where Dr. Berger's sutures have been placed in the end of the pancreas, holding in the drain. You can see the leaking pancreatic juices around the partially digested sutures. Not only did the pancreatic juice digest Dr. Berger's stitches, and the drains, but it digested the patient himself. The patient was literally eaten alive."

"Do you feel that the leaking pancreatic juice around Dr. Berger's sutures and drains is responsible for Victor Dawson's death?" Collins pressed.

"As you can see here," the pathologist continued, "the heart, while showing some moderate amount of arteriosclerosis, does not have any acute blockage. The lungs were also clear, and the carotid vessels. The patient did not have a stroke. I would say that the death was related to the disease — a very sick pancreas — and . . ." — he paused briefly — ". . . to the stress of the surgery."

Collins stood up. "That's what I thought. The question is: Was the surgery appropriate? Should it have been done at the time it was? Or could the patient have been handled better by treating him more conservatively with intravenous fluids, plasmanate, antibiotics, and waiting for a more appropriate time to do surgery?"

"All things considered," Dr. Stein interrupted, "I

believe I would have opted for more intravenous fluids and antibiotics, and waited it out."

Dave stood up. "It was my judgment that this was the time to operate on Victor Dawson."

Collins smiled thinly. "That's the question, Dr. Berger — it was your judgment. Was it the right judgment? Or should Dawson have waited to have the surgery? We all know acute pancreatitis, when operated on, might well kill the patient. In this case, it seems that it did."

"Victor Dawson needed the operation!" Dave shouted. "It wasn't my surgery that killed him. I believe, Dr. Collins, you and others in this room know what did!"

There was a shocked silence as everyone stared at Dave.

"What do you mean by that?" Collins was on his feet now.

"I never went back into the patient's room," Dave said. "Someone else did. And the chart was doctored to make it look as if I had. Whoever was in Victor Dawson's room, whoever stopped the IV's and the post-op fluids that were so necessary for his life — whoever pulled the plug in this case — is the one who killed Victor Dawson, not my surgery."

Half of the committee began busily looking over the papers in front of them, while the others continued to stare at Berger.

"This is a most serious charge, Dr. Berger," Collins said finally. "The committee will have to discuss it in private session after you leave."

Dave tried to ease the knot forming in his stomach. He concentrated on the reflections that danced across the polished tabletop between Collins and himself.

"Let's go on to the case of Dr. Winston for the moment," Collins said. "In the matter of Dr. Winston's death, there was a question of adequacy of preoperative workup and operative behavior."

"When you came on the scene," Dave replied, "the patient was already in surgery. But where were *you*, Dr. Collins, when we tried to page you from the emergency room for over an hour? I couldn't get you, the nurses couldn't get you, and —"

"Hold on!" Collins shouted. "We're not here to discuss my performance. I happened to be on the way into the hospital; it was a rainy day and the freeway was a mess. I got there as fast as I could. My beeper wasn't working. The battery was dead."

"We tried to get you for over an hour. I only took Dr. Winston to surgery to save his life."

"Well, you didn't exactly prolong it, did you, Dr. Berger?"

"Emily Harris, the ER nurse, was there. She'll tell you what happened."

Collins turned to Emily, who shifted uneasily and didn't look up.

"Tell us what happened, Miss Harris. Tell us what happened that morning. Was there trouble getting me? Did Dr. Berger perform adequately?"

Emily spoke in a low voice. Dave could tell what she was going to say before it came out. They had reached her, too.

"Dr. Berger had had a long evening, he had worked the entire night shift, and, frankly, his nerves seemed a bit on edge. He was abrupt with a few of the patients. At one point he screamed at me. I think the long emergency shifts may have —"

"May have what?" Collins said. "Hampered his judgment?"

"Well, maybe —"

"How dare you?" Dave demanded. "How dare you say that! You know what happened, Miss Harris! We couldn't get Collins. We tried and tried."

"Is that true?" Dr. Stein asked.

"I . . . I . . . really can't recall," Emily said. "It . . . everything happened so fast. I just can't recall. I do know that Dr. Collins did arrive and did perform the surgery after Dr. Berger had taken the patient to the OR."

Dave jumped out of his seat again. "A total lie!"

"Sit down, Berger!" Collins shouted. "You have now heard what the nurse on duty has to say about the case. I don't know why I should have to explain my actions to you. I did what I could for the patient, and I didn't think your workup and preparation of Dr. Winston for surgery were at all adequate. I personally would have done a pre-op IVP going in to evaluate the kidney and the bladder better. You did know the patient had an avulsion of the renal vessels, Dr. Berger? Tore them right off the main trunk, like a fine razor. And bled to death, right in our operating room!"

"The patient needed emergency surgery. I did what I could to save him," Dave said firmly. "There was no time for fancy X rays. I was sure he also had brain and heart damage from the accident."

Dave sat back, mortified. He was being set up. They had even gotten to Emily Harris. It was all a lie, and there was nothing he could do.

Collins continued. "The patient got the best care this hospital had to offer, the best care, and he died."

Dave sat there as doctor after doctor, witness after witness, spoke up.

They said he was working the ER shift too often. Several physicians, whom Dave had never seen but who were on the hospital staff, talked about the value of having only board-certified surgeons operating on major cases.

"At best," they said, "those doctors without boards should be proctored and watched by a more *senior*, more *responsible* physician."

Dave thought ahead to his own boards. Only two days away now.

Dr. Curtis finally stood up. "I feel I have to speak up for Dr. Berger. I know Dr. Berger; I trained with him. He was always an excellent doctor, and I feel he's being treated unfairly now."

"Dr. Curtis, when we want your opinions, we'll ask for them," Collins said coldly. "You're in the family-practice department here, with two years of residency in family practice behind you. I don't think that makes you exactly an expert on what other board-certified surgeons think of Dr. Berger's performance. Let's leave it to the experts."

"Experts, my ass," Curtis said. "Dr. Berger is a better doctor than any of you here."

"Any more outbursts and you'll be asked to leave," Collins said. "And may I remind you that your privileges at Beverly Hills Hospital are only temporary, Dr. Curtis, and subject to review, including your right to assist in the OR."

As Curtis sat down, Dave shot him a look of appreciation. At least Curtis tried to stick up for him. But they had him, too — by the balls.

Finally, Richard Horn, the hospital administrator, stood up. "I feel that from the administrator's point of view we must say that Dr. Berger, who was originally hired by Dr. Winston to work in the ER, has done a good job . . . on the whole. Of course, there have been certain incidents —"

"Incidents? What incidents?" Dave cried.

"Please, you'll get your chance, Dr. Berger," Horn said. "Well, like the shouting at nursing personnel, like losing control on certain occasions in the ER. I realize Dr. Berger is under great stress studying for his boards. The emergency room nurses often had to prod him away from his notes and journals to get him to see their patients. I believe there was a certain discomfort, a certain feeling that Dr. Berger wasn't always sure of what he was doing."

Dave stared at the administrator. He remembered the first time he met him in his office. "*We* know how to handle problems with doctors," Horn had said.

Dave had noticed the *we*. The administrator thought he was a doctor or even more than a doctor . . . that doctors should be under his thumb.

"We can move them off the Wilshire corridor, we can move them out of the hospital — we can do what we want with them," he had said.

Dave had been horrified. Like some sort of giant game of chess. War games. Moving doctors here or there. Looking for their vulnerabilities, then trying to destroy them.

He remembered seeing a picture on Horn's desk of his wife and two children with a bunch of fish on the front lawn.

"You know, son," Horn had said, "the doctors are really into financial games. I've seen them come into the valley. Within two years they have a Mercedes and a new house and a swimming pool. I've seen it all. But that's not what's important. Here's what's important." He had then pointed to the picture of his two kids and wife, with the fish on the front lawn.

"Oh, yeah," Dave had said, "families are important. Someday I'd like to have one of my own. I think a family is very important."

"No . . . no . . . " Horn had said. "Not the family, the fish. Look at those fish, boy. I love to fish. Gimme a weekend with the old trout line up there in the lakes, just half an hour from here. It's the fish that are important."

Dave had been appalled.

"You'll have to come up with me some weekend, meet the family. We'll do a little fishing. What do ya say, boy?"

Dave had nodded.

He was nodding now, as Andrew Collins again got to his feet. "The board will entertain a motion that Dr. Berger's privileges be limited to this hospital in the following way: He must require a board-certified surgeon to be consulted on all surgeries he takes to the operating room."

Dave started. This would be like kicking him out of the hospital. What surgeon could get referring doctors, including GP's and internists, to send him cases when another surgeon would have to be checking them?

"And," Collins continued, "I feel that for the first dozen or so cases, Dr. Berger should be proctored by a second board-certified surgeon, that he should *not* be allowed to operate without a second surgeon being there."

Now Dr. Curtis jumped up. "That would make it impossible for Dr. Berger to practice. I like to assist on my own cases. In fact, my patients insist on it. It would mean that I would have to call another surgeon rather than Dr. Berger."

Collins smiled smugly. "I'm sorry that it would be inconvenient for you, Dr. Curtis, but I must consider the safety of the patients and the reputation of the hospital. Due to Dr. Berger's performance, and being without boards, I think these precautions would be in the patients' best interests."

Patients' best interests, hell! thought Dave. It was in the interest of Andrew Collins, it was in the interest of Dr. Stein, it was in the interest of the other surgeons around the table.

"Why does all this have to be done now?" Dave asked. "I'm taking my boards in two days. I may well be board-certified in a few days. Couldn't it wait a week?"

"No!" Collins said. "I think we've waited long enough. We must consider the safety."

"Bullshit!" Dave snapped. "Safety, my ass! The bot-

tom line here is bucks — you know it and I know it, Dr.
Collins. Every case I do is a case less for you."

"I do not need your cases, Dr. Berger. May I remind
you that twenty-five percent of the elective surgery done
at this hospital is on my *private* patients? Any more outbursts and you'll leave the room. We're trying to do this
in a civilized way, doctor to doctor."

Doctor to doctor, Dave thought. *Civilized, my ass!*

"Do me a favor, Dr. Collins," Dave said. "Don't
lock me out of my office. I am not a Dr. Klein."

Collins flushed. Dave had finally hit a sore spot.
"You bastard . . . you incompetent failure! I'll —"

Collins was on the verge of losing control. Red-faced,
he resumed his seat and nodded at Dr. Stein, signaling
him to take over the meeting.

"Dr. Berger, I believe it is time to discuss these matters with the surgery board," Stein said quietly. "Thank
you for attending. The committee will let you know the
results of our discussion and vote."

Dave slowly walked out of the room. He had to go to
the travel agency and pick up his ticket for Palo Alto.
The last thing he wanted to do now was to take his
boards. Whatever little confidence he had had was shot.
He was feeling as low as he'd ever felt, and those
bastards knew it. They had planned it that way.

"Executive board meeting on Monday," Stein said as
Dave was leaving. "To hear the appeal of Dr. Berger
and his attorney. That's Monday at twelve."

The same time I'll be taking my boards, Dave
thought. *Monday at twelve.*

Chapter Thirty-nine

Passersby hardly noticed the solitary figure trudging up Wilshire Boulevard. He seemed to be staring ahead aimlessly, barely cognizant of traffic signals at the crosswalks, or of the shoppers hurrying in and out of Saks and Bonwit's. As he neared the Beverly Wilshire Hotel he had to stop for a large group of foreign tourists who were piling out of three stretch limos. They were all chattering, laughing, and gesturing as they entered the hotel with their shopping bags and parcels.

Dave Berger watched them for a moment, managed a half smile, and turned to look at the displays in the windows of the hotel's corner bookstore. The latest in the trendy "literature" of art, travel, fitness, and business dominated the windows. The piles of books seemed to promise beauty, joy, and success at a price. Harold Robbins's new best seller filled an entire window, a veritable wall of books. In front of the stacks a beautiful mannequin was sprawled, seemingly asleep.

Dave couldn't see the face, but she was so lifelike and real that he was mesmerized. Her figure was draped in a diaphanous negligée, and her long blond hair spilled out all around her head, hiding her face. One hand stretched forward, a handwritten letter crumpled in it. Nearby, on a low side table, was a bottle of Dom Perignon in a silver ice bucket, and a single crystal goblet, half empty. He could hear Streisand singing "Memories."

His eyes misted. Dave jammed his hands into his jacket pockets and gritted his teeth. His stomach began to ache. And then he began to cry, quietly at first, then in deep, racking sobs. A young couple nearby stopped and the girl whispered something.

Dave groaned and turned away from the window. No one else seemed to notice him. He walked briskly past the hotel's entrance. At the next corner, El Camino Drive, he turned right and began to jog. Soon he was running like a marathoner, throat rasping, chest heaving, tears still running down his face. Everything was a blur. Like driving in the rain with faulty wipers. A vision of Shana's smiling face was clear, however, superimposed over the fleeting images of cars and buildings and people as he ran. She was murmuring his name over and over.

He didn't know why he was running, but he had to. Was he running from something? Retreating? Escaping? Or was he chasing something? Trying to win?

His apartment, he guessed, was nearly two miles away.

Dave was strangely exuberant when he reached his building. He was perspiring heavily and his feet hurt, but he felt alive. Just hours ago, in front of Collins, he had wondered if the numbness he felt was anything like the approach of death.

When he opened the door to apartment 4E he was hit with the smell of stale coffee and the familiar musty odor of the old carpet. He had once figured out that it was a combination of cat piss and cabbage soup, with a touch of cheap incense. "God, what a mess!" he muttered, gasping. "How can a bright young surgeon live like this? Shit!" He propped the door open with a newspaper and opened the windows in both rooms. There was hardly enough breeze to move the curtains.

Everywhere he looked there were piles of books, papers, dirty clothes, and boxes of every description. His whole life seemed to be made of papers and boxes of papers, and books and tapes, and files, and clippings. His desk was a morass of paper, too. Journals and books, some open, some closed. Colored pencils and pens, paper clips, old mail and bills. Streaks of yellow- and red-marked pages torn from magazines. Dirty coffee cups and nearly illegible notes completed the composition, as if an art director had created a scene of academic chaos. Not an inch of the desk's wooden surface was visible.

In the bathroom Dave stared at himself in the soap-spattered mirror. He was still flushed and sweaty, his hair matted and wet. He tore off his damp clothes and entered the shower stall. It was going to be a long night. Hot and cold showers would help. Along with that crazy Hawaiian coffee and some jazz piano on the tape deck. Then, tomorrow, boards.

Dave combed his hair, shaved, and splashed himself with his birthday bottle of Aramis. Then, wrapped in a nearly threadbare old terry-cloth robe stolen from a health club, he checked his image. Dr. David Berger, man of medicine. With bloodshot eyes and blistered feet. He looked at his hands. Surgeon's hands, shaking only slightly.

As he stared in the mirror he thought about tomorrow. What he looked like wouldn't matter. It all centered on what he remembered and what he would say. They wouldn't look at his hands. They couldn't see into his head. They couldn't know what was in his heart. And they couldn't judge his guts. Damn! All these years of work and study . . . boiled down to a bunch of chicken-shit questions.

Dave went to his slide machine and turned it on. It hummed softly, and immediately a large fungating cancer, growing out of the kidney of a child who had died, showed on the sheet that served as a makeshift screen hanging on his wall.

"Wilm's tumor of the kidney," he recited aloud. "Lethal. Patient dead nine months after parents noticed a lump on the left side of his belly."

Dave pressed the button on his machine and the next slide appeared.

"Parathyroid gland," he said. "Four little specks of orange-tan tissue, each no bigger than a pea, and hiding from the surgeon deep in the tissue planes of the neck. . . ."

The professor in Chicago had summed it up well: "These glands control the calcium level in the body. The surgeon must find all four of them at surgery. A tumor or cancer in any one of them can cause the calcium in the body to go sky-high. A level of twelve or thirteen milligrams can kill a patient, can cause calcium crystals to be deposited in the pancreas, intestine, and even skin, and can cause ulcers, and kidney stones. . . ."

Dave could see the professor's slide in his mind as he prepared a cup of coffee. He could hear that voice of authority booming over the audience, each student straining to absorb every word and fact.

With coffee in hand, Dave slumped into his old easy chair next to the slide projector and continued his review of tumors. With each slide he would recite his knowledge of the subject like an automaton. When he completed one carousel of slides, he would run it through again, faster, trying to imprint the images onto his brain.

He would close his eyes tightly to see if he could recreate the shapes and colors in his imagination, and link the necessary verbal description to the image.

After two hours, Dave fell into a deep sleep, the images of deadly tumors giving way to brilliant sunsets, sunny seashores, and verdant meadows. And Shana. The droning of his own voice was now overdubbed by Shana's throaty whispers. He could even smell the perfume she wore, L'Air du Temps. He could feel her hands rubbing his neck and shoulders. It was magical. All his senses were awake to her presence, yet he knew it was a dream.

The hum of the slide projector was the only reality he was aware of. He knew he should snap out of this adolescent reverie and run through all the slides again before reviewing his journals. But the dream was so soothing and sensual that he fought any thoughts of breaking away from the sweet escape. Now he could even feel Shana's face next to his, her breath on his mouth as she kissed him ever so lightly. *God, if this is heaven, to hell with boards.*

The loud click of the projector startled him. The humming stopped, too. His eyes opened to total darkness. The dream collided with reality. There was someone here with him. His heart raced. He stopped breathing. Shana! He reached out to see if he might really be awake, and grasp reality. His head struck something soft, and it moved. And giggled mischievously. It was Shana.

She turned on his desk lamp and seemed to glow in the ring of light it cast. Dave was afraid to move, afraid to spoil the moment, ruin the dream. Then the dream rushed to him and hugged him.

They kissed. And held each other for a very long time.

Dave was nearly overcome with happiness, yet confused by the surprise. He was suddenly unaware of time, yet he knew he'd have to leave for the plane to Palo Alto within hours. He was also embarrassed by the disgusting condition of his apartment, and the skimpy robe he wore.

Shana saw the confusion on his face and said, "I know, I shouldn't have come here. But I was worried about you, David. I thought I might be able to help you in some way. I know what it's like during those last-minute cramming sessions. Come on, let's run through these slides and then we can taken a break."

Obediently, Dave snapped on the projector and fell into his study position. Shana hovered behind him, massaging his neck, temples, and shoulders.

"Are you expected to know *all* those things?" she murmured.

Dave thought she regarded him with a new sense of respect. Or was it worry? He couldn't be sure.

"Yes, all of it," he said. Then he recited, "The parathyroid glands can be found anywhere. From the neck to the back of the esophagus . . . to the chest and even on to the heart."

She seemed interested, so Dave began to explain in even greater detail.

Dave told her all about the way it was with the tumors and cancers surgeons had to hunt down, wading through the body's subtle clues and, like a master detective, finding the villain.

Then the radiologist would join the search, with his barium enemas, IVP's, CAT scans, ultrasounds, and angiograms. And then the pathologist, with his blood tests and cultures and biopsies.

The bottom line was to find the cancer and cut it out. Or to try to melt the cancer with chemicals and X rays. It sounded like such a big responsibility. Human life. And it was up to him and surgeons like him all over the world to know about the body, and about tumors, how they grew, how they spread in the body, bones, lymph nodes, blood vessels, in the brain.

It was awesome. There was so much to know. And it was always changing.

The state of the art in medicine was ever-changing. And he, a candidate for the boards in general surgery, needed to be aware of it all.

"What are the clues that the body puts out for the doctors?" Shana asked.

"Biological markers, we call them," Dave said. He pressed the button and a silver-stained tumor about the size of an acorn appeared. It had deep purple lines throughout. "Pheochromocytomas," Dave said. "Rare small tumors of the adrenal gland that put out two chemicals, adrenaline and nor-adrenaline. We can measure them in the blood and urine."

Dave felt proud to use the collective "we," which included him and all the other doctors in the world, including Stein, Collins, Niles Kelly, and the professors who would soon be questioning him on his boards.

"Once the surgeon makes the diagnosis . . . then, where the hell is the damned tumor?" Dave continued. "Ten pecent of these are bilateral and will be found in both the right and left adrenal glands."

"Where do these tumors come from?" Shana asked.

"They begin when we are only three or four weeks old in our mother's uterus," Dave said smartly. "They arise from the primitive nervous tissue in our body. And go anywhere . . . adrenal glands, spinal cord, chest, neck, and even the bladder."

Shana was fascinated. "What will these chemicals do?" she asked.

"High blood pressure is one of the early signs." He recalled a handful of reported cases in one of his journals. "One surgeon actually found three of these pheochromocytomas growing in the bladder. Every time the patient took a piss, his blood pressure rose from one-twenty to two-twenty . . . over a hundred points, and he turned cherry-red in the face, sweated like a skunk, and fainted.

"X rays, IVP's, CAT scans, and ten thousand dollars later in the workup, the doctor found the cause of the problem. This damned tumor was sitting on the patient's bladder. The surgeon cut it out and the patient was cured. He pissed happily ever after."

Shana sat back and sipped her coffee.

Dave said, "Other patients were not so fortunate. I recall one poor soul who didn't have his tumor discovered till autopsy. His doctor found him in his hospital gown slumped over the toilet, dead. He had had a severe attack of high blood pressure and simply stroked out. Ironically, the Cat scan, the specific test that would make the diagnosis and tell the surgeon where to cut, would have been done the next day."

"How terrible!" Shana said.

"And in the past two or three years, as if there wasn't enough to learn and memorize, a whole new field of tumors and cancers has come to be known. They're called apudomas, of all things, and they all come from the basic nerve tissue that's present in all of us when we are still in the uterus."

Shana put in, "And each of these has its own biological marker, I suppose."

"Yes," Dave said, turning to the next slide.

This time, a silver, red, and pink slide with a cluster of dark, evil-looking dots running throughout the pink part of the slide. "Those tiny dots are the cancer," Dave explained. "Carcinoid. Tumors of the gut or intestinal tract either in the small bowel or the colon. A few have even been found in the rectum. They will spread undetected to the liver, the heart, the lungs. They will cause strokes and sweating and nausea, and fainting, and weight loss, and even death, if they're not found in time."

Shana stared at the dark specks. . . .

"How do we find this?" Dave said. "We measure the . . ." He picked up the SESAP book. "Here's a question on the exact same thing that was asked on the boards. We measure the five-OH, IAA, the five-zero-hydroxy indole acetic acid in the urine, for these tumors put out serotonin, which breaks down in the urine to five-OH IAA."

Shana said, "That's the oddest description of anything I've ever heard. All this detective work would kill me long before I ever put it together. I don't think I'd be very good. My, how hard, how very hard it all is."

"And there's more to it," Dave said. "There are now new tumors of the pancreas; ZE syndrome, WDHA, and insulomas, where the patient's blood sugar drops down to twenty and he faints on the street."

"MEA's one, MEA's two." Dave was about to go on.

"Wait! Wait!" Shana said. "Please, it's too much for me. It seems like another world."

Dave smiled. "In a way, it is. Studying for boards is like another world. In a way, Beverly Hills Hospital is like another world, and working in an emergency room, and seeing the patients there, is still another world." He held out his hand and grasped Shana's. "In a way, you're like another world, too — a new and better world."

She smiled and finished her coffee.

Dave pressed the projected button and the next slide flashed on the screen. It was a thick yellow inflamed organ. "The pancreas." Dave held Shana's hand tighter. His mouth suddenly felt very dry. "Acute pancreatitis," he whispered as he and Shana exchanged glances.

"Like Victor Dawson." Shana Winston nodded.

Dave felt his hands sweating profusely. Symptoms: pain in the abdomen radiating to the back, worse on consumption of alcohol and rich foods.

He stared into Shana's eyes. "Usually, superimposed on a chronic condition from years of drinking."

He withdrew his hand from Shana's, and continued weakly. "Diagnosis . . . CAT scan, ultrasound serum blood amylase and white count . . . Treatment of choice . . ." Dave hesitated as Shana put her hand back into his. "Conservative intravenous fluids, antibiotics, close observation. When the patient develops clinical signs of sepsis, with an increased blood count, the surgeon should be aware of an acute catastrophe, an acute necrotizing pancreatitis."

Dave flipped to the next slide and an intense green, hardly recognizable dying pancreas came into view.

"At this point the treatment of choice is surgery. Debridement, clean up the dead pancreas tissue, drainage, and get out."

Dave held Shana's hand in a viselike grip.

"Perhaps I was wrong, Shana. Perhaps the surgery on Victor Dawson was too much. Perhaps a more mature, board-certified man would have waited, would have —"

"Nonsense," Shana retorted. "David, you must believe in yourself. You did what you thought was right. Just because the patient was Victor Dawson —"

Dave pressed the button and another dying pancreas appeared on the screen. "Complications," he continued. "Abscess formation and death. Mortality, over fifty percent." He shut off the machine.

"David," Shana soothed, "you adhered to every one of the principals on your boards with Victor Dawson. You did everything by the book. The book doesn't mention someone sneaking into a patient's room and stopping his life fluids."

Dave turned on the machine again. "Treatment of pancreatitis, IV plasma, a definite life-saving measure for the patient. IV plasma. Without it to support the patient's own body fluids, the patient was as sure as dead."

He and Shana stared at each other and went on to the next slide.

Dave saw pieces of a ragged liver and spleen obviously smashed in some sort of a high-speed collision.

"Trauma," Dave said matter-of-factly. "Automobile accident. Torn liver and spleen. The principals here: Save the spleen and debride and remove the dead torn pieces of liver. Here is the kidney from the case. Contusion, severe with the blood vessels torn right off the . . ." He looked over at Shana, who had turned pale as the next slide flashed on the screen.

Then he stopped. Shana grabbed his arm tightly.

"Like my father," she whispered, "like the blood vessels that tore off my father's kidney when he died in surgery."

Dave shut off the machine. "Shana . . ." — he held her in his arms — ". . . about your father. I did everything I could."

"I know," she replied stiffly.

"I've sat up all night thinking about the preoperative X ray, the IVP. Would your father have been saved, like Collins said, if —"

"Don't, don't," she interrupted.

"Please! I've got to! I've wrestled with it every night since it happened. I can't sleep, I . . . there simply wasn't time, Shana!"

"It wasn't your fault," she said sadly. "I guess it wasn't anyone's fault, but I still believe my father would be alive today if you, not Dr. Collins, had operated on him —"

"I'm not sure."

"And Victor Dawson, also. Your operation was the

right one for him. Somebody slipped into his room and killed him, David!''

"Well, the hospital committee will handle all that. What we've got to try to do is turn it around. I've got to pass my boards. I've got to show them all, Shana! I simply must do it!''

"What are these?'' she asked, picking up several tapes that lay next to his scattered medical tapes.

"Oh, those.'' Dave seemed a little embarrassed. "Those are my Al Jolson tapes.''

"Oh.''

"Want to here them? I play them just to relax. My father always liked those songs, and I guess I just inherited the feeling.''

Dave turned on the tape deck and Al Jolson's voice filled the room.

"California, here I come . . . !''

"How appropriate,'' Shana said. "California . . . right back where I started from . . .''

After a moment she looked at Dave and said, "Why don't you lie down and let me massage your back? You're still very tense. Jolson doesn't seem to be relaxing you. And that coffee isn't helping any, either. Go on, stretch out on the couch while I get something more appropriate on the radio. I see you don't have much of a tape collection.''

"Yeah, my tapes aren't exactly top of the charts or state of the art. Mostly lectures and dictation.'' Dave laughed. "And Jolson's tape is getting a little worn.''

Neil Diamond's "Love on the Rocks'' drifted across the room as Dave cleared his journals off the couch and collapsed on it with a groan.

Shana knelt next to him and began gently to stroke his back. Her hands then kneaded his buttocks. "Hey!'' Dave yelped. "That hurts! Besides, I'm not used to having my ass grabbed.''

"I know, but it'll ease things up. Also gotta work on

your legs. You should be doing more running and walking. How can you go to Palo Alto like this? You're one
step from being a cripple. I can tell. Hold still, and
stretch out as much as you can. Your arms up over your
head. Stretch your feet out, your toes. Now relax and let
Shana make you feel better. I wish I had some massage
oil. Got any?"

"Only Mazola," Dave cracked.

"Well, we'll just have to improvise." Shana laughed.
"We gotta get you in shape for Palo Alto. Do you know
it's three A.M. already?"

Dave groaned and tensed. Shana smacked him sharply
on the buttocks. "Don't worry, David, your mind is in
great shape, you'll remember everything. But your body
needs some attention. Just relax, close your eyes, let go,
let go, let Shana put her holistic therapy to work on you.
That's better. I can feel the tension melting. Just let
go . . . let go. . . ."

Dave awoke suddenly to the sound of water running. He
was in bed. Naked. Only a sheet over him. His mind was
a jumble and for a moment he wasn't sure where he was
or what day it was. The early morning sun that usually
awakened him was blocked by a window shade and curtains. He never used his shades. And the running water.
What the hell is this? he wondered. He sat upright and
assured himself that this was, indeed, his bedroom. The
digital clock on the dresser blinked nine-oh-seven A.M.
*God, I overslept! Today is boards! I didn't finish my
journal reviews. Oh, shit!*

The water stopped. The shower door slid open. And
Dave remembered. Shana. *Oh, God!*

It wasn't a dream. *Oh, God!*

Shana stepped into the room and, smiling sweetly,
said, "Good morning, David. How do you feel?"

Dave groaned and shook his head, rubbing his eyes.

"That tough, huh? You've been alone and working

too hard too long, David. But you're an amazing man. You can somehow operate in the waking and sleeping worlds, and both at the same time." Shana stood there, brushing her hair, smiling wickedly, and wearing Dave's old robe. "I guess we'd better do something about breakfast. I'm famished."

"But how did I . . . I mean, what did we . . . how did you . . . oh, God, Shana!"

"I'll tell you over breakfast, David. Here's a towel. Get yourself showered while I see what's in the refrigerator besides moldly cheese. . . . Oh, I have some funny things to tell you about your talking in your sleep, David. Not to mention your sleepwalking." Shana laughed. "My massage really loosened you up. I got a little untethered, too, I'm afraid. C'mon, get up, you've got to pack and everything. And I've got an appointment later myself."

Dave sat, stunned by it all. Shana's surprise appearance last night, today's flight to Palo Alto. He could only stare at Shana and shake his head in disbelief. This was not the script he had written.

"David, do I have to come and pry you out of your trance?" She walked over to him and took his head in her hands, almost as if he were a child.

"Shana, I don't know what to say, or do. What *did* I do? What happened?"

Shana sat on the bed and embraced him, laughing softly and saying, "Well, it started something like this, once I got you relaxed."

Shana kissed Dave on the neck, on his cheeks, and on his mouth, as they fell over together in a warm and lingering embrace. Dave held her so tightly she had to plead for breath.

"David, you're tensing up again. Let's relax. Let me get this silly robe of yours off. It's cutting into my armpits."

Shana rolled off the bed and stood up, her mane of

blond hair askew. The robe fell to the floor and she just stood there looking at Dave, trying to finger-comb her hair into some semblance of order.

Dave marveled at her body and her complete lack of self-consciousness for her nudity. Her legs were even more beautiful than he'd imagined. Like a dancer's, sleekly muscled. Her stomach was soft and rounded, with hardly an extra ounce of weight anywhere nearby. But Shana's breasts were her glory, twin perfections, delicately tipped. Now they were bouncing as she struggled with her long hair.

Dave leaped from the bed and embraced her. He kissed her eyes, her nose, her mouth, and said, "Shana, you're so incredibly, wonderfully beautiful, I want to remember you in this moment forever. I want to hold you like this, our hearts and bodies as close as humanly possible. You can't imagine the powerful feelings I'm feeling for you. It's more than I can stand, yet I don't want to let go and lose the moment. It doesn't seem possible that . . . that you might have some feeling for me as well. Oh, God, Shana, you've got to be here when I get back. If it were any day but today, I'd never leave."

Dave caressed and stroked Shana's back and waist. He grasped her buttocks firmly, squeezed them slowly and gently, then massaged them in erotic patterns. Never was anything so silkily, velvety smooth and warm, and responsive. Shana duplicated his every move. While their hands rubbed and slid and explored each other, their lips locked in kiss after kiss.

As if by a prearranged signal they pulled apart, then held hands while they looked at each other adoringly, happily. "David, you look so much better without clothes," Shana whispered.

Dave laughed and pulled her to the bed, where they fell into each other's arms. Dave slid down to nuzzle and tease Shana's breasts, kissing them and fondling them until she could no longer endure the sensations he was causing.

"David," she whispered, "let's love each other long and lazily now. I don't want to rush this beautiful morning. I'll help you pack and get you to the plane on time. This is more important than another review of those damned papers. You know your stuff. I know you do. I want you to know me. . . ."

Chapter Forty

Palo Alto, Sunday, November 18 (One Day Before Boards)

Dave took the late-afternoon plane to San Francisco; from there, he would take a taxi to Palo Alto, checking into the hotel at approximately six o'clock with the other candidates. He had been told it would be best to get a good night's sleep, that last-minute studying wouldn't help. But he knew he would stay in his room, going over those damned books, tapes, journals, and slides until the very last minute.

After checking in at the airport, he discovered that his flight would be delayed by an hour and a half. He sat there, with his suitcase, a folder bulging with journals and papers, and his small tape recorder sticking out of his pocket. He felt awkward and out of place among the tourists and commuters.

He thumbed through a few of the journals to kill time.

"What's Ahead with Cancer of the Colon?"; "Stab Wounds of the Liver . . . New Approaches"; "Gunshots to the Stomach."

Case reports — a hundred cases, a thousand cases; retrospective studies; prospective studies. He suddenly felt panicky. He should have read more references. Surely they would ask him about some of the newer operations.

He remembered his past mistakes, on questions about cancer of the breast and repairs for hiatal hernias of the stomach that bulged into the chest. Dave hadn't been able to answer because he wasn't up on the literature. He should have read more.

But there were so many journals. Stacks and stacks of them, still piled high on his dining room table, on his bedroom dresser, in the bathroom, and strewn around the living room floor. A mass of color and information to be mastered, digested, and spit back on the boards.

However it came, whatever the color of the journal or the size of the magazine, thick or thin, it represented the latest factors and operations and nuances of technique that he might be asked.

He recalled the professor in Chicago saying, "There are no hard-and-fast laws in reading the journals, but if I were a candidate, I'd be familiar with the literature for the past three years, at least, every article, every change. The standard textbooks are not enough! Your examiners will want to be assured that you're keeping current."

Keeping current! Dave's stomach muscles tightened. It was almost impossible. He had tried to read through it all, but every month the piles got higher. Some journals did contain important articles on changes in surgery; others gave a few isolated case reports. And some were just outright wrong. But all had to be read. He had been doing it for months now. For years.

He thought about his apartment, the dirty coffee cups, stained counters, and spilled sugar he didn't have time to clean up. And he thought about his slide machine, and all his books and reports and journals and tapes, and pictures of ovaries, kidneys, cancers, bladders, lungs, tuberculosis, infections, and abscesses. Night after night, week after week, he had gone over them again and again.

He had been like a prisoner. He had been totally isolated. His body had gone to pot; he had gained twenty pounds. He felt sluggish and old. Even his hair was starting to gray. How had it all come to this? he wondered. He had had such a good start. Why did he feel so alone? Where were all the people whom he had been so kind to, whom he had helped over the years? Was this thing with Shana the real thing? Or just a passing fantasy?

Dave's eyes were closed in deep thought as the taxi made its way toward Stanford University. He thought back to his other two trips to Palo Alto — as a college student at the Princeton–Stanford game fifteen years ago, and for a medical meeting four years ago.

But he was not at Princeton, nor was he attending a meeting. For David Berger, it was all on the line. He had to meet the monster in his den. He had to pass his boards!

He thought back to the phone call he had gotten from Dr. Curtis just after Dr. Stein had asked him to leave the meeting. He remembered Curtis's tone on the phone: "Yes, it was tough. Collins brought all those people to the meeting, those orthopods, his own special cronies."

"Yes?"

"They stacked the committee! Eveyone voted the way Collins wanted."

"And Nino? Didn't Nino speak up for me?"

"No. He wasn't there. They said he had an emergency surgery at another hospital."

"And you, Joe?"

"I showed up, but they wouldn't let me vote. Said family-practice people couldn't vote on general surgical matters. And Stein was there, too, but it looks like they pushed it through. They had the votes, they stacked the committee. They want you out. The executive board will meet on Monday and consider your appeal. Your attorney is to represent you since you'll be taking your boards.''

Would anyone in this country believe that doctors so highly trained — so specialized, in whose hands was the care of patients — were actually playing war games?

We'll drive him off the Wilshire corridor, we'll push him into the mid-valley. We don't want his *kind practicing around here.*

And it was all done legally, through committee, through the hospital boards — but for the wrong reasons. And who were the people who survived? The Andrew Collinses, among others.

It was a horrible thought.

A chilling thought.

When Dave checked in at the hotel in Palo Alto, he wished he could change places with the woman at the desk. She seemed so peaceful, with such a simple, uncomplicated life.

"Is there any room service?" he asked.

She smiled with a trace of motherly instinct. "Yes, up to eleven o'clock. Will you be ordering up to your room?"

She knew why he was there; she understood.

He went to his room, unpacked, set up the old tape recorder, and spread out his papers and journals on the bed. He knew he wouldn't have time to read them all. He knew he should concentrate on getting a good night's sleep, and not think about all these things, not worry. But he couldn't help it.

He called room service and ordered a steak, medium-rare, broccoli, and a vanilla milkshake for extra energy, he told himself.

He pinched the small roll around his belly and was disgusted with himself. He felt lethargic and old. He felt like a failure. He didn't know how he would face the boards in the morning.

He ate the food and drank the milkshake while listening to a tape. "The aneurysm of the aorta will increase in size after five centimeters," the voice droned.

Godamned aneurysms! he thought.

"They should be resected even in the elderly by six or seven centimeters in size, because of the high incidence of ruptures. Patients may bleed out and die at home or in a taxi, if this bubble breaks. Very few will leave the hospital alive. Those who do must be taken to surgery right away, worked up on the operating table, and put to sleep as soon as possible. Otherwise, death is certain!"

The tape went on to describe how the young surgeon could make his diagnosis: the clue, calcium in the wall of the aorta, deposited over the years. . . .

Dave tried to concentrate. Then he looked at his watch. There was still so much to do. It was ten o'clock already. It had only been nine a short while ago. He must have dozed off after the milkshake. High blood sugar. Shit! He had lost precious time.

He splashed cold water on his face and urinated. Then he listened to another tape.

He needed a break.

He called Shana. She was warm and friendly, but her voice held none of the intimacy she'd shown last night at his apartment. And rather than helping him to relax, she made him more nervous by reminding him of the board meeting at which his suspension would be decided.

Then just as he was about to hang up, she surprised him by saying, "I'm not going to wish you luck on the boards because you don't need it. You've got all the skill and knowledge it takes. When the time comes, you'll use it.'' Her voice was husky as she added, "I told you I could love you, David. I meant it. When you get back to L.A., I'll be here. . . .

He was elated when he hung up and tried to return to his studying, but he couldn't concentrate. He was getting confused; his thoughts were disjointed. He went over the eight causes of pancreatitis: gallstones, alcohol, drugs, trauma . . . No — trauma was the Winston case. Then he found himself mixing up the parathyroid and the pancreas.

He put away the papers and the tapes and looked in the mirror. His eyes were red. He knew he shouldn't go to the test tomorrow with red eyes.

He took a shower and climbed into bed. At two o'clock he was still tossing and turning. To get his mind off the boards, he thought about the hospital, about the doctors who had hurt him, excluded him, and now turned against him. Dave had gone to Stein twice, asking if they could set up an hour where they could just talk over melanoma, Stein's specialty. "Sure, sure," he had said, "I'll get around to it. I've been real busy building that house up in the country." When Dave asked a third time, Stein had said abruptly, "I just don't have time, Berger. Get off my back!"

Dave tossed and turned some more. Now it was three o'clock and sleep still eluded him. He remembered Niles Kelly, who would go whichever way was best for him politically. "Sure, I'll help you. Gimme a call in a couple of days and we'll get together," he'd said to Dave. Dave had called twice; Kelly had never returned the calls.

He tried to shut out these thoughts, but he couldn't.

And Sandry Coyle, who had referred a gallstone case to him for surgery. When she realized he didn't have his boards, she withdrew the referral and sent the patient to another surgeon.

It had a mushroom effect. The doctors thought less of him now; soon the patients would begin to believe it.

He *had* to pass his boards!

He thought about Shana. She'd said she could love him. But would she? If he flunked his boards and was suspended from the hospital, would she turn against him, too?

He looked at the clock. It was five o'clock. He could see the morning light coming in over the mountains. He got up, opened a window, and felt a breeze from the north.

As he began to brush his teeth, he looked in the mirror at his red eyes, wondering how he was going to survive, let alone answer the questions.

Chapter Forty-one

Monday, November 19

Dave walked out into the early morning sunlight. An old, distinguished-looking man, with immaculately groomed white hair and wearing matching sport jacket and bow tie, was walking several feet in front of him. Dave recognized him as the doctor who was conducting the boards — a distinguished surgeon who'd had a brilliant career and who in his later years had been given this little pearl, this little gem, to instruct the candidates and run the boards. Of course, for a free trip to California and a proper fee. It was the American College of Surgeons' way of saying thanks to one of its grand old men.

Dave let the sun bathe him for a few moments, allowing himself this last luxury before following the old man into the large room.

The old man stood at the podium and stared down from that vantage point. "Well, what brings you all to Palo Alto today?" he asked. There was nervous laughter among the fifty or so candidates in the room.

Then the room became strangely quiet as the old man continued. Dave looked around at the other candidates, surprised to see the Iranian from Chicago sitting in front of him. Their eyes met and they nodded at each other.

Strange, Dave thought, as he turned back to the old man, this test was such an isolated, personal experience, not to mention traumatic, that he hadn't even talked to any of the other candidates since his arrival.

"I'm going to pass out your schedule for today's program," the old doctor was saying. "As you know, there will be three separate rooms for you to visit, and in each room you'll be quizzed by two surgeons. One is from the American College of Surgeons; the other is a board-certified surgeon from California. These men know their business. They sit on the national boards that make up these questions and many have written the definitive articles and books. So don't try to bullshit these men. They can each ask you and me a hundred questions we couldn't begin to answer."

Dave's heart was pounding. God! Just to get it over with! At least there would be no more books, coffee cups, and journals and tapes. At least . . . at least . . . oh, shit!

"Here is one good piece of news," the old man said. "We have asked that the experts who will be quizzing you not concentrate on their own field; in other words, don't be surprised if the guy who did the original experiments on porta-cava shunts for cirrhosis of the liver asks you about cancer of the stomach, or the guy who did major research in surgery on dog hearts asks you about fluid levels of potassium in the newborn. In other words, you guys are in the hot seat, and anything is fair game."

Dave tried to be calm. At least he wouldn't be tied to his damned tape recorder anymore. At least he would have time to go out and do things — anything but this.

He thought of Shana, of her warm lips against his mouth.

"You have all been through your training now," the old man continued. "What we will ask you today is what you have been doing and, hopefully, learning, and what we have been teaching you for years. You are our children, and we want you to pass. I repeat, we want you to pass. If you fail, we fail." The candidates looked around nervously. "And I know fifty percent of you will not make it today, and will be invited back next year. You have all passed your written exam. That was your ticket to get here, but it's up to you now."

Dave felt his throat constricting and suddenly found it difficult to breathe. Al Jolson was in his head. He thought of Little Duck and Big Camel. He thought of the course in Chicago. He had to take a piss.

"And for some of you this will be your third and last time, and there will be no more invitation to boards. Anyone failing three times must return to his residency, must interrupt his private practice and take an extra year of training at the chief resident level. I'm sorry, but that's the way it is. We're not giving anything away. This is life, and you guys are going to earn your union cards today."

He was tough. He was right. He was putting it on the line. No free trips.

Dave knew he would have to earn it right here; there would be no tomorrow.

He thought of the committee at Beverly Hills Hospital, probably just now getting ready to meet, as the professor called the candidates one by one and handed them their admission cards to boards.

Dave found the professor breathing down on him, looking directly into his eyes. "Good luck, boy," he said. "Good luck." He handed him his card.

Dave thought of Shana again as he looked over his

schedule. He wondered if the old man knew he was a two-time loser.

Room one . . . Damn! He was shaking so much he could hardly see who he had. Dr. Zites. The endocrine specialist who had actually discovered those damned apudomas and had collected the first fifteen hundred of them. Why hadn't he read more about apudomas? Shit! Well, maybe Zites wouldn't ask about that.

Dave tried to appear calm as he stood outside the first closed door. He could hear the muffled voices of the candidate and the examiner inside, but he couldn't make out what they were saying.

Dave hoped the candidate was really screwing it up. It would make him look better by comparison. No. No! He wasn't hoping that.

He stared at the closed door. He couldn't control his racing heartbeat. His pulse was rapid and thready. He wished he could be calm. He wished he could stop sweating.

The voices stopped and Dave held his breath. He heard footsteps, saw the door open and the candidate before him. The Iranian came out smiling. Shit! He must have done well.

For the very first time, Dave heard the Iranian speak. "Tough, Zites was tough," he said, but he kept on smiling.

Dave wanted to say, "What did he ask? Tell me the questions. How was it?" He knew better. He wished the Iranian had looked more upset. Dave wondered how *he* would look to the next candidate.

The door shut again, and the Iranian walked away. Dave faced the closed door. Then he heard footsteps again, and the door opened and a hand was thrust out at him.

"Good morning," said the hand. Dave looked straight into the eyes of Dr. Zites. "My name is Dr. Zites. Would you come in, Dr. Berger?"

Dave extended his hand. Oh, God, he had forgotten the handkerchief! His hand was wet and limp. He walked into the room.

"And this is Dr. Callahan. Dr. Callahan is chief of surgery here at the university."

Dave tried to pay attention. He slipped into his chair and sat facing Dr. Zites and Dr. Callahan. He was drenched with sweat and felt very weak, and in that one panicky moment he was sure he had forgotten everything he'd ever known — not just about medicine and surgery and boards, but *everything*.

Why hadn't he brought the handkerchief? He was happy he had remembered his name. He thought about the Iranian again, and Little Duck and Big Camel, and Al Jolson, and Shana . . . and Victor Dawson. . . .

Shit! Concentrate, Dave — gotta concentrate. Please, God, make him ask an easy one.

"Well, Dr. Berger," said Dr. Zites, taking the lead, "hope you had a nice trip up here."

He's trying to relax me. He's only making it worse. Please, please ask me something easy.

"Well," Dr. Zites said, "shall we plunge into it?"

Dave scarcely breathed as the doctor took out a little pad and began to take notes.

"Tell me, Dr. Berger, how would you fix a Colles fracture of the wrist?"

Dave just sat there and didn't move. There was a painful silence. He couldn't speak. He thought of the candidate who had fainted. He saw the eyes of Dr. Zites and Dr. Callahan on him. He knew they were thinking: *How much does this son of a bitch know? Can he practice safe medicine in the community? Is he able to go out there and do it? Should he be board-certified, or should he be sent back for more training?*

Oh, God! They probably knew he had flunked the boards twice; they knew he couldn't do it. Colles fracture. Why would Zites, the father of apudomas, who had discovered all those little bastard endocrine tumors, ask him about fractures? This wasn't an orthopedic boards; he wasn't a damned orthopedist.

"Well, Dr. Berger?" Dr. Zites seemed a little uncomfortable, and repeated the question: "How would you fix a Colles fracture of the wrist?"

Dave thought back over the years to his rotation on orthopedic surgery. He had done at least a dozen Colles fractures. Stretch the damned fracture site for length! And then it began to come back: Colles fracture . . . dorsal angulation . . . get length. He remembered his orthopedic resident telling him "You've got to put traction on two parts, get length, get angulation."

Dave reached out to an imaginary hand and started fixing an imaginary fracture. No, no, that wasn't it; he had to talk, to tell Dr. Zites just how . . . he had to name the bones and tell what he was doing.

Miraculously, it came back, and Dave recited what the Colles fracture was and how he would fix it, then added, "And I would put it in a cast."

"What kind of cast?" Dr. Zites pressed. He was looking at Dave closely now.

"A . . . plaster," Dave said.

"I know plaster. From where to where? Above the elbow or below?"

Shit! Dave hadn't thought of this in years. He remembered his orthopedic resident telling him, "Joint above, joint below," and he said that.

"I would put it joint above, joint below."

"Fine," Dr. Zites said. "But where? Where above and where below?"

Dave thought the man was trying to be patient. Above the elbow or below? Dave took a deep breath and tried to appear confident. He had been told that guesses were frowned upon, but he took a guess anyway, and said, "Above the elbow." Dr. Zites made notes on the pad.

Was he right? Was he wrong? Damn! Dr. Zites wasn't talking.

"And how far down would you put it? Below the metacarpals or above?"

Again Dave took a deep breath. "Below."

Again Dr. Zites jotted notes on the pad. What was he writing? Was Dave right? Did his pass? How was he doing? All Dr. Zites showed was a poker face.

Then Dr. Zites said, "All right, we have a twenty-five-year-old white male who was riding his motorcycle, was hit by a car, and comes into the emergency room complaining of pain in his mid-abdomen. His vital signs are stable, his belly is swollen, and bowel sounds can't be heard at all. What would you do, Doctor?"

Blunt trauma to the abdomen flashed through Dave's mind. He thought back to the Chicago course and the six immediate steps the professor had told him to do. He thought back to the hundreds of cases of blunt trauma to the abdomen he had seen himself in the ER and had treated himself, but nothing came. He drew a blank. He couldn't remember what to do.

Dave panicked. He was failing again. His whole medical career was going down the drain. His whole life. Shit!

"Doctor, blunt trauma — what would you do?"

Dave thought again, and still nothing came. Then suddenly, from deep down . . . from somewhere, he heard, *Examine the patient, Dave . . . examine the patient.*

And he said, "I would examine the patient."

He felt Dr. Zites was trying to be patient. "Yes . . . well . . . ?"

And suddenly Dave got into the flow of it. "I would

be very careful taking a history of what kind of accident it had been, and then I would —"

And then it came suddenly and he remembered what he would do — he would order an X ray! Of course, he would order an X ray of the abdomen!

Dr. Zites jotted down something and smiled thinly. "The X ray shows a mild ileus pattern of bowel loops; there is no free air under the diaphragm," Dr. Zites said. "Now what would you do, Doctor?"

"Abdominal tap, abdominal lavage! I would run in a liter of Ringer's lactate through a paracentesis needle," he said.

Dr. Zites smiled. "Good," he said. "All right, your abdominal lavage comes back five hundred red calls per high-power field, five hundred white cells, and amylase on the fluid is up three times normal."

Dave felt more relaxed now. "I'd get the patient ready for surgery, sir. The finding you cite would tell me there was trouble inside his belly. Maybe a ruptured liver, or ruptured spleen, due to the red cells."

Dr. Zites had what he wanted. "Fine," he said. Again, poker face jotting down notes.

"You would take the patient to surgery?" Dr. Callahan asked staring straight ahead.

Dave nodded.

"All right," Dr. Zites said, "at surgery you find that this young man's spleen has been severed in two, a good chunk of the spleen cleanly sliced off. What would you do now, Doctor? Take out the spleen?"

Dave was ready now. He thought back to the professor in Chicago: *Save the spleen.* He thought back to Jaspar Jarvis. Save the spleen, save the goddamned spleen! Suddenly Dave felt euphoric.

"I would make every effort, sir, to save the spleen," he said. "I would use gauze compresses, pledgets. I would try to use gel foam, avitine, anything to stop the bleeding so I wouldn't have to take out the spleen."

"Oh? What's wrong with taking out the spleen?"

Dave closed in on Zites now and went into the high incidence of pneumococcal sepsis and infection, especially in young people, pointing out literature that showed the spleen was necessary, and bringing in the immune system, and the one young patient he had seen die.

He felt good; he was talking about what he had studied. Thank God for the Chicago course. Thank God for the professor. Dave knew all about the spleen. But just when he was ready to pour out his heart on it, giving the gist of the five articles and the literature, Dr. Zites cut him off.

"Tell me about Zollinger–Ellison syndrome," he said.

Dave was caught short. Then he thought back to the professor: *Answer the exact question asked.*

Zollinger–Ellison — this was the endocrine stuff. This was apudoma, Zites's specialty.

"Total gastrectomy used to be the treatment of choice," Dave said. "Now, with H_2-Blockers, a tablet that blocks histamine release and acid secretion in the stomach, I would have more time to work up the patient. Diagnosis, increased gastrin levels, increased overnight acids in the stomach. High gastrin, high acid." Dave spouted it back just as the professor had spouted it to him. He could almost see the slide from the Chicago course in front of him now.

He was ready to go on to tell Zites about the five ways of diagnosing Zollinger–Ellison and the surgery he would do, and how ten percent of these tumors could be found in the sub-mucosa of the duodenum and how —

"Fine. You have taken out the total stomach of this patient," Zites said. "How would you hook it up?"

Dave felt weak. He knew all about Zollinger–Ellison syndrome. He remembered all the professor had told him, all he had studied and read about it. He could see the slides before him; he could see the pages of the book — he could even tell Zites what page it was on. But how to hook it up — he hadn't thought about that. Shit! How would he hook it up?

Dr. Zites's next question: "And let's say you find a big hematoma, a collection of blood behind the duodenum, in the right gutter in the area of the kidney. . . ."

Dave stared at Dr. Zites. The area of the kidney — why was he asking him this? Was it still about Dr. Winston? Did the hospital committee tell him that he, David Berger, had been responsible for Dr. Winston's death?

Was Zites working with the surgery committee, and Andrew Collins and Tony Manchester and Bill Benedict and the others? Was it all some horrible conspiracy against him?

"Well, what would you do, Dr. Berger?"

Dave was snapped back into the reality by Dr. Zites's voice. No! No! He was just being paranoid. Zites could never know. It was just a coincidence. He was here taking his boards, his final chance! It was a good question. Legitimate — trauma to the kidney. Zites *couldn't* know about that awful morning and the ambulance and Dr. Winston.

"Again, I would get control of the renal pedicle, control of the circulation," Dave answered slowly, watching Zites's eyes, "before the patient bled to death."

He saw Zites writing down words on his pad. Was it the right answer? Did Zites think he should have gotten preoperative X ray and IVP? Would Zites be calling up Collins and the surgery committee afterward? Dave couldn't be sure.

After a painful silence, Zites said, "All right, Dr. Callahan, what would you like to ask Dr. Berger?"

As Callahan began, Dave felt a fresh wave of anxiety. Had he answered the questions right? Had he told Zites enough about Zollinger–Ellison syndrome? There was so much more he had wanted to say, but Zites hadn't given him enough time.

Callahan's questions were a blur to Dave. Something about a breast lesion. Something about a melanoma. Something about blood transfusions and fluid balance. Something about obstruction in the GI tract in the newborn. Then suddenly Dave was shaking hands again, a little more strongly than before, and walking out of the room.

Out in the corridor, a pale, scared-looking candidate was waiting. Dave managed a weak smile, but no words came to his lips.

Had he passed? He wished he had remembered more about Colles fracture. Why hadn't he thought of abdominal tap right away on the blunt-trauma question? Why didn't he order an X ray? He must have done it a hundred times in his own practice; it was an easy question. He must have looked like a real dummy to Zites. He knew they were in there, grading him, talking, and looking over their notes.

Dave suddenly thought of the conference at Beverly Hills Hospital, where the board was sitting down now, going over . . . Oh, God! He was losing it on all fronts. He was losing it here — failing his boards. And he was losing it at the hospital, too.

Dave felt terrible as he walked toward the second room. There were tears in his eyes. He wished it were all over.

The second room started out a little better than the first.

Dr. Marshall, a renowned professor from the East Coast, who had pioneered one of the surgeries of the pancreas, met Dave at the door. There was some discussion of ultrasounds and biliary tract disease and even the pancreas.

Then Dr. Marshall popped the question. "You have a

coin lesion of the lung. It shows up on a routine job physical X ray of the chest. Turns out to be a smoker. How would you handle that, Doctor? Coin lesion of the lung.''

Dave blurted out, ''I don't do that. I don't do chest surgery.''

His heart stopped; he thought he saw Dr. Marshall scowl. Had he made a mistake? But it was true — he hadn't done any chest surgery since his residency, five years ago.

Why would Marshall ask him something he hadn't done in five years, or wasn't doing in his practice now? Marshall knew Dave was a general surgeon. Did he also know Dave had flunked his boards twice? The examiners were not supposed to have any previous knowledge about any candidate.

But Marshall knew, Dave was sure. He was just trying to get him. Maybe he was friends with some of the doctors at Beverly Hills Hospital. Maybe it was a conspiracy to get him.

These thoughts were going through Dave's mind as he muddled through an answer on coin lesion of the chest and watched a scowling Dr. Marshall scratch notes on his pad.

Then a second examiner, a Chinese physician, began to speak. ''You have a patient, Doctor, with a blockage in superficial femoral artery on left side and deep femoral artery on right side, and there is history of pain in right toe and dorsum left foot.''

Dave was stunned. He leaned forward. He didn't understand what the Chinese doctor was saying. Left foot? Right foot? Blockage? Where? The Chinese doctor was speaking in a low voice, and his accent threw Dave. He couldn't even visualize where the vessels were blocked.

Again he remembered the professor saying, ''Make sure you answer the exact question.''

Dave couldn't even understand the question.

"Would you please repeat the question?" he said and immediately sensed they were annoyed with him.

The Chinese doctor went through the question again, but Dave still couldn't quite picture the situation he described. Finally, the Chinese doctor said, "Okay, tell me about gunshot injuries in the liver."

Dave talked about gunshots to the liver, feeling more confident in this area. He recited how he would handle several such cases, and the Chinese doctor seemed satisfied. But he feared he had gotten a zero for the vascular surgery question.

Dave felt very awkward and uncomfortable as he left the second room.

Chapter Forty-two

Although it was twenty minutes before the pathology slides were supposed to be shown, all the front seats were taken, so Dave was relegated to one of the last three rows.

Damn! I should have gotten here earlier. It was important to sit up front so he could see the intricate little black marks and dots and subtleties on the slides, which often indicated whether a lesion was cancer or whether it was invading a capsule. Whether it was spreading to a bone or what the hell it was doing. . . .

Finally, the slides were flashed on the screen.

"First slide," the examining doctor said. "Here's a smoker who comes in with a twenty-pound weight loss and hemoptysis. Coughing up blood."

The slide showed a big fungating cancer in the middle of the lung.

Dave thought back to the question about coin lesion of the lung. Why had they asked him that? What an easy slide. He couldn't imagine even a med student missing it. He wrote *cancer of the lung* in his diagnosis block.

The second slide flashed on. Dave saw some sort of yellow tumor sticking out of an area of pink tissue that he recognized as the colon. He squinted, unable to see the screen clearly. What was it? Were those malignant cells? Was there capsule invasion, or was it benign?

The old man continued: "Here is a patient with sweating and hypertension and flushing, and was found to have this tumor. This was the specimen at surgery."

Dave looked around. The other candidates seemed to know; they were writing their answers.

"And here are the microscopic slides of the tumor," the examiner said, flashing a set of pink tissues with little silver and black dots.

Dave thought back to his slides at home. He had seen that slide in his collection at least a hundred times. What was it? Cancer, colon, diverticuli, ulcer, inflammation? No! No! Carcinoid, apudoma . . . a bloody apudoma! Excitedly, he wrote *apudoma*. Then he crossed it out. Carcinoid — it was a specific type of apudoma. He wrote *carcinoid of the appendix*, as the professor flashed the next slide on the screen. And so it went.

Dave was never quite sure of his answers and never had quite enough time.

After the fifteenth and final slide had been shown, Dave handed in his paper and walked out of the room.

He was conscious of the talk around him.

"God! That must have been a cancer of the pancreas and not fat necrosis," one of the candidates was saying.

"Are you sure? I thought it was carcinoid myself. What about the one of the appendix?"

"Hell! That wasn't the appendix — that was the salivary gland."

Goddammit! Dave thought. He must have gotten two wrong. At least two out of fifteen. He felt panicky again, and nauseated.

"God!" another candidate was saying. "Zites was a bear — asked me about fractures."

"Really? I thought it was easy. When I left the room, he shook my hand and said, 'You did fine, son, no problem.' "

Dave felt even worse. Zites hadn't said anything like that to him, nor had Dr. Marshall.

It was unfair of the examiners to have asked him about chest and vascular. He didn't do those. Sure, he was responsible for them, but if they wanted to know what he did on a day-to-day basis, they could call Beverly Hills Hospital and Andrew Collins would tell them what he did. He would tell them what he did to Dr. Winston and to Victor Dawson. Yes, sir, Zites and Mashall could hear it firsthand from Collins and the others at Beverly Hills Hospital.

Dave felt relieved as he entered the third room. Whatever happened — good, bad, or indifferent — he would walk out of this room free — free and finished.

But room three went better. The questions began to come Dave's way. Cancer of the colon. Easy. "How would you prep the colon for this, Doctor?"

He was ready. He recited just how he would do it. He felt more confident now.

"Endocrine. Pheochromocytoma. What is it, Doctor? How would you diagnose it?"

Dave thought of Shana for a moment, and felt a surge of elation. He answered accurately and succinctly.

"Dr. Berger, can you name the causes of acute pancreatitis?"

Dave launched into his carefully memorized list. "Alcohol, gall stones, iatrogenic, mumps, morphine, trauma."

"And what is the leading cause of pancreatitis, Dr. Berger?"

He thought of Victor Dawson. "Alcohol. Drinking over long periods of time with continued acute episodes."

Dave remembered the first time Victor Dawson came into his office. He could still see his face as he looked up at him from the examining table.

The examiner's pencil danced over his paper. "All right, Dr. Berger, and how would you treat pancreatitis in the patient who suddenly came to you with acute pain in his belly after a period of intense drinking?"

Dave was startled. Why was he being asked this? His mind flashed back to Victor Dawson lying helpless in his bed looking up at him.

Do people talk in their sleep, Dr. Berger? I don't want anyone with me in the operating room. Not Andrew Collins. No one.

Why did Victor Dawson want Andrew Collins, the chief of surgery, out of the room? Why?

"I would give IV fluids, antibiotics, and use a conservative approach," Dave emphasized.

"And say the patient is getting worse with your treatment, Dr. Berger. The white count is up, the amylase is up, he's in much more pain. *When do you operate?*"

When, indeed! *When do you operate?* David thought. When had he operated on Victor Dawson? Had it been too soon? Had his judgment been right? Were Andrew Collins and the surgery committee right? Had he made a dreadful mistake? No!

He thought back to Victor Dawson's eyes and the ring on his finger and Melissa Baxter and Emily in the emergency room, and Shana Winston. No, he had done the right operation. He had done what he thought was right. Someone — someone had stolen into Victor Dawson's room and turned off his intravenous lifeline and killed him.

When he left the room, he had a firm handshake and a dry hand, and both examining doctors seemed pleased with his performance.

But Dave left the room with mixed feelings. He was

elated and relieved that the nightmare was over, but terrified, too, that he hadn't passed.

Everything he had said during the day — every question, every pause, every answer — was acutely painful to him now.

He went to his room. The litter of journals just didn't mean anything to him anymore. He gathered them into a pile, then sat on the bed, limp and exhausted.

He looked out the window of his hotel room and saw the sun dipping below the horizon. From fourteen stories below came the sounds of people and cars, together with the sounds of birds singing in the palm trees.

God! He had had such a good start at Princeton. He thought of his first year and his final philosophy exam. He had done really well. He had smashed the course, as they used to say. Big four. A winner! The professor had asked about Plato and the dialogues and Plato's theory of justice, and Dave had been right on the money.

He remembered signing the Princeton Pledge: *I pledge my honor as a gentleman, that during this examination I have neither given nor received assistance.*

He had had such a good start. He remembered how good he felt walking down the path, watching the moon rise over the early June evening at Princeton. Life was sweet then, and there was hope in the air. How had it all come to this?

Downstairs, he knew, the examiners for the American College of Surgeons were talking over the candidates and evaluating their performances.

Once again he heard the words of the professor in Chicago: "You'll all be rated on a one-to-ten basis. For those who are seven and above, there will be little discussion. Anyone who has four or below will be discussed, and anyone taking his boards for the third time will automatically be discussed because it is his last chance, his last hope, before going back to residency."

Dave shuddered. Such a good start. He recalled his first year at med school, remembering how proud he had been after his first anatomy exam, on which he had gotten a B+. He had even recognized the ligaments and tendons, which were so hard to visualize, around the shoulder.

He remembered the bones of the wrist and the memory device he had used to ice that one. "Never Lower Tillie's Pants . . . Mother Might Come Home." Never — navicular: Lower — lunate; Tillie's — triangular; Pants — pisiform; Mother — greater multangular; Might — lesser multangular; Come — capitate; Home — hammate. . . . Goddamn! After all these years!

After that exam, flushed with success, Dave had gone to see *Tender Is the Night*, with Jennifer Jones. He remembered seeing Jennifer Jones making love to her psychiatrist in a posh hotel on the Riviera.

"God, I want to be like that," he had said to himself. And he had always carried that thought with him. . . . It was one of the things that had made him plug on even harder and become a doctor.

God, he had had such a good start. How had it come to this?

Dave imagined they were discussing him now. Again he berated himself for the long pauses, the hesitant answers, the blanking out on certain questions.

In fact, Dave *knew* they were discussing him; this was his third and final time.

Then the phone rang, interrupting his meditating. It was his attorney.

"How did it go?" Dave whispered, afraid of the answer. There was silence on the other end of the line.

Then: "Don't worry, Dave. They stacked the executive committee against you. But we'll appeal it — we'll take it all the way. We'll fight those bastards. They can't do this to us.''

To us! Dave thought. The bastard at the other end of the phone draining him at a rate of one hundred dollars per hour. *To* us *shit!*

"What happened?" Dave asked.

"The executive committee turned you down. Collins apparently was the big factor. He insisted that you need two board-certified surgeons — one to evaluate you preoperatively, and one to scrub with you in surgery."

Dave felt like ripping the phone out of the wall. But he was too tired — and too tired to fight.

"Isn't there anything we can do?" he asked weakly. "It's so unfair."

"We'll fight those bastards, Dave. Right now I've got calls in to several people. Several prominent people, I might add, who have to a lot to say about the running of Beverly Hills Hospital. We'll appeal the executive board decision."

"But what about my surgery privileges?" Dave asked.

"Well, for the moment we'll have to go along with them. But we're getting together a list of general surgeons who will cooperate with us, so don't worry, Dave. You've got friends. . . .''

Dave hung up. He felt so isolated, so tired. Sure, friends. Where were they? The people he had been kind to, now that he needed them, now that he was too tired to fight himself? They were all gone.

Dave walked to the window. A cool breeze wafted in, and he shivered. The sun had disappeared below the horizon.

He was devastated. Locked in at the hospital, unable to operate without two board-certified surgeons scrubbing with him, helping him, treating him like a surgical cripple. An expensive attorney to appeal surgery boards' decisions. If they were all so firmly against him, maybe they were right. Maybe he shouldn't be doing surgery. Maybe he shouldn't be doing anything at all.

Dave looked down fourteen floors to the street. The wind was blowing harder now. He ought to step back and close the window, but he didn't move.

Downstairs, the doctors from the American College of Surgeons were discussing the candidates.

"I don't know about Berger," Dr. Zites said. "I just don't know. He seemed preoccupied, almost at a loss for words. He was in some kind of fog. I mean, we didn't ask him hard stuff — abdominal trauma, Colles fracture. Your bread-and-butter stuff. We were trying to be easy on him."

"And it was his third time," said Dr. Chin, who had given Dave the vascular question. "I'm sorry we had to ask him things on vascular and chest, but after all, the candidates are responsible for that material."

"Now, he did have a good residency," Dr. Schwartz said.

"He did," Zites responded. "We checked his credentials. He had good training, he has passed the written, so we know he has the knowledge, but this is his third time on boards. He just didn't seem to have the confidence, like someone had torn out his heart or something."

Upstairs, Dave remained at the window. The news from Beverly Hills Hospital was sinking in. He would never be able to practice there. His few referring doctors would leave him now. They would all leave. He was alone.

Downstairs, the surgeons were finishing. David Berger was their last candidate.

"Let's call for a vote," Dr. Zites said. "I mean, he seemed to do well in the third room — he got three sevens and an eight. And he did pass the pathology — missed only two. I gave him a six, myself."

"I gave him a three," said the Chinese doctor. "He just didn't seem to know the vascular stuff, or coin lesions of the chest."

Dave just stared at the street. He wasn't even aware of the wind now. He thought about Little Duck and Big Camel. What would they have done? He thought about Al Jolson. . . . *When there are gray skies, I don't mind the gray skies, I still have you, sonny boy.* . . .

He thought about Shana.

He leaned closer to the window ledge.

Downstairs, the vote was in.

The American College of Surgeons broke up and the doctors prepared to leave Palo Alto. They had done their duty.

Another group of candidates had come and gone. Some had made it; others hadn't and would be invited back. Others would be going back to their residency for more training. It was all in a day's work.

The phone rang. It was Dave's attorney again. "Concerned about you . . . you didn't sound good. I'm just waiting for a few answers."

David put the phone down and went back to the window.

"Hello? Dave, are you there?"

Dave stared out the window. The wind was strong now; it sent cold chills down his spine.

He thought of his empty apartment, his tapes and journals, dirty coffee cups. And Shana Winston.

Chapter Forty-three

The call from his father-in-law had annoyed Andrew Collins. This was a hell of a time for Tony to insist that Andrew drive out to the studio to look at rushes. Andrew had personally supervised every important surgery scene in the next three "Medicine Men" episodes, and they were all medically accurate.

Andrew needed to keep an eye on things at the hospital until he was absolutely sure Dave Berger could find no way around the obstacles he and Bill Benedict had set up.

"Can't it wait until Tuesday?" he had asked Tony.

But Tony had been insistent. "No. Some questions have come up about one scene, and if it's wrong, it'll have to be reshot today. I can give you an hour to get here, but no more."

Before hanging up, he had told Andrew which screening room to report to, because it would not be posted in the front office.

The guards at the front gate now recognized Andrew on sight, and they waved him on through with a smile. He still felt a thrill of self-importance each time it happened. The film studios were no longer the grand little monarchies they had been in the early days of Hollywood, but they were still the only royal kingdoms America possessed, and passing through their gates freely was the equivalent of knighthood. Of course, it never occurred to Andrew that deliverymen and messengers had the same access and got the same smile.

His ego was so assuaged that by the time Andrew arrived at the screening room, his annoyance had faded. Once inside the gates of a film studio, the anxieties of the real world faded into insignificance, and make-believe became much more important.

He was only a few minutes late, and the projectionist was waiting patiently in his small, darkened room behind the screening room, with his door open, as usual. It was customary to treat projectionists with deference, but Andrew was always uncomfortable with them. He forced himself to say hello when he came in and thank you when he left, but that was about all he could manage, and they remained equally reserved with him.

He waved to this projectionist today and received a nod of recognition in return.

Tony Manchester was already seated in the screening room, next to a woman. Only after Andrew had slipped into the seat beside her did he realize it was Alice.

She smiled faintly — almost apologetically — at him. But Tony beamed in his most infuriatingly magnanimous way and said, "Alice happened to stop by the studio, and I thought she might be interested in seeing this footage." Then he looked at his watch and added, "You're late."

Andrew started to reply acidly that he hadn't been

given much warning, but he caught himself and ignored the barb.

It wouldn't have mattered anyway. Tony was oblivious to anything Andrew might feel. He twisted in his seat and called to the projectionist, "We're ready to begin anytime you are."

There was a brief, uncomfortable pause before the projector was turned on. In that moment, Alice asked, "How are things going at the hospital? I haven't seen much of you in the past forty-eight hours." There was a strange edge to her voice, and Andrew couldn't quite grasp what it meant.

"It's okay," he said as the tape bagan. "Hectic."

Andrew's mind did not immediately grasp the images on the screen. His throughts were on Alice. Why was she here? And why the strained, solicitous, almost pitying looks from her?

The room that appeared on screen had a certain familiarity, and the woman was quite obviously Lina Lathrop. Andrew expected to see a familiar setting, and it certainly wasn't unusual for him to view footage of Lina.

Then, the action and the identity of the other actor registered. Andrew was looking at a pornographic scene, and the man undressing himself on the bed was . . . Andrew's eyes strained and he could hear his heart pound. *This was the videotape Lina had made of the two of them making love.*

For a moment, Andrew was simply too stunned to react. He felt his face grow hot as anger and shame enveloped him.

Neither Tony nor Alice spoke, but Andrew knew what each was thinking. Tony had gotten his son-in-law where he wanted him and was laughing delightedly, while Alice was careening between hurt, mortification, and disgust.

For some reason, Andrew was more outraged over the fact that Tony would permit his daughter to see these acts than over the fact that Tony had possession of the tape and wanted to hurt Andrew by showing it.

Finally, he exploded. "You crazy bastard! What the hell is this all about?" he screamed at Tony, leaping to his feet. "Shut that thing off!"

"Sit down and shut up!" Tony said firmly. "You're going to watch every bit of this."

"All right!" Andrew shouted back, but his voice broke. "But does Alice have to watch it? This isn't anything for her to see."

"Yes, it is," Tony replied calmly. "It's time she saw what's been going on behind her back."

Lina was now on top of Collins, her legs straddling his face, her head between his legs; they were performing acts that Alice would never even have considered doing. As far as Andrew knew, she barely knew they existed.

"You son of a bitch!" Collins screamed, lunging at Tony. "I'll kill you!"

He grabbed at Tony's neck, but only for an instant, because Tony was on his feet quickly, fending Andrew off. Trying to fight across Alice, who had stood up in alarm, and in the tight space between the rows of seats, Andrew lost his balance. One hard blow from Tony sent him sprawling across the rows of seats in front of them.

He struggled clumsily and painfully to his feet, intent on fighting back, but then the overhead lights snapped on and two men — the projectionist and a security guard — rushed at him.

He tried to shake them off, but they were far stronger than he, and he was easily subdued. His humiliation was complete, but it was not over. He was forced to stand facing his wife and father-in-law while his shame still played faintly on the screen behind him, until Tony Manchester could squash the last ounce of his dignity.

Tony adjusted his jacket and shirt collar and relaxed back into his seat, triumphant. "This is a very marketable little piece of tape," he said smugly. "If you aren't willing to listen to reason, there are quite a few movie theaters and porno shops willing to run it all across the country." He paused to allow Collins to comprehend his meaning fully. "That's one way of getting what I want. But of course I'd rather not have to resort to that."

"What do you want?" Collins asked shakily.

"I knew you'd be cooperative. I'd like you to agree to two things. First, I want you to give Alice a divorce."

Until that moment, Alice had remained silent and expressionless, but now — before Andrew could respond — she broke in. "What makes you think I want a divorce?" she cried.

Tony looked at her in surprise. "Surely after seeing this bit of tape you will. Won't you?"

"I don't know. I'll have to think about it." Then she gave him a very hard look and added, "But that's a decision for me to make, not you."

Tony dismissed her resistance. "I'm sure after you think about it you'll realize it's the only sensible course."

"Perhaps. But this is a very cruel thing you've done, Dad. I didn't know you had it in you, and I don't understand why you had to do it this way." She scowled. "In fact, suddenly I don't think I understand you at all."

Tony was immediately puzzled and dismayed. "I had to do it this way, sweetheart," he said gently. "It was the only way you would realize what kind of man he is. Eventually you'll understand I did it because I love you."

Tears began to well in Alice's eyes, and she shook her head violently. "No," she said. "You couldn't possibly do something like this if you loved me." She paused to wipe tears from her cheeks. "In his own odd way, I wonder if Andrew doesn't love me more than you do."

Her kind, gentle words stabbed Andrew with a force he hadn't thought possible. When Tony first mentioned divorce, Andrew's initial reaction had been relief. Divorce was what he had wanted. He would gladly give Tony that so he could have Lina. But, while father and daughter had been speaking, doubt had assailed him. How had Tony gotten his hands on this tape? How had he even known it existed? As producer of "The Medicine Men," Tony was Lina's employer, but could he have even more control over his employees than Andrew had thought? Could this possibly have something to do with the reason why Lina had suddenly left Los Angeles without so much as a word to Andrew?

But it was the depth of Alice's feeling for him that troubled him most. She should have felt outrage and hatred for him after seeing the tape, but she semed less affected by it than Tony and Andrew were. Her feelings for Andrew hardly seemed to have suffered. That show of love and faith threw Andrew right off course.

He was afraid to allow the conversation between them to go too far, afraid that Alice might persuade her father to withdraw his demand for a divorce.

He interrupted, demanding, "What's your second requirement?"

Tony stared blankly at him. *Andrew Collins must have ice water in his veins*, he thought.

"You said there were two things you wanted," Andrew prodded. "The first was for me to give Alice a divorce. What's the other one?"

"I want you out of Beverly Hills Hospital," he said, his voice as cold and hard as Andrew had ever heard it. "I want you to submit your resignation, to be effective immediately."

"Why?" Andrew asked, genuinely perplexed. "You no longer have an interest in the hospital."

Tony smiled. "That's not quite true. If anything, I have an even greater interest, since I'm going to be running the Betco Corporation."

Andrew, whose first instinct was to believe him, panicked, but then he quickly told himself Tony was bluffing. "That's impossible." He laughed nervously. "Bill Benedict will be running Betco now that Dawson's dead."

"Maybe that's what you think," Tony said easily, "and what Benedict thinks." He smiled broadly. "But Dawson made certain changes in his will the night before he died. I'm in control."

"You can't be! You're just trying to bluff me."

"I'll tell you what," Tony replied, sarcasm tingeing his voice. "If Benedict controls Betco, you can stay at the hospital. If he doesn't, I want you out." Then, as an afterthought, he added, "And I want you to drop your complaint to the surgery committee concerning Dave Berger. You know and I know it has no basis whatever."

By this time the two guards had softened their grip on Andrew, though one still kept him firmly in check, as the tape finished and the projectionist had to leave briefly to shut off the machine.

"All right," Andrew agreed reluctantly, still suspicious. "*If* you manage to gain control of the hospital, I'll be glad to submit my resignation." Then he smiled nastily. "It might interest you to know that I don't like you any more than you like me." He glanced at the guard, who remained at his side. "May I go now?"

"Of course," Tony sneered. "You've always been free to go."

Andrew moved toward the door.

However, as he cleared the row of seats, Tony called out to him, "Just a moment. There's one other thing I think you ought to know. Lina Lathrop isn't going to marry you. She doesn't give a damn about you. As far as she was concerned, this was just another job.''

Andrew was dumbstruck. ''What do you mean?'' His ears were ringing.

''I mean,'' Tony gloated, ''Lina was nothing but a whore from Las Vegas. A high-class, expensive whore. I made a deal with her: I'd make her a star if she would do a bit of acting on the side for me. You won't be able to see her again.''

Andrew didn't answer. There was nothing he could say. He had no idea whether there was any truth in what Tony was saying. Anything was possible. As for Lina, he suddenly realized he couldn't honestly judge. He turned and left the screening room.

He was only a few paces down the hall when Alice called to him. He stopped and turned as she ran to catch up. ''I need to talk to you, Andrew,'' she said quietly. ''Could you manage a few minutes for coffee or a drink?''

''Sure.'' He shrugged. ''But I need to make a couple of phone calls first.'' He hesitated, then said, ''Listen, Alice, I'm sorry about this. I never wanted to hurt you like this.'' He shook his head. ''Not like this.''

''I know,'' she said softly. ''In fact, I know you a lot better than you think.''

She waited patiently while Andrew found a pay phone. Alice always waited patiently.

Andrew desperately hoped he could reach Bill Benedict.

Chapter Forty-four

Bill Benedict felt good as he hitched up his shorts and entered the jogging track at Beverly Hills High School. He always felt good at this time of evening. It was about eight o'clock, and the moon was just rising above the two skyscraper towers of Century City, a few blocks away.

Everything else seemed dwarfed — Beverly Hills High School, the Hollywood hills off in the distance, the Century Plaza Hotel, even Bill Benedict himself. The light from the now-deserted twin towers, where only hours before office workers had scurried about, cast eerie shadows along the jogging track.

Bill Benedict had made this early evening run part of his routine for years. Victor Dawson knew it. The whole organization knew it. Bill Benedict was probably the best athlete on the staff, and certainly the best runner. He was in such good shape that he could do five miles a day and barely break a sweat. It was fortunate, he thought, that he had found a place to jog so close to their hotel. During the long negotiations for Beverly Hills Hospital, between all the politics and the meetings and the socializing, he could always find an escape here.

Benedict felt his heart pounding as he rounded the far end of the field near the third-base side of the diamond. He felt his hips tensing as he ran over the track. He loved the feel of his lean body while he was running. He could feel the pulsations within. . . .

He thought about the women he knew — and the women he would know. His former wife came to mind, and Shana Winston, and Alice Collins. Benedict thought of his status as the new boss of Betco. He would have a wide choice of women. Ever since the night of Andrew's party, he had secretly hoped for a private meeting with Andrew's wife. He hoped Andrew would leave Alice Collins behind.

Benedict was so busy fantasizing about the new conquests he would make as the boss of Betco that he failed to notice a car pull up at the other end of the field. Two men got out of the car and headed toward the jogging track.

It wasn't until he saw that the car was actually blocking the fence across the entrance to the high school that he became concerned.

The men had separated and were walking slowly toward him. He suddenly realized who they were, and looked for a way out, but there was none. The track and the car and the men stood between him and the exit.

He thought of yelling for help, but there was no one around.

He began to sprint toward the other side of the field, away from his pursuers. He felt perspiration drenching his forehead and his body as the men behind him broke into a run.

The men gained on him and finally they caught him at the far end of the track, where it was dark.

"Keep away," Benedict said, panting. "I'll go to the police."

"We don't think so," one of the men said.

Benedict shrieked in terror. "It wasn't me! It wasn't me! It was Collins!"

"We know who it was," the man said. "The boss knows."

"Please! Please!"

"Sorry, Benedict. It's been tough with these hospital negotiations and surgeons, and doctors. The boss doesn't want any more trouble. In fact, he thinks you need some surgery."

"Please! *Please!*"

The men threw him to the ground in the hedges behind the third-base line and pulled down his jogging shorts.

One held Benedict's arms over his head. The other man spread Benedict's legs wide and kneeled across both of his shins.

"Yeah, the boss thinks you need surgery of your own," the man repeated.

Benedict stared in horror as the kneeling man unsheathed a long knife.

"No!" Benedict screamed and bucked, but he could hardly move.

"You won't be needing these anymore," the man said. "Sorry, Benedict."

The last thing he saw was the sharp edge of the knife gleaming in the light reflected from the towers of Century City, as his penis and testicles were expertly removed with one sharp slice.

Benedict was found two hours later, lying in the shallow left field of the Beverly Hills High School baseball field. He was in shock from extensive blood loss, and was taken to Beverly Hills Hospital, where he was placed in the intensive-care unit.

Benedict remained in shock for twenty-four hours,

never fully regaining consciousness. He did wake up once, long enough to realize what had happened to him.

He shrieked in agony and went into a coma at the horror of what he saw when he looked under the sheets and realized what had happened.

Benedict remained alive for another twenty-two hours. He had the best care that modern medicine and Beverly Hills Hospital had to offer. He was placed on a Swan Ganz catheter, which monitored his heart, and he was given intravenous fluids and antibiotics and treated for shock.

A Foley catheter was placed through the area of his missing penis into the bladder to monitor his hourly urine output. Benedict awoke again, due to the intense pain when the urologist attempted to pass the Foley catheter through the gaping hole.

"Oh, my God!" he screamed, and fainted. He never regained consciousness.

He was taken to surgery, where debridement of the area of his missing genitals was performed. He was given six pints of blood in transfusion, and soft Penrose drains were installed.

After surgery, Benedict was returned to the intensive-care unit. He continued to bleed from his genital area and required two more units of blood. At five in the morning, he stopped breathing and a bright orange tube was placed in his trachea.

He lay there, alone and helpless, in a sort of twilight zone of consciousness, only aware of the beeping and clicking of the respiratory and cardiac machines around him.

When he developed cloudy infiltrate in both lungs during the next twelve hours, his dose of antibiotics was increased. When his blood pressure began to fall, he was given a massive dose of steroids through his intravenous lines. His lungs continued to fill up with a white frothy foam, and he lay there, choking and drowning in his own body fluids.

He died in the intensive-care unit six hours later. Autopsy showed the classic signs of "shock lung." His lung tissue was white and firm and swollen like a soggy baseball. His chest and abdominal cavity were filled with a dark bloody fluid, which was sent for culture and analysis.

The next day a Beverly Hills High School grounds-keeper found Bill Benedict's genitals near third base. They were sent back to Chicago and were buried with him, three days later.

Chapter Forty-five

Dave Berger sat facing the executive committee. He scarcely dared to breathe. This was the big day, the final appeal to the executive committee and the day his letter was due to arrive with the result of his boards. Dave stared around the room as Tony Manchester, the new chairman of the executive committee, stood up and cleared his throat. He noticed Andrew Collins sitting next to his father-in-law and staring straight ahead at him. To the other side sat Dr. Nino and the rest of the executive committee. He glanced toward the door. Shana said she'd rush over with the morning mail as soon as it arrived. Where was she?"

"Dr. Berger."

Dave stood up. He felt his knees go weak as Tony Manchester began. "The executive committee has received your appeal. We have talked it over with the attorneys for Betco and the hospital."

There was a knock on the door and Dave was relieved

to see Shana enter. She was carrying an envelope in her hand. The results from the boards!

"Excuse me, Mr. Manchester," Shana said, "I hate to interrupt the executive committee, but I think this could be important." She walked quickly to Dave and handed him the envelope.

Tony Manchester looked at Dave, as did Collins and the rest of the executive committee. Dave cradled the envelope in his hand. He stared at the return address: American College of Surgeons. Boards!

Tony Manchester nodded. "As I was saying," he continued, "the executive committee is waiting. Needless to say, Dr. Berger's reinstatement with full privileges is contingent on his passing the boards."

Dave scarcely heard Tony Manchester's voice droning on as he nervously tore open the envelope.

"Well, Dr. Berger?"

His eyes blurred, his hands trembled. His palms were perspiring more than they had been while he was taking the boards. He felt Shana's breath on him as she looked over his shoulder. He thought of Victor Dawson and Winston and Collins and . . . and Dr. Zites and Little Duck and Big Camel. Everything flashed before him as he opened the letter and read his fate.

Dear Dr. Berger:
    The American College of Surgeons is happy to inform you . . ."

Dave didn't need to read on. "I did it! I did it!" he shouted. "I passed the boards!" He turned to a tearful Shana, reached out, and hugged her.

Tony Manchester stopped speaking. The entire committee waited.

"I knew it, David!" Shana cried. "I could see it through the envelope. I held it up to the light."

"Well" — Tony Manchester looked from Dave to Collins — "I guess this about clinches things. I think our business is completed here."

Chapter Forty-six

Beverly Hills, One Year Later

Her husband was annoyed as not being able to watch the ball game on the big TV, but Melissa didn't care. There were things in this world more important than ball games, things more important to her survival. Chuck could watch the game on the little black-and-white in the bedroom. Melissa had been waiting to see this television movie for months.

It was something called "Gibson's Girls," and it starred a new young actress who had been getting an enormous publicity buildup by Tony Manchester Productions.

Her name was Lina Lathrop, and few people knew what Melissa Baxter knew about her. Few people had any idea how much she had affected the lives of others.

It had been over a year since Melissa had first heard the name Lina Lathrop, and even then she had been curious to see for herself what this young woman was like.

Over a year. It was incredible to think that all the

trouble at Beverly Hills Hospital was now past, that, indeed, so many had survived, that the hospital itself had not come crashing down around their heads.

There hadn't even been a hint of scandal in the press. No suggestion that either Phil Winston or Victor Dawson had been murdered. Bill Benedict's death had also been reported.

The Betco Corporation hadn't wanted a scandal, so Tony Manchester and Phyllis Dawson had said nothing either to the police or to the press.

To Melissa's knowledge, no one knew that Bill Benedict had arranged for Phil Winston to meet her at the emergency room that morning.

Tony and Phyllis — they were quite a team. Even now Melissa couldn't quite understand what was going on between them. Certainly, both had a great deal to gain by cooperating closely. Phyllis controlled the Dawson stock, and Tony ran the corporation at a big profit. But Melissa was sure there was more to it than that. She had had her contacts working on it for a long time, but so far none could prove that Manchester was sleeping with Phyllis Dawson. Eventually, however, Melissa was sure she could find out the truth. She always did, sooner or later.

That would be the only thing that could possibly explain how Tony Manchester had survived the loss of his own daughter.

To Tony's amazement, Alice Collins had left Los Angeles with her husband. Even Tony hadn't been able to understand the kind of woman Alice was. That was because there weren't many women like Alice anymore, women who wanted to love and care for one man for a lifetime, through thick and thin.

Her decision had not caused Tony to change his demands. Andrew had been forced to drop his charges against Dave Berger and to resign from Beverly Hills Hospital.

Andrew Collins — that was a pitiful sight. Only Alice Collins could love a man like that. Of course, Melissa hadn't seen him in over six months, since he had given up his meager practice in the valley and moved on, first to try to establish a practice somewhere in Arizona; and now — as far as Melissa knew — he was struggling along in a town in upstate New York.

Andrew Collins wouldn't change. He'd still try to make a big show of prosperity and success, concentrating more on that than on caring for his patients. He'd still sleep with anything he could get, only to return home to a loving wife whom he couldn't possibly understand.

Dave Berger had been the big surprise to Melissa. She hadn't expected that at all. Not at all.

If she had realized how Berger would have acted under the stress of his boards and the hospital committee, perhaps Melissa would have behaved differently. She might have taken him into her confidence; she might have worked it out with him. But how could she have known?

Melissa had no time for regrets. A person couldn't survive with regrets. But, if she had had regrets, that would have been one of them — that she had taken her stand against Dave Berger. Well, not precisely against.

It had almost proved to be a mistake. If she hadn't made her phone call about Bill Benedict, she could easily have lost everything. Of course, she hadn't wanted to do it, but she had had no choice. And Benedict had died, and no one had ever suspected her.

Anyway, Melissa hadn't lost, though she had never been able to get back on good terms with Tony Manchester. Perhaps he suspected something.

It had floored Melissa completely when Tony Manchester had put together his little scheme to get rid of her and Maturity Medical Services. But Tony — even with all his power — had been no match for her.

Somehow, they had managed to get a full list of her clients, and they had written to all of them, offering — on behalf of Beverly Hills Hospital — to provide the same services she provided, free of charge.

But Melissa's patients were loyal. They knew her and they trusted her. She was much more human than a big modern hospital. Fewer than a dozen had taken Tony up on his offer, and even those few had returned to the fold when Melissa threatened to sue them for breach of contract.

Melissa could never be friends or partners with Tony, but they managed to get along. Melissa was a power with which the hospital had to contend. Tony needed her business, and that was as it should be. Melissa could keep him in check when she needed to.

No, her business was thriving and would continue to do so as long as she was around. Maturity Medical couldn't survive after she was gone, of course. Melissa knew that. Chuck could never carry on in her place. She doubted if anyone could. Chuck wasn't a survivor. Melissa was.

Melissa suspected, from what she had heard, that Lina Lathrop was also a survivor. That was why Melissa wanted so badly to see "Gibson's Girls."

It was almost time.

Melissa turned on the TV, turned down the lights, and picked up her knitting. While the preliminary commercials ran their course, she began to knit and purl, keeping her hands busy.

Then the film began, with the credits flashing onto the screen, accompanied by one clip after another of a face Melissa knew had to be Lina Lathrop's. It was a fantastic face and confirmed everything Melissa suspected about the young woman.

The face was beautiful, but its beauty was not the empty, transient beauty of most of the manufactured, lookalike television stars. Hers was a striking individual beauty — soft, gossamer red hair, done up in the Gibson style, a lustrous, creamy complexion, with just a trace of freckles, and eyes that said it all. The eyes revealed that the beauty might fade with time, but the zest for living and the determination to success would never pass.

Yes, Melissa smiled to herself, Lina Lathrop was also a survivor. Melissa wished she were young enough to be around long enough to watch the new star's progress. Twenty years from now that young woman might just own the whole town.

WAYNE D. OVERHOLSER

WESTERNS

HERE IS YOUR CHANCE TO ORDER SOME OF OUR BEST

HISTORICAL ROMANCES

BY SOME OF YOUR FAVORITE AUTHORS

____ **BELOVED OUTCAST** — Lorena Dureau   7701-0508-4/$3.95

____ **DARK WINDS** — Virginia Coffman   7701-0405-3/$3.95

____ **KISS OF GOLD** — Samantha Harte   7701-0529-7/$3.50

____ **MISTRESS OF MOON HILL** — Jill Downie
                7701-0424-X/$3.95

____ **SWEET WHISPERS** — Samantha Harte
                7701-0496-7/$3.50

____ **TIMBERS AND GOLD LACE** — Patricia Werner
                7701-0600-5/$3.95

____ **TIME TO LOVE** — Helen McCullough
                7701-0560-2/$3.95

____ **WAYWARD LADY** — Nan Ryan   7701-0605-6/$3.95

Available at your local bookstore or return this coupon to: